Discovering Grace

*A story about family
and the redemptive
power of forgiveness*

DAVID TEMPLE

ST SIMONS PRESS

Published in the United States of America

ISBN: 978-0-615-41675-5

Published by St Simons Press
www.StSimonsPress.com

Book designed by Ken Magas,
www.KenMagasDesign.com

Book photography by Lindey Magee,
www.LindeyMagee.com

Audiobook recording provided by
www.GroundcrewStudios.com

This book is dedicated to my parents, Edward and Barbara, for they are my inspiration and the inspiration upon which I based Grace's parents. Dad and Mom showed such love for me as I was growing up, and I can safely say that without their gracious direction my life would not be as well grounded as it is.

To my sisters, Alice Kay and Barbara Ann, for the loving support and continued encouragement they have shown me every step of the way. They helped me to keep the belief that I am a writer with something to say.

And finally, to my brother Jonathan Edward, whom I have always admired and whose love for me has stood the test of time. There are influences in this book that reflect the love that my brother and I share.

"Treat a man as he appears to be, and you make him worse. But treat a man as if he were what he potentially could be, and you make him what he should be."

– Goethe

Discovering Grace

PROLOGUE

A MAN IS FACE DOWN on the bed, motionless and breathing heavily. He wears shorts and a faded golf shirt. The bed, large and ornate, is carved with scenes of the Deep South. An overhead fan spins slowly, stirring the drapes. Shades half-drawn darken the room, filtering the harsh afternoon sun. A clock chimes three times in the distance. Oblivious to the sounds of the children outside, the man doesn't stir.

Suddenly, a screen door flings open, slamming against the house, followed by the shriek of a young girl.

"You're it, Grace!" the children shout.

Her older brother Christopher chases her. Their younger brother David jumps on his back and quickly sidelines him. The children cheer Grace as they pile on Chris, tackling him. The momentary distraction allows Grace to capture the lead. Angela sees her nine-year old "birthday princess for the day" run into the house. She smiles and returns to her novel. Her husband Jonathan sleeps on a nearby lounge, uninterrupted by the children's voices.

Grace sticks her head out the door, checking on her brother. Seeing that Chris has dumped his brother, she slams the screen door and darts across the huge living room, stopping at the entrance to the kitchen. Her grandmother holds up a hand.

"No you don't, Gracie," Daphne says. "Nana's cleaning. Now run along."

Grace giggles then darts in the opposite direction as Christopher enters the living room. She runs down the long hallway, her small hands gliding along the walls for balance. The sound of her shoes on the wooden floors becomes muffled when she reaches the antique carpet. At the end of the hall she looks one way then the other.

Christopher is quickly approaching so she runs toward the guest room at the end of the house, stopping at the doorway.

The room is quiet and dark, a sharp contrast to the bright outdoors. Her eyes quickly adjust as she nears the four-poster bed. Christopher enters breathing heavily and stops to catch his breath.

Shaking the sleeping man, she shouts, "Wake up, Uncle Carter!"

He doesn't move.

"Don't bother him, Gracie. He's taking a nap."

Thirsty, she sees a glass of water on the bedside table and picks it up. Christopher notices a vodka bottle at the back of the nightstand.

"Stop, Gracie! That's a grown-up drink."

She takes a gulp then quickly spits it out. "Yuck!"

"I told you. C'mon, let's go back outside. It's your turn to be 'It'."

"Why do people drink that stuff?"

"Makes them feel good, I guess. I don't know. C'mon, let's go."

Grace plans her escape, then reaches to shake her uncle once more. He doesn't move.

"Let's go," Christopher whispers.

As she turns to leave she sees something nearly hidden under Carter's pillow.

"Chris! Look what I found."

He sees that Grace is holding a large gun.

"Grace, put that down!" he gasps. "It's dangerous!"

Waving it around, she says, "Hey, let's play 'Cowboys and Indians'. This time, you be the Indian and I'll be the Cowboy!"

Panicked, he slowly starts toward her.

"C'mon, Gracie. Stop playing with that thing and come play with me." Hoping to persuade her, he starts to leave then hesitates and turns back.

Grace has turned the gun and is looking down the barrel.

Terrified, he shouts, "Grace, put it down. Now!"

Startled, her hand slips.

BANG!

CHAPTER 1

SUN SPARKLES THROUGH CENTURY OLD oak trees and their leaves dance in the breeze. Children play in the yard, their laughter echoing through the neighborhood. Chasing one another they are happy and carefree. Their world is an imaginary fortress, a castle, a western frontier or anything that their imaginations create.

The season is perfect. People relax more, stress less. Children play more, fight less. Families vacation more, work less. And everyone naps more. Nothing seems better than a long nap on a lazy summer afternoon.

Jonathan and Angela relax in matching lounge chairs, embracing the time off—a gift enjoyed all too rarely. Angela reads a summertime novel, her perfect recipe to escape the pressures of the day. A floppy hat shades her bright blue eyes and protects her complexion from the afternoon sun. She loves getting lost in romance novels for they offer things she secretly dreams of. She is happy but longs for the kind of passion that seems to have faded with years of marriage. After nearly 20 years she still deeply loves her husband, but with three children and the responsibilities of their pastoral calling, private moments have become rare.

She gently pats her sleeping husband's arm. He doesn't stir. Jonathan could easily pass either as an athletic trainer or a professional napper— if there were such a competition! His mower cools nearby. Mowing is a chore Jonathan enjoys, the simple pleasure of time alone. No children's chatter, wife's "honey-do" lists, or phone calls—nothing but the throaty roar of the powerful mower and the smell of freshly cut grass beneath his well-worn sneakers. But for now Jonathan is oblivious to the world as he sleeps beneath his old straw hat.

Angela's sundress drapes a slim figure that reflects extra hours in the gym. Sandals reveal manicured toes that wiggle as she reads. Though she looks like "Glamour" magazine, her life is more like "Family Circle." She puts her book down and pours more lemonade from the pitcher on the table between them. "*Summertime and the living is easy*," she hums. She sees the children: her sweet three, the next door neighbor's friendly four and another neighbor's ferocious five. Their happy voices provide the perfect backdrop to an idyllic day. Breathing deeply, she smiles. Their laughter is enchanting, their inhibitions unrestrained. Their minds are open to all that life offers, unspoiled and innocent. These qualities are her deepest joy.

Suddenly the sound of a gunshot pierces the afternoon silence. Angela drops her book, looks at the children and then the house. A scream from inside makes Angela's blood run cold.

"Christopher," she shrieks, gasping for air.

The children stop, looking at one another with panic.

"Grace!" she shouts in fear.

Time seems frozen. Terrified children cry. Angela stands, a frightening pain pierces her heart, and she runs toward the house. The children huddle, hugging and crying. She tries to comfort them but only for an instant.

"Shhh…. Stay here and I'll be right back," then she runs toward the house.

Daphne opens the screen door as Angela nears the bottom step. Panic races through her as she sees the horror on Daphne's face.

The earth seems to shift beneath Angela's feet as her heart falters.

CHAPTER 2

FALL IS TRYING FOR AN early return, as noted by the trees changing colors. Perhaps the gray sky is reflecting the sorrow felt at this moment. Heaven's head seems bowed as one family mourns in deep despair, their sunshine having left with no warning.

A fine mist falls on the mourners. The group encircles the tiny grave. Pastor Jonathan Matheson, his wife Angela, and their two sons, Christopher and David are silent, heartbroken. Angela seems years older than she had a week before. Christopher gazes into the distance, expressionless. Younger brother David holds his mother's hand, squeezing it tightly, quietly crying as he looks at her. Her face has a vacant look of disbelief that such a terrible thing could have happened. She tries valiantly to smile and comfort David. But comfort doesn't come easily.

Jonathan stands in silence for a seeming eternity before he speaks. All eyes are on him.

"Thank you for coming here today. You are a blessing and comfort to Angela, me and our boys. What happened last week was a tragedy. Some say an accident. But certainly a tragedy."

He sees his brother Carter standing across the way. Carter appears 20 years older than Jonathan, though he is only 11 years his senior. Carter is motionless, staring at the grave.

"Only God knows for certain," Jonathan continues.

Their eyes meet. It is only after Jonathan looks away that he continues speaking.

"Grace was a very special little girl. An angel sent to us from God. In a family with a long history of boys only, it was not only a miracle, but also an honor and blessing to receive our daughter into the Matheson family. She certainly was the apple of *our* eyes." His arm encircles Angela.

Carter sees Christopher staring at him in quiet rage. Christopher's jaw is taut, his hands clenched. Carter drops his gaze, looks at Jonathan, then away.

Jonathan continues, "Grace had a unique ability, a special gift that caused everyone to feel special, as though they were the only one in the world. We loved her so very much. We all did. She will always be in our hearts and our thoughts."

Angela looks into the faces of her friends. Then her eyes meet Carter's. He slowly shakes his head. After a long time, almost imperceptibly, she nods. He manages a pained smile. Turning to Christopher she sees the brothers are trying to be strong for one another. They stand close. Christopher has his arm around David who smiles. David tugs on Angela's sleeve. She looks at him saying, "I love you."

"Please join me in prayer," asks Jonathan.

Angela notices that Carter has left and turns back to Jonathan. He has been with the congregation for many years and they love and trust their pastor. It is evident in their faces. They stand with heads bowed.

"Dear Father in Heaven, thank You for friends and family who love and support us in our deep need. We embrace one another." Glancing up, Jonathan notes that Carter has disappeared and he frowns. "And Lord help us, no matter the circumstances, to trust their love for us. Thank You for loving us and for forgiving us our sins. Help us to forgive those who have sinned against us."

He continues, "We commit Grace into Your hands, Father, and we pray that You will forever keep her close to Your heart, as she is in ours. In Jesus' name we pray."

Everyone responds, "Amen."

Carter stands at a distance. He feels the pain that he has caused. It is etched on their faces. He is nearly breathless from the crushing guilt that rests on his shoulders. He looks from one family member to another. Innocent David, still in shock, won't fully comprehend the gravity of the situation until much later. Brave Angela, the good wife and mother, watches over her family. Jonathan, a good man, a stalwart in the community and a strong brother is now a broken man. He is trying to ease his family's agonizing pain and yet cherish these last moments remembering Grace.

Carter and Christopher lock eyes. Carter can feel Christopher's anger penetrate him. As Christopher's girlfriend hugs him he slowly positions her so that he can watch Carter. But Carter is now out of his range of vision.

Christopher looks at his dad who responds with a small smile and wink. Christopher manages a faint smile, seeking to hide the guilt that he feels.

Friends approach the family and share hugs, a squeeze of the hand, a pat to the back—anything to show their love for their pastor and this family who have given so much to the community.

As the crowd begins to leave Jonathan whispers to Angela, "Hang in there, dearest. I'll be right back. I love you." She smiles.

He excuses himself and crosses to Carter who stands with his back to the thinning crowd. He is finishing a cigarette as Jonathan approaches and taps him on the shoulder. Carter turns.

"What are you doing here?" Jonathan asks.

"What do you think I'm doing here, Jonathan? I'm mourning the death of my niece."

"How can you stand here, knowing the pain that you've caused our family and this church? A church, may I add, that you've never stepped foot in since I've been pastor."

"Someone was best man at your wedding, remember?" Carter asked.

"You know what I mean."

They stare intensely at each other.

"Today's a tragic day and you're being smart with me," said Jonathan.

Carter breathes deeply and after a long pause looks into his brother's eyes and asks, "Has it occurred to you, for even a moment, that I am hurting also?" Carter pauses. Then he adds, "I've suffered a great loss also."

"Sure, it has occurred to me. But something else has also occurred to me. To all of us, I might add."

Carter says, "I'm listening."

"That this is your fault."

They glare at one another. Carter grits his teeth. The veins in his forehead look as though they may burst.

"That's not fair."

"But true."

Carter leans near his brother's face. "Listen to me. You may be a great pastor, a loving husband and a good father, but you're a poor excuse for a brother."

Jonathan turns to leave, stops and faces Carter again, "I may understand how you feel Carter, but frankly, if it weren't for your drinking..."

"Me?"

"Yes, you," Jonathan comes closer. "You are a hopeless drunk. Just like Dad. And frankly, you both disgust me, hiding inside a bottle."

"I seem to recall one brother who not very long ago joined this hopeless drunk for a lot of drinks."

Jonathan stands tall, trying to intimidate Carter. "Maybe you enjoyed several but not me. I don't have the ability to handle it like you and Dad."

"You were handling them pretty well that day," growled Carter.

"Stop," Jonathan says. "We could go in circles like this all afternoon but my family needs me."

"What about me?" Carter blurts. "I am part of that family."

Jonathan stops. "After what you allowed to happen—on your watch?" He waits a long moment then adds, "Not anymore."

Carter is speechless. The pain of his brother's words ring in his ears. He watches Jonathan join his family. And one by one they enter the family car and drive away.

The mist that had fallen during the service has finally stopped. Carter sees a break in the clouds that reveals a patch of blue sky and a single ray of sunshine. His eyes trace that ray to where it rests on the tiny grave. He picks a yellow rose from a nearby wreath and lays it gently on the mounded earth.

"I'm so sorry, Grace," he whispers. He wipes away the foreign tears and leaves.

CHAPTER 3

INSIDE THE FAMILY LIMOUSINE IT is silent as the family sits lost in sorrow. In the back is Jonathan and Angela. On one side is David and his best friend Russ. Opposite the two boys are Daphne and Stuart, Angela's parents. With their back to the driver are Christopher and his girlfriend, Kym. Each passenger silently remembers Grace in their own way.

Angela: *"Grace, my baby girl. You were my joy. How I wish that God had given us more time. I so miss your sweet smell. It seems only yesterday that I was carrying you. I'll never forget the day you were born. You came kicking and screaming into this world. Little did anyone know that your big personality covered such a gentle, sweet spirit..."*

Jonathan: *"I know I'm supposed to be strong, God, but why my baby? Why Grace? How could you let this happen? I wish Dad could have met her. Damn him. And Carter, that rotten apple fell right off the old man's tree. It will be a cold day in hell before I let that drunk off the hook. I know this isn't right, but..."*

Christopher: *"Why couldn't I have been the one to be 'It', Gracie? I should have set David down. I could have gotten to you sooner. I could have taken the heat. Oh, God, it is not fair. You are not fair. Grace was my best friend. What are we going to do without her? She was the glue that kept us together. And Carter? Damn him. If I had my way...I don't know..."*

David: *"Dear God. I'm sorry. My family hurts. They hurt and I hurt. Why did You allow this? Why do we believe in You if You allow such a horrible thing to happen? Grace was so sweet and she never hurt anyone. Look at Christopher. He's a mess. It is my fault. I should have been the one tagged. I should have been the one! I think I'm going to throw up…"*

Daphne: *"Dear Heavenly Father, please heal our family. Heal my daughter's heart. We don't know why You chose to take our angel, but we have to rely on Your wisdom. It hurts. We hurt. I hurt. Please, help us heal, Lord. Help us heal. I know that You said in Your word that we can lean on You. I'm trying to lean but help… help… please help."*

Stuart: *"Lord, please help us get our hearts into the right place to better understand You. I have no idea what You're up to, but look at our family…we're dying. If You hear my prayers, even though I don't pray much and I'm sorry about that, but if You would help this family, then just maybe…"*

The car turns the corner, passing through the gates, up a long drive and into a lovely development. The small enclave of homes represents both history and influence.

The Matheson's home has been in the family for over one hundred years. Stuart and Daphne inherited it after his mother passed away. They had raised Angela and her brother Fairfax here. After building a smaller but very handsome home on the back acreage, they gave the family home to Jonathan and Angela as a wedding gift.

CHAPTER 4

THE EARLY MORNING DRIZZLE GAVE way to a light fog that now slowly drifts across the mountainside, hanging in trees and floating along the fields. It appears and disappears like a mysterious vapor. The leaves of fall have begun to fill the small front yard. A modest log cabin is tucked against a great expanse of woods. Smoke rises from the old stone chimney. Inside the curtains are partially drawn, adding to the darkness of the day. A black jacket and tie are over the back of a chair and a crumpled memorial bulletin peeks from the breast pocket. Across the room Sampson, the old chocolate Lab, lies sleeping by the fireplace. An antique mission lamp's glow matches that of the fire.

The seemingly cozy room is not that at all, for it houses a broken spirit and wounded soul. Carter is in an old leather chair by the fireplace. A bottle of scotch, a half full glass, a box of bullets, a gun cleaning kit and two guns are lying on the side table. He stares first at the weapon he's had since entering the service. It's a 9-mm Glock; the weapon that took his niece's life. The other, an unregistered 44-magnum Smith & Wesson Revolver, has a slightly shortened barrel and custom teak grip. A rubber cushion is embedded into the underneath of the grip which buffers recoil; however, there is no safety which makes it particularly dangerous in the hands of an inexperienced person. He sits in silence for a long time, then picks it up and meticulously checks it over, examining every part of it. First through the sights, then down the barrel. He turns it over and spins the chamber, checking for bullets. It is empty. He slowly shuts it and places it on the table, startling the dog who raises its head.

"It's nothing, boy. Just the old man digging around the pain barn again."

Sampson goes to Carter and waits for a head rub. Carter obliges and the dog lies down at his feet. "At least you still love me, old boy."

Carter picks up the glass of scotch and takes a long sip. He studies a framed picture of the Matheson family taken several years ago during happier times. In the picture Carter and Jonathan are standing by a grill in the back of Jonathan and Angela's home. Christopher is bouncing a basketball.

Angela, very pregnant, stands smiling at her son. Her hand rests on her tummy. Her best friend, Cheryl Franklin, is next to her laughing and pointing at Angela's baby bulge. "You are soooo big," The memory of her voice echoes years later.

Carter recalls that Cheryl's husband Ricky took the picture. He knows exactly what Ricky was saying as the photograph was taken.

"Jonathan, what in the world are you going to do with a GIRL? I mean, if she doesn't play catch, climb trees, or hunt and fish...you won't know what to do. Speaking of fish, if she doesn't shape up, will you throw her back?" Their laughter echoes in his memory.

Carter returns the picture, takes another drink and picks up the weapon. Suddenly, in one blazingly fast move, as though he'd done this a thousand times, he disassembles it. Then instantly reassembles it and takes one bullet from the box. He loads the revolver, spins the chamber, and without a moment's hesitation puts it to his temple and pulls the trigger.
CLICK.

He freezes. In what is a seeming eternity he breathes deeply and lays the weapon down. Once again, the sound startles Sampson. Carter smiles at the dog and says, "Not today, buddy." He looks into the fire and pats Sampson's head.

"Guess hell's not ready for me yet."

CHAPTER 5

THE STREET IN FRONT OF the Matheson home is lined with cars. In the front several children sit and quietly talk. In the back tables are laden with food and friends are gathered. It looks like a church picnic but is much more subdued. Inside, the Mathesons are accepting condolences from a host of their friends. They are gathered in the front rooms, talking softly and eating food brought by a caring community. On a large wall in the living room a family portrait has been taken down, making room for the slide show being displayed there. David oversees the pictures that are going through a laptop computer and a digital projector, then onto the wall. Images of Grace and the family slowly dissolve from one photograph to another. Quiet piano music plays on the stereo.

Jonathan pats David on the back, saying, "Nice work, son."

David responds softly, "Thanks, Dad."

At that moment a photograph of a laughing Grace dissolves onto the screen. She is being held upside down by Jonathan. David smiles, "I remember that day."

"Yes, summer vacation. She loved our trip to Disney World."

Angela comes, puts her arm around Jonathan and smiles at David. "You've done a really nice job, son. Grace would have loved it."

David smiles, "I think I'm going to get something to eat. Nana in the kitchen?"

"Yes. And do eat," Jonathan says, "I have it on good authority that she has biscuits with your name on them."

Joshua and Deanna Ridge come in. Dee hugs Angela and Josh puts his arm around Jonathan's shoulder.

"Nice service, Pastor," Josh says. "Your family is blessed with a great many friends."

Jonathan, obviously moved, replies, "Yes. It's at a time like this when you appreciate the support of your closest friends."

One by one others approach Jonathan and Angela, hugging them, sharing words of encouragement and their favorite memories of Grace.

Jonathan sees Christopher leaning against the wall, eating a sandwich and talking with his friends. His girlfriend Kym catches Jonathan's eye. She smiles. Christopher attempts a smile. He is distracted by chuckles from his friends who are looking at a photograph of him playing airplane with Grace. He sees the image, smiles and looks at Jonathan who winks at him. Christopher nods and returns to his friends. Angela whispers to Jonathan, then faces the group. She says, "Friends." The room becomes hushed and attention turns to her.

"Thank you so very much for being with us today. This means the world to us. It would have meant the world to Grace also. She loved you all. Just as we do." She pauses. "I'm so thankful to have friends like you." She looks at each one. "I speak for all my family when I say that without your support we could not have made it through our pain. A part of our hearts has been torn away. Your friendship, love and prayers will help us heal. I believe this."

Sniffs are heard throughout the room. Several people have come from outside and are quietly taking their place among the group.

Jonathan puts his arm around Angela. "And we promise, we will all get through this." He takes a deep breath, "Now, if you knew Grace you know that she would want this to be a happy time. You know how much she loved it when we all gathered."

At that moment he sees the image that fills the wall. Grace is bouncing on a trampoline.

"See what I mean?" Looking at the ceiling, he says, "Nice timing, baby!"

They all laugh.

"Now, please eat. There is plenty for everyone, thanks to all of you."

Daphne comes into the room, an apron around her waist and a

wisp of hair in her face. She pushes the hair back.

"Daphne has blessed us with her famous biscuits." He pats his stomach. "As you can see, they're popular with our family." The group enjoys that.

Christopher and his friends are on the front porch as a car slowly approaches the house. The driveway is crowded and Christopher watches as the car comes up the driveway and into the grass. Its back tire catches in the ditch causing the tire to spin. This in turn digs into the lawn. Frowning he mumbles, "What the…"

Carter steps out, tosses a cigarette away, straightens his tie and starts toward the house.

Christopher, obviously not happy, goes inside and directly to Jonathan. With urgency he says, "Dad."

"What is it, son?"

Christopher leans close, "Carter's here. He just drove in."

Jonathan whispers to Angela, "Dearest, I have to…"

Before he can finish Carter comes in and trips over the door mat. Jonathan and the others turn.

"Hey, bro," Carter slurs, "Thought I'd come by and pay my respects."

Jonathan tries to smile, approaches Carter and takes him by the arm. The squeeze is tight enough to be uncomfortable but not so strong as to begin a confrontation. Although Jonathan felt that to be a distinct possibility.

"For the love of God, Carter, can't you see…"

"Of course, I can see, Jonathan," Carter cuts him off, "I'm not drunk."

Jonathan is furious. "That's perfect. Talk about pouring salt into a wound…" Jonathan feels all eyes are on him and he tries to calm the situation.

To those gathered Jonathan says, "Everyone, you know my brother…Carter."

Several nod knowingly, others look with disdain while others have no idea of the situation. Daphne assembles a plate of food and quickly yet discretely crosses to the brothers. Jonathan has not removed his grip on Carter's arm.

Daphne smiles, "Hello, Carter. Nice to see you. I have some lunch for you."

"I like you, Daphne. Thank you."

He takes the plate and looks for a seat. Jonathan anticipates this and says, "Let's go outside…around back…to the deck. You have always enjoyed the deck."

"Wait a minute! Everyone else is watching the slide show. I want to."

He tries to walk away forgetting that Jonathan still has a firm grasp on his arm. He is yanked back. "Let go of my arm," Carter says roughly.

Jonathan shakes his head. "No. Let's go outside."

"Not before I pay my respects to Gracie," Carter mumbles.

Jonathan is simmering. "Really? Your respects?"

Carter leans closer, his breathing heavier. Jonathan smells the alcohol.

"Let…go… of…my…arm," Carter says in a gravelly whisper. "Now."

Hoping to keep things calm, Jonathan releases his arm. "Just behave. That's all I ask."

Carter lightens up a bit. "Your wish is my command, sir," he slurs. Then he makes his way to the center of the room and sits in the middle of the couch. This causes the two women who are sitting there and chatting to shift to the end. He nods.

"Ladies." He pretends to tip a hat. "May I join you?" He picks up one of Daphne's biscuits and says, "My favorite."

One woman smiles but the other shakes her head.

Jonathan is watching in obvious disgust. Angela joins him and says, "Breathe deeply. In. And out. It will be fine. Breathe."

Jonathan smiles at Angela and says, "You are an angel."

Christopher is seething as he stares at Carter. Under his breath he murmurs, "If it's the last thing that I do..."

His girlfriend Kym asks, "What is that, babe?"

"Oh, nothing. I was just saying...there's one last thing I need."

"What?" she asks.

Daphne passes by carrying a plate of biscuits fresh from the oven. He takes one. "Just one more!" She pretends to slap his hand, smiles and continues on.

In the living room the slide show has stopped and David quickly attends to the laptop. He taps at the keyboard as Carter approaches. David looks up and says, "Hey, Uncle Carter."

Carter rubs the top of David's head and exclaims, " You are really growing up. Look at you. You are going to be tall!"

"Are you kidding me? Christopher's the tall one. I get the brains, and he gets the girl."

Carter chuckles. "Be glad you got the brains. Girls are a dime a dozen."

David continues working on the laptop. A new series of images begin with slightly livelier music. The group notices and looks at the images. David beams as he sees their smiles.

"Yes, I guess," David continues, "I like girls. Kinda. But I like books and computers better."

"Smart boy," Carter says as he scans the room. "I am parched."

"I'll get you some of Grandma's sweet tea. That'll do the trick." David says and he's gone.

"Not exactly what I was thinking," Carter mumbles. He looks out the window and spots an oversized cooler on the back deck.

Making his way out he grabs a deviled egg and shoves it in his mouth. Then he takes a second and a third, wiping his hands on his jacket.

Officer Mahler, the local sheriff, comes to Jonathan with his cap under his arm.

"Hello, Johnny. Good to see you. I am so sorry for your loss." He shakes Jonathan's hand and clasps him firmly on the shoulder.

"Thanks, Danny. Good of you to come."

Jonathan sees another large image of Grace appear and he motions toward the display. "She was something else," he says. "I need you to do me a favor."

"I'm one step ahead of you, friend," Mahler interrupts. He scans the room, catches a friend's eye, smiles and nods then returns to his conversation. "I've done some research," he says, lowering his voice, "and I think I may have a way to…" he pauses, watching Carter who is making his way through the crowd, "how shall I say… eliminate a problem," he finishes.

Jonathan is puzzled. Danny motions for Jonathan to follow him to a corner where no one is standing.

"Two words. Negligent homicide."

"What?" Jonathan says, not able to hide the shock on his face.

"We both know your brother's a drunk. Just like your old man was."

"But, Danny, he's not…" Jonathan interrupts.

"I'd be lying if I said that I haven't, on more than one occasion, had to haul him in for disorderly conduct or public drunkenness."

"Yes, but he's not a killer! Sure, I hate him right now…" Jonathan stops, taking a deep breath, then continues. "For *accidentally* killing my daughter or for…" he hesitates, "for allowing her to accidentally have her life taken." He stops. "You're killing me, Danny," he says very quietly.

Danny says, "Sorry. Sorry. You're right. I'm being insensitive. Sorry, I'll drop it. I was just trying to help."

"And I appreciate it, Danny. You and I go a long way back. You've always looked out for me and my family, but…" He shakes his head, "I just don't know about something that severe. There must be a better way."

A crashing sound comes from the backyard and several people look to see what happened.

"What the…?" Mahler asks.

Christopher approaches with fire in his eyes. "Dad, it's Carter. Again. He's out back. Having a few. He fell flat! He will never stop, will he?"

Jonathan feels deeply for his son. He pats Mahler on the arm, nodding for him to follow. "Come with me, please?" Jonathan asks.

Christopher starts to follow but Jonathan stops him, saying, "Son, please. Stay here and keep everyone calm. I'll take care of this."

"But..." Christopher said.

"Please? Get your mother," he hesitates, "and let's start easing this along. It's been a long day. Please?" He smiles.

Christopher sighs and nods, "Yes, sir."

CHAPTER 6

JONATHAN AND DANNY GO OUTSIDE just as Carter is getting up from the ground. His trousers are grass stained, his tie askew and blood is on his lower lip. Sam Lowell is the local high school football coach, Navy Reserve representative, and a man whose hefty size is to be reckoned. He looms over Carter. His fists are at the ready for another punch.

"It's his fault," Carter shouts. "I just wanted another beer and he punched me."

Jonathan looks questioningly at Sam.

"Pastor, do I look like someone who goes around picking a fight?"

Jonathan sees his fists, turns to Danny and says, "Well…"

"What I mean is, you know me…" He relaxes his stance. "I'm not a trouble-maker. But I don't like being pushed! And I really don't like my girlfriend being hit on." He glares at Carter.

"Give me a break, Sam." Carter brushes his jacket, straightens his tie and runs a hand through his hair. He says to his brother, "Sure, I've had a few. It's been a tough time. For all of us, but…"

"Carter, just…leave," Jonathan interrupts. "I'll walk you to your car." He grabs Carter's arm.

"No!" Carter shouts and jerks his arm away. "I'm not leaving. And…" he turns toward Sam's girlfriend and adds, "I wasn't hitting on you, I was reaching for another beer." He moves toward the cooler and mumbles just enough to be heard, "Although, I'd gladly snag her from grandpa!"

Sam goes for him. Danny jumps in as Sam starts to swing. Jonathan tries to restrain Carter as he is also winding up.

WHACK! Carter connects with Jonathan's jaw. Jonathan falls to the ground. He lifts his head to check his lip. It's bleeding. Jonathan stands, heading for Carter, but is intercepted by Danny and Sam who have double-teamed to keep the brothers apart.

"Okay, okay," Danny shouts. "I think we've all seen enough. Jonathan, go back inside to your family." He grabs Carter, pushing Sam aside. "And you! Let's take a walk!" Danny smiles his best. Several friends are trying to keep things civil and are ushering onlookers inside.

Jonathan is livid. He and Carter duel with their eyes.

"Pastor, I'm sorry," Sam says. "I mean it. I was out of line and shouldn't have let this... loser get me riled up. Should've known a man who lets his niece die would disgrace her wake."

Carter breaks free from Danny and attempts to hit Sam with a flying right hook. He trips on a loose board in the deck and accidentally connects with Jonathan.

WHACK! Carter connects a second time. This time it's Jonathan's eye. Jonathan falls back and into the arms of Sam who catches him before he has a chance to hit the ground.

Mahler shouts to Carter, "Get off of him and out of here." He grabs Carter with his huge hands, spins him around and in one move handcuffs first one wrist, then the other.

Carter shouts, "Get your ..." Danny slams his hand over Carter's mouth, muffling the angry words.

Sam helps Jonathan up as Angela and her father run outside.

"What in heaven's name is..." She sees Jonathan and gasps, "Honey, what is going on?"

Jonathan stands with the help of Sam and uncovers his left eye. Angela gasps again. "Oh my! Let's get inside..."

Jonathan interrupts, "It's okay. I'm alright." Angela swings into action. She gets a nearby towel, opens the cooler, wets the towel and wrings it out. Then she folds ice cubes into it and places it on Jonathan's eye as he sits on a nearby chair.

Stuart looks first at Jonathan then Carter and sternly says. "I cannot believe that two grown men, brothers no less, would be so insensitive as to allow this to happen at…" He looks at Jonathan, "at his daughter's…" and turns to Carter, "…and his niece's wake!" He continues, "This is simply not acceptable. No matter the reason." Stuart nods for Danny to take Carter away.

Danny escorts Carter across the lawn to the squad car. He shouts over his shoulder to Jonathan, "I'll catch up with you later."

Sam sheepishly says to Jonathan, "Sorry again, Pastor. I'll see you on Sunday." And with that, he and his girlfriend are gone.

The other onlookers have left and now only four watch. They are David, Christopher, Kym and Jimmy.

Daphne comes with a first aid kit. She shakes her head and looks at her husband.

Stuart looks at Jonathan. "I know this has been a sad day, a heart breaking day, but you should set the example."

Angela holds the cold compress on Jonathan's eye.

"You know it's his fault, Stuart," Jonathan says. "He is like a volcano that's ready to erupt at any moment."

A short distance away Christopher's best friend, Jimmy, has relished the entire scene. "Nice party." He pauses. "Rough, but nice."

"Settle," Christopher says—without emotion, or even turning his attention away from his dad.

Daphne unwraps a large band aid, which Angela applies to the side of Jonathan's eye.

"Guess it's not a real party until somebody gets hit," Jonathan says. Daphne suppresses a chuckle. He then adds, "Twice."

"Who'd ever think a pastor could turn a wake into a brawl," Angela said.

David and Christopher watch as Carter is being driven away in the sheriff's car.

Officer Mahler cruises down the road with an angry and drunken Carter Matheson handcuffed in the backseat. Danny checks the rearview mirror and grimaces.

"What are you looking at?" Carter asks with disgust.

"Not much," Mahler returns. "Not much at all," he adds.

They drive the rest of the way in silence.

Twenty minutes later they arrive at the station. Danny opens the back door and takes Carter by the arm. "Watch your head," Danny says absently, more from routine than from concern.

With his arms handcuffed behind his back, Carter slowly maneuvers out of the car. They go into the building. Danny nods at the officer on duty.

"Got a live one," Danny says. "Put him in Number Three to cool off."

The officer nods and pushes a button. A loud buzzer sounds and Danny escorts Carter down a short hallway. He opens the door to a small cell and directs Carter to a wooden bench in a windowless room and pushes Carter's shoulder down, forcing him to sit. He then locks his cuffs to a bar behind his back where he will be forced to sit upright until time to leave.

"Make yourself comfortable," Danny growls, shuts the iron door and leaves. A second cell door slams in the distance.

Carter mumbles, "Not exactly the day I had planned."

CHAPTER 7

CHRISTOPHER STANDS AT HIS BEDROOM window overlooking the backyard. Kym sits quietly with her hands folded in her lap and after several minutes she asks, "What is it, Christopher?"

There is no response.

"What has you so angry?" she asks.

"Isn't it painfully obvious?"

"I understand your sorrow for the loss of Grace. But please hear me out before you react; it was an accident. He didn't actually pull the trigger."

He asks, "Are you serious? Accidents don't just happen. Events are put into place by the hand of each of us. Either consciously or unconsciously we create what happens." He turns back to the window.

"Haven't you thought about God in all of this?" Kym asks.

He quickly turns to her, "Do NOT start with that, Kym. Did you see my father out there today? Do you hear him in the pulpit talking about forgiveness, but then he doesn't live it? Just don't..." He stops, suppressing both anger and tears, and turns back to the window.

"Okay." She pauses, "But Chris, he's a man—not God—just a human being...like all of us."

He remains silent.

"Look," she sighs, "I cannot imagine what you're going through. Truly, I can't. I mean, as much as my little brother drives me batty, if I lost him..." She catches her breath. "Well, I...just can't fathom that sort of pain. I'll not pretend to even understand. All I'm saying is this, your dad's just a man and he's suffering as are the rest of us. And as for God's plan, I guess I just think that His hand is in

29

everything and He allows things to happen. His plans are for good and not for evil..." She fears that he doesn't want to listen.

"To give us a future...and a hope," he whispers.

She joins him at the window. Taking his hand she whispers in his ear. "Greater is He that is in us than he that is in the world."

He looks into her eyes and takes her face in his hands. He kisses one cheek, then the other and then her lips. "I love you, Kym."

"I know," she says. "And I'm here for you. I will always be here for you. No matter what."

He looks on his desk at a photograph of him and Grace playing in the yard, turns back to the window and looks toward the distant woods. He finally speaks and tears are in his eyes.

"I suppose I just want someone to take the blame and be punished. And that person should be Carter. It was his fault. He wasn't thinking clearly. Because he's never thinking clearly."

Self-conscious, he wipes away the tears. "I'm not going to cry anymore. In fact, never again. Never."

Kym hugs him. "Chris, crying is okay. Men can cry. It takes a bigger man to cry than not."

"Well, I'm not. I have to be strong. Buck up and take responsibility. Unlike some people."

He becomes even angrier and shouts, "Damn Carter." He goes to his desk, sits in the chair and changes his shoes, trying to mask his emotions.

"Dad told him before, and I heard him, to never ever bring a gun around this house. I understand that he suffers from what happened to him in Vietnam. I get that. But this is America, land of the free and home of the brave." He walks back to the window. "Besides, this is the south. The only people that are going to come out of those woods and shoot us are...well, there aren't any."

"True," she says quietly.

"Well, except maybe the rednecks from way over in the valley."

"What?" she asks, and laughs.

They laugh together now, for the first time all week.

CHAPTER 8

JONATHAN AND ANGELA SIT WATCHING David as he plays with some of his buddies in the backyard. They're riding skateboards up and down a ramp that Jonathan built for the boys two summers ago. Jonathan has a cold compress on his eye. Angela looks through a photo album with pictures of Grace, Christopher and David. Deanna sits next to Angela and comments from time to time about a picture.

"I love this one," Deanna says, laughing. "I remember the vacation. We all went to Myrtle Beach." She tries to recall something. "Oh, yes. You and I had a romance novel spree, reading them one after the other."

"Yes. We thought that they were so steamy," laughs Angela.

"And Josh and I played volleyball with some local high school kids," Jonathan says from beneath the icepack. "We got so sunburned. What were we thinking? Trying to look like bronzed lifeguards?"

"Or impress the girls. Which you did," Deanna pipes in.

"Yes. And you two impressed us," Angela laughs.

Stuart and Daphne come out to say that they are leaving.

"We are heading home. The kitchen is cleaned," Daphne says. "And there are plenty of leftovers."

"You'll be eating mighty fine for several days," Stuart chimes in.

"And dearest," Daphne says to Angela, "please try to keep your boys in line!"

Stuart says to Jonathan, "Hey, Ali, how's your speed bag of a face?"

"Very funny," Jonathan says, lifting the ice bag. "Very funny, indeed. You saw him, I nearly..." He stops, thinks about it, sees that they're not buying that and lets it go. He replaces the icepack.

"Profound," Stuart says.

Jonathan stands as Stuart prepares to leave and Josh walks over to join them.

"Let me ask you men something." Jonathan nods toward a corner of the yard, "Come over here please."

Josh and Stuart join Jonathan. The girls watch for a moment but Angela waves them away.

"Man stuff," she says.

"Whatever," Dee adds.

Jonathan faces the men. "What do you think?" he finally asks.

Stuart and Josh exchange looks, then both turn to Jonathan. "What?" They ask in unison.

"Do you guys think I should press charges against Carter?"

Josh shakes his head.

"You're kidding, right? Son, you can't press charges for an accident," Stuart says firmly.

Jonathan says, "Hold on. Hear me out." He motions for the men to move away from the deck where the girls are sitting.

Christopher and Kym have joined the others.

"I don't want them included right now," Jonathan says softly. "It's too sensitive."

Josh starts to speak, then stops.

"What?" asked Jonathan.

"Look, Johnny, I know your heart. You're a good man. You love your family more than anything. And your church nearly as much. With that alone you shouldn't give this another thought. Think about it. A pastor pressing charges against his own brother...for a death that the brother did not commit?"

Stuart nods in agreement. "He is exactly right. You have your family to think of, your reputation to consider and the effect that it would have on your boys." Stuart looks in the direction of David.

"I know. It's just that..." Jonathan stammers.

" And Christopher?" Stuart states, "You know he's raw right now. He'd likely hold the rope if you chose to hang Carter but that's partly because of his anger. He has lost his baby sister. And his anger is also partly because of...you."

Jonathan is surprised.

"Right. He looks up to you and he wants to pattern himself after you. Maybe not today, or next year, but you know as well as I do that he is forming the man he will become. If you do something that sends this sort of a message...well, I'm just afraid that..."

"No. I get it," Jonathan says. Then he adds, "Although Carter was clearly at fault, I guess I should..."

"Practice what you preach?" Joshua asks.

Stuart and Joshua both nod in agreement.

"I keep thinking that the discipline of jail time would do him good. I know that sounds harsh but it would keep him out of trouble. Danny says that he's had his hands full from time to time with Carter who has been a loose cannon since coming home from Vietnam."

"Just think hard about it. The ramifications could be long lasting," Joshua looks to Stuart for support.

Stuart agrees, then checks his watch.

"Alright. Settled. It's been a heck of a day. We have all had about as much as we can handle. Here's the bottom line. Think of your family first. Then consider the feelings of anger and animosity that you hold against your brother."

"Let's also not forget to be praying for him," Josh suggests. "He's got a sickness, Johnny. And it's likely the same disease your father had."

They start toward the house.

"Jonathan, you're like a son to me and you know that I have your best interest in mind. But think about it. Pray about it. And don't do something you'll regret later," Stuarts says, wrapping his arm around Jonathan's shoulder.

"Vengeance is mine. I will repay, says the Lord," Josh adds.

"Now, pack up the day, put your feet up and be in the moment. Those boys of yours will be grown up and out of here before you know it. Spend time with your family."

"While it's yours to have," Josh adds. All three nod in agreement.

"Besides, it won't bring Grace back, son," Stuart adds.

Jonathan nods. "Thanks, you're right. I couldn't have two better friends."

They wave the boys over as the families prepare to leave.

In moments, the sounds of the day will echo into the trees and the last rays of sun will be swallowed by darkness.

CHAPTER 9

CARTER CONTORTS HIS HEAD TRYING to see his watch that is behind his back. It is eight o'clock. He has been in the holding cell for nearly four hours. He has tried to be patient, however the booze is clearly wearing off. He has an intense need to use a bathroom, he is hungry and decides that it is time to make some noise. He shouts in the direction of the office. "Somebody! Anybody...I have to use the can!"

He waits for a response. Nothing. "I've been in here all afternoon and I have no idea why I'm here," he shouts.

No response, nothing but a phone ringing in the distance and the faint sound of someone tapping at a keyboard.

Officer Danny Mahler has heard him. The other three officers in the station have heard him. It would be hard not to—it's a small station, in a small town with a small staff. And a small diversion makes for entertainment at this late hour.

"Guess you should've thought about that when you were getting sauced at your niece's wake," Mahler snorts.

Officer Reddick adds, "I heard that." A sly grin spreads across his face. He looks look like the Joker from a Batman movie but minus the makeup.

Mahler grins. "Hey, just watching after my friend. And this one," nodding in the direction of the shouting voice, "is nothing but trouble."

"As I always say, trouble is as trouble does." Officer Reddick grimaces.

"Hey, I'm gonna go right through these cell bars if one of you don't help me out," Carter shouts.

Mahler pushes back from his desk and says, "I'm pulling a double and I have to put up with his mouth!"

Reddick grunts, "What's he actually charged with anyway?"

Mahler looks from Rorie to Reddick, "Actually, nothing. I mean, he did hit Pastor Matheson. Twice. I am thinking drunk and disorderly conduct." He seems as though he isn't sure and adds, "Barely worth the hassle."

Office Rorie says, "Make it something worth the hassle or you really should cut him loose."

Reddick nods and his same wicked grin is back as he looks at Rorie and shrugs. "He's right. I guess. Besides, cut him loose and one of us can go. It's deader in here than…" He looks at Mahler and catches himself, "Sorry."

Mahler takes keys from the board and says, "It ticks me off that Jonathan's brother can cause so much turmoil…when he was the one who…" He stops, deep in thought.

"Hey, Mahler. Come on, you know you got nothing. Let me outta here and I'll be on my way. Promise I'll be good." He laughs.

Mahler shouts, "Hold on." He tosses the keys to Rorie, "Take him to the john. I just thought of something. Go ahead. Let him go. Then you can go."

"Sweet," says Rorie who tosses the newspaper on his desk and goes to Carter's cell.

Mahler looks at Reddick and quietly says, "Hang on. I got an idea."

"What?"

"You're bored. You'll like it," Mahler jokes.

Reddick shrugs.

A fresh-faced rookie named Scott comes in. He has an oversized thermos in one hand, a briefcase in the other and a crossword puzzle book tucked under his arm. He nods to Mahler and Reddick. Mahler looks at the clock. It's 9:55.

"What's up?" Mahler says as he punches in a phone number.

Officer Scott shyly returns, "Time to play cop."

36

Mahler leans back and speaks into the phone, "Hey, it's me."

"Third shift's a bore. Have fun." Reddick says, gathering his things.

Mahler says into the phone, "Wanted to see how you were." He motions for the others to be quiet.

Officer Scott whispers to Reddick, "I like this shift. It's quiet."

Mahler continues, "I have an interesting idea that could help your situation."

CHAPTER 10

ANGELA AND CHRISTOPHER SIT AT the kitchen table. Jonathan is at the sink, talking on the phone.

"What situation are you talking about?" Jonathan asks.

Listening intently, he looks at Angela. Smiling, he gives a thumbs up and waves for her to go back to her conversation.

"Yes, I'm here. We've just finished a very late dinner."

Angela motions for Christopher to follow her to the living room.

"Yes, been a long day alright." He pats Christopher on the head and Christopher throws a fake punch to Jonathan's face and chuckles.

"Yep...I'm here. Yes, Mama Daphne's pie for dessert."

Christopher follows Angela, looking at Jonathan who smiles at him.

Lowering his voice, Jonathan continues, "If I know you, you're up to something."

Officer Mahler's tired eyes watch Rorie as he escorts Carter from the restroom back to his cell.

"Hey!" he loudly whispers to Rorie and waves him over. Back to the phone, he says, "Sorry. Just wrapping things up at the station. Look, Johnny, I know it's been a long and painful day, so I'll not keep you. Go be with your family. Get some rest. We can chat tomorrow."

Jonathan is puzzled, but compliant. "Sounds good. And thanks for being there and helping today. Your friendship means a lot to me. Goodnight."

"Was that Danny?" Angela asks as she comes back into the room.

Jonathan nods.

She looks at her watch, "What was that about…at this hour?"

"He's just concerned," Jonathan replies, "That's Danny watching out for us."

"He's a good man. Ready to go to bed?"

"Let's call it a day."

She turns off the lights, "It's a day."

"Corny. But so cute."

They head upstairs.

CHAPTER 11

AT THE STATION OFFICER MAHLER motions for Carter to sit in the chair next to his desk. "Look, I'm sorry about all that nonsense today. I was just doing my job," Mahler says.

Carter frowns. "Your job is to incarcerate a family member at a loved one's memorial service?"

Danny leans back in his chair, "One that's been drinking and starting fights, yes."

Carter leans forward, "Hold on just a minute."

Danny puts both hands up in mock surrender, "You hold on. You were out of line. I could have arrested you for assault and battery."

Carter replies, "Whatever."

Danny adds, "Or for drunk and disorderly conduct." He pauses for effect. "The third time."

Carter is silent.

Danny continues, "But, instead, I thought it would be best for all parties involved to simply bring you here, let you dry out and cool off. Which I see that you've done. And now, go home and get some rest."

Carter stares at him.

"And let bygones be bygones. I'll let it go if you will." Danny says, through a forced smile.

Carter squints at Danny, "Okay. I see your point. Probably not the worst idea on your part." He rubs his wrists and says, "But, the handcuffs? For nearly the whole afternoon? A little much, don't you think?"

Danny leans forward, extending his hand to shake. "I suppose so. Sorry. Truce?"

Carter says, "Alright." He stands, pats his pockets and asks, "My car keys? Heck, my car. Where did I…" he trails off.

Danny nods at Reddick.

"You'll recall, if you can," he smiles, "that we drove you here? Your car's still at your brother's house."

"Oh, yeah," he mumbles, "Maybe I did have a few."

"Officer Reddick is going to drive you back to get your car."

Reddick motions toward the door and Carter joins him.

Mahler adds, "I need you to promise me something, Carter."

Carter asks, "What's that?"

"Go home. And don't go knocking on your brother's door."

Carter starts to say something but Mahler interrupts, adding, "Or his face."

Carter chuckles and holding his hand replies, "Boy Scout's honor." He goes outside.

Reddick waits for Mahler's directions. Mahler opens the door and shouts to Carter, "Get in the middle car." Then he says quietly to Reddick, "Take him over to Johnny's…"

He watches Carter reaching for the back door. Mahler shouts again, "Carter. Ride up front. You're no criminal."

Carter gets in the front seat.

Mahler continues, under his breath, "…then, ask him if he'd like to head over to Mack's for a nightcap. Tell him you're sorry about the rough housing. Tell him that you're off duty, and it has been a long day, and how about we stop and have just one drink."

Reddick grins and nods. "Done."

Mahler adds, "You got the idea."

Then, more loudly he calls to Carter, "See you, Carter. Take care!" He waves.

Reddick gets in the car and they leave.

Mahler checks his watch. It's 10:30. He then shouts, "Officer Scott, batten down the hatches, stay alert and we'll see you in the morning. I'm out of here."

Scott salutes, "Yes, sir. Thank you, sir."

Mahler gives a half salute and leaves.

In the car he makes a call, listens for a moment and says, "Hey buddy. Just wanted you to know that I have your back covered. Not to worry about anything. I'm taking care of it. Later."

CHAPTER 12

THE MATHESON HOME IS QUIET. Jonathan makes his rounds downstairs, checking doors and turning off lights. All is in order and he goes upstairs. He sees light under Christopher's door. He first stops at David's room and peeks through the partially open door. He's out cold. A book is open and spread across his chest. Jonathan goes in and stands at the foot of his bed, smiling at his sleeping future professor. He picks up the book and lays it on the desk. As he reaches to turn out the light he sees Angela smiling in the doorway.

She joins him at the bedside and whispers, "What a smart young man he is."

Jonathan nods, "Yes! Takes after his mom."

She playfully swats at him and goes into the hall.

Jonathan turns off the light and closes the door. He whispers to Angela, "You go ahead. I'll check on the musician now." She covers a yawn, blows him a kiss and tiptoes toward their room.   He taps on Christopher's door.

"Come in," he mumbles.

Christopher is stretched out on a bed that is covered with several CDs and the ever-present iPod.

"I'm getting ready to hit the hay. How about you?" Jonathan asks.

Christopher stretches, yawns and says, "Yeah, in a minute. Just listening to some music I haven't heard in a long time. Some of Grace's favorites." He sighs.

There is a long silence, then Christopher says, "I only wish that the last image I have of Grace wasn't the one I see...every...single... night." He lies motionless, staring at a homemade CD with Grace's handwriting on it.

Jonathan nearly chokes. He pauses for a long moment before saying, "I can't imagine, son. I really can't. And I'm so sorry. She was so special."

Christopher nods. "I really miss her," he says quietly. "The spoiled little brat!"

Fighting back tears Jonathan smiles, thinking how young, innocent and scared he looks. The image of the headstrong, cocky teenager is silent...for now.

Christopher breathes deeply then nervously starts sorting through the other discs.

At the window Jonathan stands staring at the full moon. The moonlight looks like a light blanket of snow on the lawn.

"Dad?"

"Yes, son."

"Why did Carter hit you?"

Jonathan quickly turns, "It was an accident. He tripped. I was just in the wrong place at the wrong time."

"But he hit you twice."

"Well, that second one was probably less of an accident."

"Really?" He grins at his dad.

"Really," Jonathan answers, without missing a beat.

Silence.

Then Jonathan says, "Don't get me wrong, son, I was angry. And I was certainly prepared to exert a little force if necessary, but I just thought..."

"If he shows up drunk, nobody would blame you if you were to swing," Christopher says.

"Something like that. My biggest problem with Carter—and it's always been—is that he..." Jonathan stops to think about it, then nods his head and continues, "You're a young man now, Christopher, I don't have to hide things from you as I did when you were younger. Or, as I try to protect David now, so..."

Christopher interrupts, "Dad, David is much smarter than I am. Than all of us, probably, I don't think you have to worry about protecting him too much. What's the saying, 'wise beyond his years?'"

They both chuckle and Jonathan says, "I suppose you're right. He did manage to grow up faster than you or Grace. Come to think of it, faster than just about all of us."

"True."

"What I was going to say is that there has always been strife between your uncle and me." Jonathan pulls a chair from Christopher's desk and sits.

"Duh."

"You and your brother were raised in such a different environment. You have had a much quieter atmosphere in which to grow and also many more opportunities than we had."

"Being the youngest, were you Granddad's favorite?"

Jonathan laughs nervously and says, "Hardly. And it's quite likely... and I don't know if I've ever admitted this aloud before...but it's likely that is what has been the main bone of contention between us. Dad liked him more. They understood one another better. And frankly, they never really made any bones about it."

Christopher is silent for a while before asking, "That hurt you didn't it, Dad?"

Jonathan sighs deeply and says, "Yes, son. I suppose it did. Maybe it still does." He smacks the bottom of Christopher's feet, "Well, let's get to bed. Been a long day, hasn't it?"

Christopher hugs his father. Jonathan is taken aback. He doesn't remember the last time his son has hugged him.

"Thank you, son." Jonathan wants to show his appreciation but knows that if he says much Christopher will retreat into his teenage shell. As Christopher moves away he says, "And you know what? It wasn't that bad. Dad was a Marine officer. Carter was in the Army. There's a certain bond between men like that." Jonathan starts to leave but not before admitting, "I guess between that and Carter being athletic and me being bookish, him being good with the ladies and me being a nerd...well, it made that much greater difference."

47

Christopher feigns surprise, "Really?"

Jonathan acts as if he's going to punch his arm. Christopher dodges and they laugh.

"Smart kid!"

"I don't remember Granddad very well but I would imagine, having heard some of the stories from Carter, that your dad had some feelings about your being a preacher too."

Jonathan replies, "Oh, you don't know the half of it." He feels the walls of discomfort closing in and changes the subject. "Well, enough of this. I'm exhausted and I'm sure that you are. And there's school tomorrow."

"Great." Christopher swaps one tee-shirt for another nearly like it and flops on the bed.

"Son, thanks for listening. I appreciate it."

Christopher nods and says, "Whatever."

"Good night. See you in the morning."

"Night, Pops."

As Jonathan closes the door, he adds, "It will get better, I promise." No response. But he wasn't expecting one. He and his oldest have just had a rare and insightful moment, one that was really needed.

At his bedroom door he hears his cell phone chirp. He starts to go downstairs to answer it but then thinks, "It can certainly wait until morning."

CHAPTER 13

THE CROWD AT THE BAR has thinned considerably. The only patrons left are two locals finishing a round of pool in the far corner, a long-time regular at the end of the bar and the "loud party" at the opposite end of the bar. It was obvious that Officer Reddick and Carter had wasted no time and appeared to be inebriated. Mahler was having another double as the bartender shouts, "Last call."

"What will it be, gentlemen?" the bartender Frank asks. He looks more fierce than he actually is. The tattooed arms, scruffy salt and pepper goatee, thick-as-a-tree-stump build and bald head make him look like a tough guy. But everyone knows differently. Frank is a family man with four kids. One is in college, one is ready to graduate high school and the twins are in middle school. At home is his bride who was his high-school sweetheart and she keeps him honest and interested.

Mahler puts up three fingers. Reddick says, "That's what I'm talking about," and he looks at Mahler behind Carter's back.

Carter waves Frank off, saying, "No way. I've had enough. And I gotta drive." He looks at Reddick, then Mahler and adds, "Wouldn't want to get arrested." The word arrested was just slurry enough to warrant a wink from Mahler to Reddick.

Frank grins, waiting for directions. "What'll it be, boys? Gotta get home to the missus."

On cue and in unison, they say, "Maybe one more." They laugh and Frank pours a round.

They empty the drinks and say in unison, "Whew!"

Strong drink has a way of distorting reality. Little do people know that drinking and driving can bring the threat of each breath being their last. And nobody knows it better than these officers. They had both seen too many highway deaths caused by too much drink.

CHAPTER 14

JONATHAN STUDIES HIS FACE IN the mirror. Lines of anxiety have burrowed deeply into his face over the past several days. He wipes his face, puts the toothbrush away and turns off the bathroom light.

Angela is peaceful as Jonathan gently pulls back the covers and slides into bed. "How's our rock star?" she whispers.

Startled, Jonathan says, "Oh, sorry. Did I wake you?"

"No. I was trying to stay awake."

Jonathan waits and then says, "He's...trying." Propped on one arm, he thinks a bit more and adds, "We had a moment. Perhaps the first in a very long time."

She turns to him and he kisses her gently on the forehead. She sighs. With great tenderness he says, "I'm so proud of you. You're such a strong mother and an incredible wife."

She whispers, "Thank you."

He kisses her and whispers, "I love you."

"I love you, too."

"By the way, in case you forgot..."

"Yes?" she asks.

"Happy anniversary, sweetheart."

"Oh, I nearly forgot. And I know that's horrible, especially for a wife, but honestly..."

"This has been the hardest time in our life. And I had been meaning to say something, but..." He hangs his head.

"What?"

"You will think that I'm awful."

She touches his face, "Honey, you are the kindest, most loving and wonderful man a wife could ever ask for. Thank you for loving me

51

through everything."

"The pleasure is mine. Trust me. And I'll tell you what..."

"Tell me!" She smiles.

"You and I are going away for a nice, romantic weekend to celebrate our years of pure bliss together." He kisses her again.

"Great! Maybe not always bliss but most definitely happy."

"I'll take happy."

"I love you so much. And despite our losses and pains, we have enjoyed some of the best moments a person could ever hope for and..." She starts to tear up. "Sorry."

"It's alright, baby."

She continues, "I would change only one thing...and we both know that is something only God has control over. But everything else has been perfect."

"I have been thinking about all the good things in our life. And... some bad ones."

"And?" Angela asks.

"It's Christopher that concerns me most."

"Why?" she quietly asks.

"Two things, really. How what he witnessed will affect him...in the long term."

"He's pretty resilient, Jonathan." She curls close to him and adds, "And, he's strong like you."

He sighs deeply and quietly says, "And..."

"Yes?" she finally asks.

"And...if he'll ever be able to forgive my brother."

After a long silence Angela says, "He will likely be watching to see what you choose to do."

CHAPTER 15

CARTER, REDDICK AND MAHLER STUMBLE out of the bar and head for their cars. Reddick's is a brand new Dodge Charger, dressed up with all the latest law enforcement details. Mahler drives the quintessential working man's truck: a Ford 350 Super Duty 4X4 with winch, light rack and all the bells and whistles. Carter's? A 1970 Chevy Impala. Classic and clean, it runs great but is nothing fancy.

The three stand breathing the night air and trying to decide if they are sober enough to drive. Mahler and Reddick watch as Carter drops his keys, stumbling slightly as he bends to pick them up.

"Okay, gentlemen. Don't know about you but I'm pretty wasted," says Mahler, laughing.

"Ditto," Reddick says.

Carter adds, "And me maketh, I mean, makes three."

Reddick nods to Mahler. With concern Mahler asks, "Can we give you a ride home?"

Carter waves them both off, "No, the fresh air sobered me up pretty good."

Reddick asks, "Sure? We can get your car tomorrow...like we did today." He grins.

Carter refuses. "I'm good. But thanks."

"Alright. I'm going home. I want to enjoy my day off tomorrow, which starts with sleeping until noon," Reddick says.

Mahler says, "You? Oh, that's right! You get the day off, while the boss here has to work first shift. And that's after working a double today." He looks at Carter and says, "Thanks to you."

Carter grins and says, "I'll see you two." He heads to his car, saying to Reddick, "Thanks for the drinks."

Mahler shouts, "Hey, Carter. Sorry again about today!"

"No biggie. You probably did me a favor." With that he lights a cigarette and drives away.

Reddick and Mahler stand watching Carter's car.

"So?" Reddick asks.

"Nice work. For Part One," Mahler says with a completely sober voice. "Ready for Part Two?"

"What do you think?"

Carter looks in his rearview mirror and watches as his drinking buddies fade from sight. "Nice guys. Right?"

Mahler asks, "See his brake light?"

Reddick sees that one of the lights appears to be out. "Yes."

"Well, I busted one out just before I joined you guys tonight."

"Oh! Really?" Reddick says.

Carter tosses his cigarette out the window, checks the rearview again and starts to whistle.

"So, why don't you give our pal there, a little taste of Part Two," Mahler says, as he gets in his truck. "And call me in the morning. I'm bushed."

"Roger. Will do."

Carter crests the hill and the lights of the bar disappear in the night. Then, as if on cue, a pair of headlights come over the hill. He steps on the gas and inches up to 60, 65 and then 70. He checks the rearview once more and, sure enough, red and blue flashing lights illuminate the dark sky.

Mahler drives in the opposite direction but not without looking at the chase already in progress. He grins. "That'll serve you right, Carter. Stay away means stay away." He shoves a plug of tobacco in his mouth, cranks up the stereo and heads home.

Reddick quickly catches up with Carter, who eventually slows, pulls over and parks. There are no lights visible for miles around. Reddick approaches the car. Carter's window is down.

"May I see your license and registration?" Reddick asks.

Carter stares and asks, "What?"

"You were exceeding the speed limit," he says with no emotion. "And your brake light is out."

Carter looks at Reddick. "You are kidding me, right?"

"It's Officer Reddick." He doesn't move.

Carter looks at the surroundings and surveys the land.

Reddick's left hand reaches in the window as his right hand touches the gun in his holster. "Come on, sir. Pass it out and we'll be on our way."

"Okay. Got it. You're a practical joker, right?" Carter chuckles. "Where's Mahler?"

"Sir, are you going to give me your license and registration or am I going to have to arrest you."

"What the...?" he snorts. "Okay, okay, hold on just a..." He reaches behind the visor, pulls out two pieces of paper and hands them to the officer. Then he looks directly into the officer's eyes and says, "Are you so bored that you..."

Reddick ignores him and walks toward the squad car. Carter watches the side mirror, waiting for him to step into the car. He flips on his high beams and revving the engine says, "And a one, and a two and a three..."

He glances back at Reddick who is now out of the cruiser.

Carter throws the car into gear and hits the gas. From behind, he hears Reddick shout, "Hey! Stop!"

In minutes, Carter is back up to 60, then 65. In the rearview, the high beams from Reddick's car nearly blind him. His flashers are going full speed and Reddick is closing in.

"Come on," he says. "I got nothing to lose."

His car reaches 70, then 75. Reddick is quicker than Carter thought. He's right next to him. Carter watches the tree line. He knows this area like the back of his hand.

Suddenly, he slams on the brakes and Reddick whizzes past. Quickly, Carter throws the car into reverse and heads down a side gravel road. More quickly than Carter had expected Reddick has turned around and is hot on his trail at about four car lengths behind.

"Just enough," Carter says. His eyes scan the dark wooded terrain. The road curves right, then left, then right again, causing Reddick to slow down. "Don't know these parts, do you, Officer Redneck?"

Carter checks the horizon and cuts down another off-the-beaten-path road, one that only seasoned deer hunters know about. Evidently Reddick didn't know, for he slowed down just enough to give Carter the chance to execute his grand finale.

At the last minute he cuts the wheel hard right and goes pummeling down the side of a mountain. He holds on for dear life.

Reddick's car slides on loose gravel and comes to a grinding halt. His front tire hangs precariously off the edge. He can't see much but he does see Carter's one brake light as the car goes bouncing down the side of the mountain. He gets out of his car as Carter's car jumps a small ravine, goes airborne, crashes into a tree and comes to rest on the edge of what looks to be a cliff.

"What the hell?" Reddick gasps. "Stupid drunk!"

He reaches in his car, clicks a button, and speaks into the microphone, "Mahler, Mahler. It's Reddick. Do you hear me?"

Ten seconds pass and the radio chirps, "Yeah, I hear you. Having fun?"

Reddick says, "Change to Channel Alpha. Gotta talk." He knew headquarters could hear their conversation, so Reddick and Mahler had a scrambled secondary channel they used for privacy.

"Roger."

Reddick turns the knob. In a few seconds Mahler's voice comes on.

"Reddick. It's Mahler. What's up?"

"You wouldn't believe it. That crazy loon had me chasing him down these back roads."

"Yeah, so?" Mahler shoots back. "I'm nearly home and I wanna catch five minutes of ESPN before calling it a day."

"Carter went off the side of a mountain."

"What?" Mahler shouts. "You have got to be kidding me."

"No, I'm serious. I had him stopped, then he handed me a bogus L and R. Before I could turn around he was gone. Flying. Into the night. So..."

"So, you did what? How did he go from sitting on the side of the road, waiting for you to haul him back and tuck him in for the nighty-night, to..."

"If you will shut up, I'll explain," Reddick shouts.

"Hold it, Dennis. Don't forget who you're talking to."

"Sorry. Anyway...he took off. I chased. He was going pretty fast. I tried to catch up. Next thing I know he pulls off onto a road that I had no idea was there. Then boom...off the side of the mountain he goes!"

"Which one? Where are you?"

Reddick looks around and then looks in his car and says, "Damn."

"What?" Mahler asks.

"First of all, I don't know this area. I've only lived here a year, Sarge. Second of all, my GPS is in the shop. I got no clue where I am."

Mahler sighs and says, "Okay. Do this. Go check on our runaway madman. I have to imagine he's pretty banged up, if not worse. Check his stats then call me back. I'm going in the house. I just got here. But call me!"

"Roger."

Reddick inches down the side of the mountain. His Mag Light brightens the path pretty well. He trips over a tree stump, falls and slides about 10 yards. Getting up he continues down the mountain side. The car is about 100 yards away. He can hear the radiator hissing in the dark.

"Damn drunk," he mumbles.

As he approaches the car he can see it must have jumped a short ravine. Then, while airborne for what looked like 20 or 30 yards, it hit a tree. He keeps walking. Approaching the car, he sees that a tree has crashed into the front window, pierced through the car and is sticking out the rear window.

"Nice work, Evel Knievel."

Something doesn't feel right. He shines the light in the car. Carter is not there. He double-checks. First the front seat, the floor and then the back seat. Nothing.

He walks to the front of the car and stops just in time. Shining the light down, he sees that the car is dangling on the side of a cliff and hanging over a lake. The lake is 200 hundred or more yards below. A lake that Reddick didn't know was there.

With heart pounding he says, "Oh, boy! That ain't good." He looks from the car to the black water below and says, "For any of us." Back at the squad car he reaches for his cell phone and dials Mahler. Two rings and Mahler answers.

Mahler is spread eagled on his bed. ESPN plays. A hound dog is asleep next to him. "Talk to me," Mahler barks.

Over some static Reddick says, "Not good."

Mahler asks. "Dead?"

"No. Gone," Reddick says.

Mahler sits up. Clearly awake he asks, "Gone? What do you mean, gone?"

Reddick's mouth is dry. He licks his lips. But it doesn't help. "What I mean is, he's gone. As in vanished. I have to imagine by the force of the crash and the fact that there's a tree shoved through his front windshield, that he's on the bottom of the lake by now."

"You have to be kidding!" Reddick holds the phone away from his ear as Danny shouts.

After a long silence, Mahler says calmly and with no emotion, "Okay. Go home. Get some rest. Needless to say, do NOT mention this to ANYONE. It is 1:30 now...I'll see you at that spot in four hours. That's 5:30 AM. Text me the...oh, your GPS...Figure out where you are and text me your location."

Before Reddick can sign off, Mahler has hung up, exhausted. He knows that it's going to be a rough night, followed by a stress-filled day. Sighing, he mutters, "So much for a day off."

CHAPTER 16

REDDICK HAS ARRIVED THIRTY MINUTES early. He wants to scout the area again, this time in the light and before his boss arrives. He needs to be prepared; his reputation is on the line and his job is in the balance. He had not known that the lake was there. He was a city boy who had relocated from Jersey. He had grown tired of the cold, especially the snow. He sips gas station coffee and it is bitter. There's a slight nip in the air at this hour. Fall is just around the corner. He thinks about how cold the lake must be. How cold it must have been last night, to a drunken old guy who had no business challenging Mahler. The good old boy network, he thinks. No different than up north. Only the accents are different.

The hillside descent goes much smoother and more quickly than last night. It helps to be able to see where you're going. The forest is peaceful with sounds of an occasional bird, a scurrying squirrel in the dense underbrush and his boots pounding the earth in rapid descent. Approaching the car he can see the exact route it took. He looks back up at his car. He estimates it at about 200 or so yards from the road to the ditch where the car... That's odd. The path looks practically like a ramp. He dismisses it as coincidence and continues his investigation.

Seeing the projection of the car was like looking at a rudimentary ski jump, rough and thick with rotted trees and leaves. He spots the broken tail light and wonders if this was such a good idea. In fact, he is beginning to wonder if this whole idea was a good idea. Sure, he was a rotten egg, but it was the way he chose to live his life. He wasn't so sure right now if the guy that he had gotten drunk last night, by the orders of his superior, was such a bad guy after all.

Carter had lost his niece. What must he have been going through, knowing that his niece died because of his stupidity. No wonder he drinks. Think about it: Vietnam Vet. Doesn't have a job. No family of his own. Seems to leave destruction in his path wherever he goes. He shakes his head, "Poor sap…" It's then that he sees something.

As he walks around the car he notices something that he hadn't last night. He had been halfway drunk, it was dark and he'd had a big scare. Leaning inside the driver's window he sees blood all over the steering wheel. Following the trail of blood spread across the dash and what used to be the windshield, he approaches the hood, careful not to lose his footing. This is the spot where he was so frightened last night. The edge of the cliff. Exactly where the car now rests. He observes the smear pattern of the blood, following it from the windshield to the edge of the hood. Peering over, it's easy to assume that he was thrown from the front seat, through the windshield and into the water below.

Or, maybe he couldn't get out of the driver's door. He looks at it. A huge rock in the lip of the cliff has the door jammed shut. Maybe he tried to crawl out, thinking he would land on the ground. He looks over the hood, being careful to hold tightly to the fender of the car. Or Carter may have dropped straight down. He estimated that drop to be somewhere around 150, maybe 200 yards. The cliff was straight down into a pile of rocks. Or, a few feet further out, he would have dropped right into the water. Carter must have smashed on the rocks. There is no sign of him now.

"Yo! Reddick!" Mahler shouts from atop the hill. Reddick turns and waves. Mahler starts the descent.

"Morning." Reddick says.

"Uh huh." Mahler replies. He rubs his left temple and stands silently.

"As you can see…" Reddick starts.

"Whoa, Boy Scout. Give me a second. My head is pounding and spinning with details, and my stomach is churning. So please give me a little time while I try to study this and figure out how we're going to fix it."

Reddick looks at him, starts to say something but keeps quiet.

Mahler walks around the car, sees the broken tail light and looks at Reddick. He notes that the car is clearly dug in yet is hanging on the edge of the cliff. Pulling it off would be possible but very challenging. He notes the trajectory of the tree and it is straight through the car.

"He must've been going pretty fast," Mahler remarks.

Reddick sticks his head in the back driver's side window and says, "That's for sure." Then adds, "And how he managed to hit this fallen tree and drive it straight into the windshield, then through the car..."

"Yeah, right. Like it was planned. That's about as plausible as..." he hesitates, looks around inside the car and frowns at him as he sees something on the floorboard.

"What's this?" he asks as he reaches in and pulls out a worn pancake holster and an empty box that used to contain hollow point bullets. He holds them up for Reddick to see.

"What have we here?" Mahler sarcastically says, "And don't tell me a holster and an empty bullet box." He walks to the back of the car and lays the evidence on the trunk. "Interesting," he looks at the woods, as though Carter could be watching them. He then walks to the driver side, looks in at the blood from this angle and his eyes follow the trail of blood to the edge of the hood.

Reddick interrupts his thought, "Way I see it is..."

Mahler returns the interruption with, "I don't want to hear your way. Give me a minute." He peers over the edge of the cliff to the water below.

"Don't see Carter." He looks back at the top of the hill and his eyes follow the path of the car to where it sits now. He looks back in the car, through the windshield, along the hood and leans back over the edge, being careful to hold the fender as he does so. He is there for a long moment.

"Yep. He's dead. There is no way in heaven or on earth that he survived this crash. If he was going as fast as you said..."

Reddick interrupts with, "40, maybe 50 miles an hour." He points to the road high on the ridge, adding, "And that's after leaving the road doing 60, maybe 65."

"Yep," Mahler grunts. "And drunk, and having just been responsible for little Gracie's death..." He looks straight at Reddick. "I don't have to tell you how that fact alone breaks my best friend's heart. And mine, for that matter."

"Understood, sir." Reddick respectfully replies.

"I was her godfather," Mahler says.

Looking confused, Reddick asks, "Really?"

"Yes. Really."

Getting back into his truck, he says, "Follow me. We've got a 'cover up' to take care of."

The bravado from last night has vanished. Reddick looks at him and softly says, "Yes, sir."

CHAPTER 17

JONATHAN SIPS THE LAST OF his coffee, places the mug in the dishwasher and stares out the window. "Looks like today is going to be a beauty," he says with a lilt in his voice.

Angela is cooking pancakes on the griddle and bacon in the iron skillet. "I think you're right, love," she says and leans over for a kiss as Jonathan starts to leave. She adjusts his tie and says, "My hero."

He smiles, "Thank you, madam."

He turns to David whose nose is buried in the newspaper. "My little professor. You are the only grade school kid I know who reads the newspaper seven days a week."

"You have to stay on top of things…if you're going to be on top of things," David quips.

"True, son. So very true. Now, where's your brother?"

"Probably still in bed. It's only 6:30. You know how he likes to push it."

"I leave at seven," Angela interjects. "If you're not ready, you're not going."

"Son, go get your brother. Tell him…" he thinks for a moment. "Tell him, Simon Cowell's at the door and is casting for the new American Idol. That should do the trick." He grins at David who is already across the room and heading upstairs.

Angela chuckles, "You're too funny."

"Got to laugh to keep from crying." He kisses her again, takes his briefcase from the counter and heads for the door. "If it weren't for the men's Prayer Breakfast…" he eyes the bacon, "I sure would have loved to devour your bacon, Mrs. Matheson."

She tosses a hand towel at him, saying, "Scoundrel!" in her best Scarlet O'Hara voice.

He catches the towel, tosses it on the table, blows her a kiss and says, "Call you later!"

"Love you!" she calls as the door closes. Through the door she hears a muffled, "Love you more."

She smiles at Christopher. David returns to his newspaper and pancakes. Christopher shuffles to the coffee maker and pours a cup of coffee.

"Morning, American Idol Man," she says to Christopher and looks at David, who grins.

"Very funny, Ma." He turns to David, adding, "Very funny, D."

"What's on the agenda today besides school…" She looks at the clock, "Which begins with or without you in less than one hour."

He sighs. "I'll be ready. Just let me have one cup of tar and a slice of bacon." He forks a slice of bacon from the hot pan, blowing on it to cool it and shoves it in his mouth.

"Ahhh… bacon tastes good, pork chops taste good," he says in a deep southern accent.

She looks at the pan, "I'm not cooking pork chops…"

He says, "No, ma. Pulp Fiction. Samuel Jackson? John Travolta?"

She is puzzled.

"Quentin Tarantino?" He shakes his head, "Never mind," he says as he heads back upstairs.

She calls, "Son, your pancakes are ready. And the bacon…"

Shouting from upstairs, "I'm jumpin' in the shower. I'll take it with me. Just wrap it up!"

"Son?"

His head pops back into view. "Please? Would you kindly wrap them up, Mother? Please?"

"Yes. Thank you. Of course."

David pipes up from across the room. "Some kids just never learn."

She looks at him and smiles. "Bless your heart, son. You're right, some never do." He winks at her just like his dad and returns to the paper.

Glancing at a photo of the family on the fridge, she looks at Grace who stands in the middle of them all. She touches her photograph and then her heart. "Bless us all," she whispers.

CHAPTER 18

MAHLER SLOWLY EASES INTO POSITION behind Carter's Impala. The enormous truck tires have left a deep path all the way down the hill. Reddick waves Mahler into position. Finally, the front brush guard of Mahler's truck locks into place in the groove between the bumper and the trunk lid of Carter's car. The sheer strength of the truck will provide enough power to push the Impala anywhere.

Forming an "X" with his forearms Reddick shouts, "Whoa! You're there." Mahler puts the truck in park, jumps out and examines where his tires are in relation to where they will be once he starts to move.

"Okay, cool. Now, here's the thing. You have to help me out here. I can see the edge but I can't quite judge how much room I have to play with."

"Got it," Reddick eagerly replies.

"I'm going to put into in gear. You're going to give me the thumbs up. I'm going to rock my truck and his car back and forth, back and forth."

Reddick nods with each description.

Mahler continues, "And then I'm going to juice it. And when I do, be sure you've got plenty of distance between the vehicles and yourself. But see this rock?" He points to the ledge that's immediately below both of the front car doors. "When my grill gets right on top of it..."

Reddick stares.

"Are you listening?"

"What? Yes! Yes! Keep going," Reddick says.

"Okay. When I hit that mark then throw both your arms into the air. Think like you're calling a touchdown. Because you are..." He looks over the ledge. "And it will."

"Got it!" Reddick confirms this with extra nods.

Mahler goes back to the truck and shouts, "Okay, here we go."

He revs the engine, sticks his head out the window to recheck his alignment, and then puts it into gear. He rocks back and front, back and front, back...and he gives it some gas. The Impala screeches across the rock ledge, then a loud snap as a tree breaks free from the earth. Mahler gives it more gas. The car inches further over the ledge. Then, as the car is almost exactly at the pivot point, the tires reach the rock ledge, Reddick throws his arms up into the air and Mahler slams the truck into park.

Silence as the car floats in space, making no sound as it falls. Jumping out of the truck and just as Mahler's feet hit the ground...as if on cue...CRASH! The old Impala smashes against the rocks below. Both men peer over the ledge as the car makes its final end-over-end crash into the lake.

Reddick says, "Damn." Patting Mahler on the back he says, "Nice work."

Mahler grins. "Not bad."

"Yep," Reddick echoes.

"And here's the best news of all, you see this cove here..." Mahler points from one side to the other in a half-moon formation, "it's hidden from view from the rest of the lake. Very few people know about it or ever fool with it. In the summer, because of the formation of the land, the air doesn't circulate much. And..." he looks up overhead to the tree line, "there's not much shadow to speak of. So, as you can imagine, it's real hot. But the best news? This cove is in the deepest part of the shoreline."

Reddick says, "Carter's car should be settling in for a nice nap."

Mahler adds, "Oh, I'd say a nice long *nearly undiscoverable* nap."

"And hopefully, for a very long time."

They shake hands, look once more into the water, and watch bubbles rise to the surface.

Mahler says, "Sweet dreams, Carter."

CHAPTER 19

PASTOR MATHESON SITS QUIETLY IN his office. It is large and handsomely appointed with rugged furniture, a worn Persian rug and a fireplace. The crackling fire is a perfect backdrop to the crisp fall day. The windows are tall with plenty of natural light and reflect the bright orange, yellow and red leaves that brush up against them. The atmosphere is perfect and it allows him to spend countless hours here nearly seven days a week.

The old leather high-back chair has seen better days but he won't give it up because of its comfort. His desk is a mahogany partner's desk that was given to him by a church member's grandfather. It was a welcoming gift his first month at the church. The desk is unique in that it allows two people to sit across each from each other and work simultaneously. There is also an old leather couch.

During his education he had felt that a double major in religion and psychology would serve him well, and it has. For nearly two decades this is the only church that he has served and the only one that he ever wants to. The church family is his family, and family is of primary importance to him.

Jonathan sits contemplating his Sunday sermon. Stacks of books sit atop the old desk. There are volumes about religion, theology, philosophy, motivation and self-help. There are books on topics ranging from inspiration, desperation, stocks and investing to literary classics and current mystery novels. Interested in technology, he has subscriptions to many periodicals and magazines. All in all the library reflects a well balanced and learned man.

He picks up a set of framed photographs. The picture on the left is a black and white picture of Grace just after she was born. She was a healthy baby with more hair than he could have imagined and the curls were abundant from day one. The picture on the right is in color and of Angela when pregnant with Grace. He looks at other photos, relishing memories. One is of Carter and him standing with their arms around each other's shoulders.

Another is Angela's best friend, Cheryl, patting Angela's tummy and laughing. He recalls the sound of that laugh. It was loud. He also recalls something that Rick, Cheryl's husband, said while taking the photo. He said he wasn't sure that Jonathan would know what to do with a girl in the family. He smiles, looks again at Carter and realizes something. He frowns, picks up the phone and punches a button.

His secretary answers, "Yes, Pastor?"

"Claire, has my brother called recently?"

"Not that I'm aware. Let me take a quick look." She flips through a notepad. As she does, Jonathan walks to her office door. "Not for weeks, actually."

"Didn't mean to startle you. I need to run out for a bit."

She shows him the phone log. "Nothing from Carter," she confirms.

"That's strange. I'm embarrassed to say that I have barely thought of him recently. Thoughtless of me."

"Not quite, Pastor. You've had a great deal on your hands with your boys in school and all that goes on here, and…well, a great deal." Catching herself, she arranges papers on her desk.

"He was becoming such a nuisance of late…" he trails off. "Then, at Grace's wake…"

Claire interjects, "I recall that." She chuckles. "Sorry."

"No, no…you're fine. It's true and he was." He hesitates. "Okay. Good enough. I'll just…Thanks, Claire." He starts down the hall, snaps his fingers and goes back. "Almost forgot."

"Yes, sir. Something else?"

"Yes. If you have time today, would you please confirm dinner reservations at Barrington's? I made them…a month ago?"

"Certainly," she responds. "If I recall it's your wedding anniversary, right?"

He smiles, "Yes. 20 wonderful years. And if you hear from Carter please have him call me. I have my cell," he pats his coat pocket. "Stepping out to chat with someone who may have seen him."

"Okay. Sounds good."

"Thanks!"

CHAPTER 20

"HEY, BABE. HOW'S THE SWEETEST one in the world this morning?" Jonathan is on his cell phone while driving through town.

"I don't know. You tell me. I'm talking to him right now," Angela says in a sultry voice.

He laughs. "Oh, girl, I love it when you sound that way."

"Listen to us. Two old married people talking sweet and sassy to one another…" She shifts from funny to sultry, continuing with, "If I didn't know better I'd say that we are still in love."

They laugh.

Jonathan is in a turn lane when he notices something. "Hon, I just wanted to call and say…"

It's a tow-truck with a familiar car on top. "…that we are still on for…" He does a double take as it passes by. Then he sees!

"Jonathan? Are you still there?"

He mumbles, "That looks like Carter's…"

A horn blows from behind. He quickly checks his rearview mirror, waves and makes a turn.

He says, "Baby, hold on a second…" He pulls into the Auto Bell Car Wash and stops, looking back just in time to see the car.

"What is it?" she asks.

"It looks like Carter's car…but I can't tell. It's covered in mud and pretty banged up, but…"

"Carter? Has he been hurt? We haven't heard from him in a few weeks."

"I was thinking that today." He is thinking about it when a car behind taps their horn.

"Sorry, honey…" he says, absently waving to the car but continuing to watch the tow truck until it's out of sight.

"Listen, the reason I called was to confirm our rendezvous tonight."

She purrs, "Ooh, tell me more. And yes, I'll make sure that Mom watches the boys."

"That would be nice. Been awhile since..." He pulls up to the gate. The attendant waves him through. He nods and mouths, "Thanks."

"...since we went out for a nice dinner,"

"Dinner? Where?" she interrupts, "Should I buy a dress for the occasion?"

He hesitates then says, "Sure. Why not?" He checks his watch. "You have plenty of time. It's not even lunchtime. Reservations are at seven. I'll be home about 5:30 and then we'll go. It's one of your favorite places."

"But I have so many favorites."

"Think top five."

She pauses, "Top five? Ooooh...Happy Anniversary!"

"Yes," he laughs.

"Honey, may I call you back? Mom just clicked in."

"Go ahead. I have to run anyway. Getting your carriage cleaned for the ball tonight," he chuckles.

"You are so sweet. Talk to you later. Love you."

"Love you too, baby."

She blows a kiss and disconnects.

At Auto Bell he nods to the attendant who takes the Escalade. Jonathan goes to the side of the parking lot so that he can hear better and makes a call on his cell phone.

A woman answers, "Mission Grove Sheriff's Department. This is Angie. May I help you?"

"Hello, Angie. Pastor Matheson. How are you today?"

"Pastor, I'm great! How are you?"

"Great, thank you. Is Officer Mahler around and if so, may I speak with him?"

"I'm sorry. He left half an hour ago. He was running errands and grabbing an early lunch. May I take a message?"

"No. That's fine. I'll catch up with him later. Thanks."

She replies, "Alright then. I'll tell him you called and we'll see you on Sunday. That is, if I can get my husband to join me."

"Thanks, Angie, we'll look forward to seeing you both."

He pays the attendant and retrieves the freshly cleaned vehicle. He thinks for a moment then murmurs, "Something isn't..." Then he checks his watch and starts in one direction, changes his mind and goes the opposite way.

CHAPTER 21

ANGELA IS PLANTING MUMS IN clay pots along the sidewalk and patio. In denim capri pants, garden clogs and her favorite floppy hat she makes even yard work look smart. A cordless phone on her belt is attached to a Bluetooth in her ear.

"Yes, Mother, I realize that. We've all been under a great deal of stress. I feel that we are just now beginning to adjust."

"Honey, stress can take on many forms. Remember how your father handled stress back in our day." Daphne sits sipping tea by the window. She continues, "You know as well as I do that Jonathan's brother has often been a bad influence on him."

A newspaper, an open Bible and a notebook lie on the table next to her.

"I know, Mother. I understand. But trust me, Jonathan has it all under control. Really. Frankly, I've never seen him so peaceful since before Grace passed away. Come to think of it, he seems to be as relaxed now as I can ever recall."

"Really? No more outbursts? Flying off the handle? Having a little too much fun with his old college chums?"

"Mom, as far as I know Johnny hasn't had a drink since he and his brother went fishing and over did it."

"See? There's a pattern, and I'm just saying..."

Angela interrupts, "Mom, I know what you're saying. I do understand. I hear you and really appreciate your concern. But what I am saying is that Jonathan isn't wired like either Carter or their father. Furthermore, he doesn't abuse much of anything. Unless you call smacking the stuffings out of a golf ball abuse. I've certainly seen that."

They both laugh.

"Okay, honey. Just watching over you. Jesus is on duty full time, but I like to keep tabs also."

"I know that, Mom. We are having a big night tonight. Johnny's going to pick me up around six and dinner's at seven. If I know him he'll have something elegant up his sleeve as a surprise. So, I have to ring off. I'm getting a manicure and a pedicure and I'd like to finish potting the mums before I get all beautiful!"

"You are beautiful, honey. Don't you worry about a thing tonight. Your father and I would love to have both the boys for a sleepover. I don't recall the last time that they did that. Do you?"

"Yes. It was three summers ago. Before they got too big and grown up for their britches. It was Gracie's birthday and Daddy rented the hot air balloon. We all went flying, or more like coasting, over the whole valley. It was simply wonderful."

"Yes, it was. And fall came early that year, so the colors were as brilliant as they are now, if not more so."

She sighs and is quiet.

"Mom, are you okay? You are mighty quiet."

She sniffs. "I'm fine. Just thinking about my granddaughter. Oh...I nearly lose my breath every time I think of her curls. And her laugh and her sparkling eyes. Honey, you go. I'll be fine. And I'll swing by around 5:30 and pick up David."

"Sounds good, Mom. Christopher may or may not be joining you. You know the phase he's in. Love you, Mom. See you soon."

Angela disconnects and looks at the sky. She says, "My sweet, sweet Grace. How I miss you ...why did you have to go? I miss you so." She fights back tears and continues to work. The melody she hums lifts into the air and sweetens the breeze. The birds seem to hold their song in hopes of hearing more.

CHAPTER 22

JONATHAN'S TRUCK BUMPS ALONG THE long and dusty drive to his brother's home. Carter purchased 30 acres when he returned from Vietnam many years ago. He followed that with buying adjacent acreage over time. His land is now about 150 acres and includes some dense woods and a lake. He still lives in the same small cabin that he started with. He had replaced the toilet, but other than that the two bedroom, one bath home's only purchases were a new refrigerator and stove. The home was like Carter, Jonathan thought, simple, rustic and distant from everyone.

When he gets out of the truck he notices dirt all over the freshly washed vehicle. "That was great timing. Good thing it was a free wash," he thinks. Carter's car is nowhere in sight and it's 11:05.

Carter has always been a creature of habit and could be found chopping wood and stacking it from 10 to 11 about every single day of every single week, except Sunday. It was not because of a religious conviction for he said he didn't have much need for God. He was usually hung over until mid afternoon on Sundays.

Jonathan checks out back where Carter sometimes hid his car. He didn't care for drop-in visitors. He often said, "Drive-bys should be like fly-bys. Both should be fast and quick to disappear." Jonathan chuckles at that even now. He feels guilty that he was so hard on Carter the day of Grace's funeral but Carter had no business showing up drunk. Forgiveness is a funny thing, he thought and it should be practiced often. Resentment percolated in his chest and anger threatened to erupt. The memory of that afternoon couldn't be erased from his mind.

He looks in the window and nothing seems out of place. Sampson jumps on the window ledge and startles him. "Sampson! You scared me!"

Inside Sampson was whimpering and running in circles. That seemed strange so he retrieved the spare key from over a front window. Inside he was nearly knocked over by the smell. Sampson flew out and ran around the yard, frantically searching, probably for Carter. Then he came back to Jonathan and jumped all over him.

"Down boy, down. How are you doing, buddy?" He rubbed the dog's body. "What is up with you? You have lost weight!" He can feel Sampson's ribs. Carter was notorious for feeding him straight from the table and Sampson had never been malnourished. Today is a different story. He is at least 10 pounds lighter than a month ago.

Jonathan goes inside. The smell is horrible. Sampson had scattered piles of excrement throughout the house. An empty, shredded bag lies on the floor, torn into fragments. It had held dog food. Jonathan stands motionless. This isn't like Carter. He may have an alcohol problem but he has never been a slob. In early childhood their father had drilled them to always keep their belongings "inspection-ready."

Randall ran a tight ship with no room for error. "A place for everything and everything in its place" was the marine officer's motto. Carter is the same. Nothing was ever out of place. This is a different story and Sampson has become very distressed. He is lying on the front porch, head on his paws, whimpering. He is pining for Carter. That means Carter hasn't been around for a while.

"Okay. First things first, Sampson." In the kitchen he grabs a mop, bucket, cleaners and gloves. As the pail is filling with very hot water, he rolls up his sleeves, takes off his watch and goes to work. It's funny, he thinks, he has spent so much time being angry with Carter that he doesn't remember the last time he said something nice to him. And here he is cleaning his older brother's house without a moment's hesitation.

Later the house is clean, aired out and smells better. He gets more dog food from a storage closet and fills up three containers with water...just in case. He feels that the dog situation is under control. But is it?

And where is his brother? Clearly, Carter hasn't been here for quite awhile. Ammunition and gun-cleaning tools are spread on a small table. Again, this is not like Carter.

No additional firewood is stacked by the house. He remembers, since recently he had come and gotten a load of wood. Jonathan had commented to Carter how nice that it was to drive just 20 minutes for all the free firewood that he could load in a truck. Carter had said that with a hundred-plus acres he would never run out of firewood. Besides, who needed a gym when you could chop and split wood and stay in shape for the rest of your life.

Jonathan suddenly realizes that he is hungry, behind in his errands and hasn't yet stopped to talk with Mahler. He calls Sampson in and shows him the fresh food and water. He says, "It may be a good idea to take you for a quick walk."

While outside, Jonathan calls the office. "Hello, Claire. It's Jonathan."

"Hello, Pastor. What may I do for you?"

"Has anyone called today? Carter, Officer Mahler or Officer Reddick?"

"No, sir. It's been quiet." Claire replied.

" If either of them call, please have them call me."

"Yes, sir."

"And two more things. First, we have a board meeting scheduled for tomorrow night that involves discussing the sanctuary expansion and its budgets," he paused.

"You need that moved," she says.

"Yes. How did you know?" he puzzled.

"I've worked for you since you've been with this church, Pastor. I know when you have something that you are, as you put it, fiercely focused on."

He chuckles, "You know me well. I need to delay that meeting for a few days. I have something on my mind that feels like a priority."

She says, "Tell me when you would like it to be scheduled, please."

"Push it to next week. Ask the members if that works for them. I'll make myself available for any late afternoon or early evening that they want."

"Will do."

"Let's see. Dinner reservations. Already mentioned that. I suppose that's it. Thank you."

"My pleasure. Will you be back in the office again today?"

"I think not. If so, it will be at the end of the day. Thank you for your help. If you'd like to leave an hour early, please do."

"That would be nice. I could certainly use an hour just for me. Thank you," Claire says. "Have a lovely evening and please give my best to Angela."

"Will do. Thanks."

Something is still troubling him.

Sampson is chewing on a stick. Jonathan says, " Come on, boy, let's head in. Uncle Jon has some loose ends to take care of."

They go back into the house. He locks the house, replaces the key and goes to his Escalade, and thinks, "Auto Bell again will make three stops on the way home."

CHAPTER 23

AN OVERWEIGHT STUDENT NAMED VAUGHAN is lying on the hallway floor of Mission Grove High School. He has an overbite and a bad haircut. A group of 15 or more students stand waiting for the next punch to be thrown. He wipes his nose with the back of his hand and sees blood.

"You were lucky with that swing, but you're about to have a taste of what Peter Vaughan can deliver." He slowly stands and the fact that he is bloody makes him look strangely cool. Several of the younger girls whisper among themselves and this feeds his ego.

Christopher stands like a rock, unmoving and unintimidated. Vaughan outweighs Christopher by at least 30 pounds, but Christopher is more agile. And smarter.

"Really?" Christopher asks.

Some of his buddies are cheering him. "Kick him, Christopher. He may be bigger but you're faster."

"You have to knock him down. Your face is too handsome to damage." Christopher knows who that is. It's his girlfriend, Kym.

SMACK! Peter connects with Christopher's face.

The crowd groans, "Ooohh..."

Christopher staggers, nearly falling, but thanks to friends nearby he regains his footing and stays upright.

"Ouch! That smarts," he says. The crowd laughs and this eggs Peter on.

Two teachers and Principal Stover approach the crowd.

"Break it up. Get on your way. Back to class, or wherever you should be," the principal orders. He has a firm grasp on each boy's arm and they head down the hallway. As the crowd disperses, Kym uses her cell phone and makes a call.

Angela is making a sandwich when the phone rings. She wipes her hands and answers the phone. "Hello, Matheson residence."

"Mrs. Matheson, it's Kym. How are you?"

"Fine, thank you, Kym. How nice to hear from you. To what do I owe this pleasure?"

"I wish it were for another reason but I thought it best if you hear this from a friend first."

"What is it, Kym?"

"A bunch of us were just getting out of class when the lunch bell rang. Christopher and I and some friends were hanging out in the hall. This kid, a jerk named Peter Vaughan, came up out of nowhere and started giving Christopher a hard time."

Angela calmly says, "Back up a second. You're telling me that you and Christopher were minding your business when a kid comes up..."

Kym interrupts, "Yes, this is still high school, Mrs. Matheson. Some of these teens are Neanderthals."

Angela smiles, appreciating Kym's sense of humor. "Is Christopher okay? At least tell me he got in a good hit." She catches herself. "Sorry, I didn't mean that."

Kym chuckles, "Yes. He may be smaller than this galoot but he's faster. Everyone knows that. Anyway, it was silly, but Principal Stover has them in his office right now."

"That can't be good."

"It isn't. Just yesterday Principal Stover said that he was, quote, 'Sick and tired of students not respecting authority and that from now until the end of the semester anyone caught fighting, skipping class or smoking in the bathroom was immediately on a 48 hour suspension,' and he was serious."

"So, then, what I'm thinking is..."

Kym interjects, "Is that Christopher has a two day mini-vacation."

Angela's tone changes, "Don't be too sure about that, Kym. Christopher's father isn't one for bad behavior especially as it pertains to disciplinary reasons. This won't be, as you put it, a mini vacation."

"Oops."

"It will quite likely be just the opposite." She pauses, "I suppose that I will need to come and get him."

"Sorry, Mrs. Matheson, but I have to go. The bell just rang and I need to get to class. Just wanted you to know."

"Thank you, Kym, I appreciate that. I'll expect the principal's call. But before you run, what was it exactly that caused this boy to hit Christopher, or for him to hit back. Was something said, or done?"

Kym hesitates. "Well…Peter's from a broken family. His father has problems, so I'm sure that's part of it."

"Kym," Angela says sternly, "what happened?"

Kym sighs, "I'd really rather not say, Mrs. M."

Angela becomes more anxious, "Kym, please. I need to know."

Kym is quiet but finally says, "Peter asked Christopher…" She pauses. "He asked Christopher…what it felt like to…see someone's head blown off."

Angela gasps and nearly drops the phone as air is sucked from her chest. Silence. She can barely breathe and fights both anger and tears, then finally says, "Oh, my Lord, that is…*awful.*"

"Yes, ma'am, it is. Which is why Christopher came unglued. And rightly so. I'm sorry I had to tell you but we're so close…and I thought it was best if you know."

"Absolutely, Kym. Thank you. As hard as it was to hear, I'd much rather hear it from you and be prepared."

"Mrs. Matheson?" Kym asks.

"Yes, dear."

"I'll be praying for you. And Christopher. I know he's really having a hard time coping with this and we all need to stick together."

"Yes, we do. Thank you for caring so deeply. You run along. We'll take care of things. Bye, now."

Angela finally composes herself, stands straight and takes a deep breath. She covers her sandwich and puts it away. She kisses her fingertips and touches Grace's photo on the refrigerator. Smiling, she whispers, "Some people have no heart, Gracie. You had the biggest."

CHAPTER 24

JONATHAN PULLS INTO THE DERBY Diner as Officer Mahler is leaving the parking lot. Jonathan calls out the window. "Hey, buddy, I was just coming to grab lunch. Had a feeling you may be here."

Officer Mahler smiles. "Yeah, my usual lunch hangout. Sorry I missed you. I mean, sorry we missed one another. Another time, maybe?"

"How about coming in and grabbing a cup of coffee. I want to chat with you about something."

Mahler looks at his watch, "I'd love to but I gotta run. Have a few things I have to take care of. We're short-staffed and..."

Jonathan interrupts, "If you're heading to the station I'll get my order to go and swing by there. Good?"

"Not really. I'm not actually going back to the station right now." He glances at his watch again. "We could catch up later, if you would like."

Jonathan hesitates. "Sure, I'll catch you later."

Mahler says, "Actually I promised Mom that I'd take her to dinner tonight. Her birthday. Gotta treat her special, you know." He nervously laughs.

Jonathan nods, "Sure, I get it. I'll try and catch up with you tomorrow."

He is ready to pull off when Mahler says, "That might work. I'm supposed to head up to Lake Mitchell but should be back late in the day."

A car is behind Mahler. He looks in the rearview then says, "Well, gotta run. Good seeing you. Take care."

Jonathan's gaze follows him down the road and he thinks, "Something doesn't feel right."

CHAPTER 25

ANGELA CLICKS THE REMOTE CONTROL and her Buick chirps that the security is set. Parked in Guest Parking at the front of the school, she breathes deeply, calming herself and tries to recall the last time she was here for disciplinary reasons. A moment later, she is greeted by Delores Franks, the administrative secretary, who approaches Angela with a smile and outstretched hand.

"Hello, Angela. So good to see you," Delores says. "Sorry that it's under these circumstances."

They embrace. "How have you been Delores? You're looking wonderful."

She basks in the comment. "I'm terrific, thank you. Things are better. No, actually, they're really good. Next month, it will be a year since Chris passed." She continues, "His health took so much away from him, that…let's just say, I'm adjusting." She is self-consciousness as she says, "Let's talk about why you're here."

She draws Angela aside and quietly says, "Forgive me, Angela. I meant to say, I'm so very sorry for *your* loss." Putting her hand to her mouth, she tears up, "It's one thing to have been married to someone your whole life and lose them to cancer, but it's an entirely different story to…" She loses her breath. "To lose a child…I'm so very sorry."

Angela is surprised at her own strength as she says, "We don't know the plans He has for us, Delores, but we do know that they are for good and not for evil; to give us a future and a hope." She smiles, "Hope. Now that's a powerful thing."

This lightens Delores' spirit and she replies, "Amen." They both chuckle.

"Delores, we've known one another a long time and you can level with me. Give me the skinny before we go in to chat with the *head master*. Not that he frightens me. I like to know all the ins and outs of a situation before I go into battle."

Delores pats her hand and smiles. "Not to worry. Well, your boy did hit our *perpetrator* back, and with force, but he was clearly provoked. I don't know the exact conversation that incited this melee. Frankly it was more of a bump in the road between classes. We have to maintain order, otherwise..."

"The natives can get restless?" Angela asks.

"Exactly."

Angela pretends to roll up her sleeves, "Let's show them who's boss, shall we?"

They walk arm in arm to the principal's office.

CHAPTER 26

JONATHAN DRIVES THE VAN TO Brown's Body Shop & Tow Service. He sits for a moment, recalling something that he hasn't thought about in a long time. He'd known Rowland Brown, Sr. most of his life. He remembers the time Carter took him there to survey a small lot of bangers. These were cars that Carter used to say were not nice enough for the average man but perfect for a kid just learning to drive. He ended up buying him his first car. It was a '69 Chevy Coupe. It was a little banged up, but fast. Carter always drove Chevys. "It's as American as it gets, little brother." Carter's voice echos in his mind. He didn't like to admit it but he was missing Carter. As angry as Jonathan was toward him right now, it didn't stop him from loving him as a brother, or wondering where Carter has been recently.

He goes to the front office. Becky, the wife of Rowland, Jr., greets him, "Hello, Pastor Matheson. What a nice surprise." Becky enthusiastically exclaims as she comes from behind the counter with her arms held wide and they hug.

"Hello, Becky. Good to see you."

"You too, Pastor."

"It's been awhile since I've seen your smiling face."

She blushes. "I'm sorry to say that I haven't seen much of you or the church lately," she says shyly. "Rowland's working nearly seven days a week and has put me to work four of those seven days, just to keep us afloat in this economy."

"No worries, Becky. I understand. Desperate times require desperate measures. However, we do have a Saturday evening service now. It started just this summer."

"Message received, Pastor. I'd like that," she replies. "I miss my friends and could really use the support," she looks around and whispers. "Things have been a little different between us lately. Stressed, for lack of a better word. It could certainly help," Becky says, with hope in her eyes.

"It would. Trust me. And please know that Angela and I are always here for you and Rowland. No matter what."

Her shoulders relax. "Thank you. You both have always been so kind to us, and to this community, for so long."

"And for the record, this visit is not about delivering a guilt trip. I have something on my mind that I want to ask Rowland about it."

"Of course. It's all good, Pastor. Come on, I'll take you around back. That will make two friends Rowland's had visit in the same day."

Rounding the building, Jonathan isn't sure whose look of surprise is more amusing...Rowland's or Officer Mahler's. They both stand next to the car that Jonathan had seen atop the tow truck earlier. Being this close to the car now, even with all the mud, weeds and damages, he realizes he was right. It is Carter's car.

Jonathan smiles at them both. "Hey, guys!" he shouts, approaching Rowland to shake his hand, "Rowland."

"Pastor," Rowland responds.

Jonathan then shakes Mahler's hand, "Danny. Good to see you again...so soon." He looks at the car and says matter-of-factly, "That looks familiar."

Rowland looks from Mahler to Jonathan. "Yeah, we think it is." He looks to Mahler for support.

Mahler kicks into business mode and says, "Looks like your brother's car. I haven't investigated yet but it does look like it." He is obviously uncomfortable and adds, "Funny thing is, we're not sure what it was doing in the back end of Lake Mitchell. Some guy was up there in the cove fishing, where hardly anyone fishes anymore, and his line gets caught on something. Well, he pulls and pulls until... according to him something didn't seem right...so his son jumps in and sees the car. It was nearly on the bottom of the lake. Strangest thing."

Becky says, "You guys have a lot of catching up to do. I'll be inside. Good to see you again, Pastor. We will see you soon. The Saturday night gathering sounds good."

Jonathan replies, "It'll be nice to see you both."

She smiles at Rowland and goes back inside.

Jonathan says, "Might be a good idea to check the car for identification."

CHAPTER 27

LEAVING THE SCHOOL ANGELA AND Christopher go in silence to her car. She starts the car then turns it off and sits quietly several moments before speaking.

"Son, I want you to know..."

He interrupts angrily, "I don't want to know what you think. You weren't there!"

She is hurt by his sudden verbal attack and quietly says, "Son, I want you to know that I don't blame you for what happened."

"You don't?"

"Not at all."

He sighs with relief as she continues, "I am proud of you for standing up for what you believe. If what he said to you is truly that, then I have all the more reason to be proud."

"How do you know what was said?" he asks. "Kym?"

"Yes."

"I wish she hadn't..."

"If it weren't for her, I would have gotten a call from the principal. That would have caught me completely off guard and upset me greatly. And, I wouldn't have been prepared."

"But I don't want my mom coming to my rescue and making me look..."

She stops him and says, "It's not like that. This is about looking out for others. Kym did the right thing. She cares deeply for you."

He toys with the strap on his knapsack. She starts the car and leaves the parking lot. After a few more minutes of silence, she says, "Now, here's the good news and the bad news."

"Oh, brother."

"Which do you want first?" she asks.

"Give me the bad first, as if it could get much worse."

"Oh, it can. And it likely will. Mainly because your father doesn't like fighting and…"

He interrupts her, "But what about during…you know…during…" He chokes up.

"Son. That was different. And it wasn't exactly his fault."

"But he's always said to stand up for ourselves. Never show weakness. And…"

"And to turn the other cheek…whenever possible. And don't get me wrong. He does say all that. However, the one thing he may have a problem with is that perhaps you could have taken a moment to think about what your testimony was saying to other people…"

"Please don't start preaching."

With an index finger in the air she says sternly, "Please stop interrupting me. I'm trying to make a point."

He sighs.

"Let's not fight. Please, son."

He wants to challenge but thinks better of it and lowers his head. "I apologize."

"Apology accepted. I'm on your side. Trust me on that. And I will always be on your side, as long as your side is the right side. Do we understand one another?"

He nods. She softens.

"Next time please think twice. Okay? Your friend, what is his name?"

"Vaughan. Peter Vaughan."

"Let me ask you. Does Peter come from a good family?"

"No."

"Is he as fortunate as you to have been raised in a Christian family?"

He shakes his head and says nothing.

"Would it be safe to assume that he is unfortunate to have not been blessed with a Christian upbringing *and* perhaps may not have parents who really care for and want the best for their son?"

"I see your point." They ride in silence and Christopher finally says, "Mom, you should have been an attorney."

She laughs. "Oh, son, you're something. Thank you for the intended compliment but I'm afraid that attorneys may stretch the truth more than I would be comfortable with."

"By the way, what was the good news?"

She is puzzled. "What?"

"You said there was bad news which we have now enjoyed thanks to your stellar presentation and there was good news. Now, what is the good news?"

"The good news is…" She turns to him, being sure that she has his attention. "The good? You got in a good punch and showed Peter that you can't mess with a Matheson and walk away unscathed."

"Nice." He holds up his hand. They high-five and he adds, "That's what I'm talking about."

CHAPTER 28

ROWLAND IS HOSING DOWN CARTER'S car to better see what may have happened. Officer Mahler walks around it, looking for anything unusual. Jonathan stands, his face blank. Rowland opens the doors letting any remaining water drain out. The smell is horrible.

"Whew! That's ripe," gasps Jonathan.

"No doubt, Pastor. Must have been sitting in the lake for some time." He looks at Mahler and Mahler looks at Jonathan. Jonathan looks at the bumper. Mahler is watching him closely.

Jonathan rubs the bumper trying to see the old sticker. Between the trunk lid and the bumper he finds what he was looking for. Jonathan says. "It's an old MIA sticker. I remember the day Carter put that sticker on. He hadn't been back in the states but about a month. He'd lost some buddies in Vietnam and he put this on to honor them."

Rowland says, "That's admirable."

"Yes. He was a POW himself, at one time. He was dropped into hostile territory, amidst heavy gunfire. He was captured and the Viet Kong held him for nearly a year, starving him and brutally beating him. He told us later that he had escaped once and lived off the land for three months before being recaptured."

Mahler says in amazement, "Wow, I never knew that."

Jonathan quietly continues, "If it hadn't been for his comrades who came back for him he most certainly would have been killed."

A ringing phone blasts over an outside speaker, jarring the men back to the present. "Rowland. It's for you. They say it's urgent."

Rowland says, "Sorry, guys. Be back soon."

Jonathan walks around one side of the car. Mahler walks in the opposite direction. Jonathan checks inside the front and Danny looks in the back. Jonathan then examines the rear as Danny examines the front.

After a long silence Jonathan asks, "Danny, how long were you going to wait before telling me that you ran Carter off the road and into the lake?"

Officer Mahler looks into Jonathan's cold stare.

CHAPTER 29

AS ANGELA DRIVES UP TO their home Daphne comes to greet her. Jackson, the family Lab, bounds from behind her and runs to greet Christopher. They romp vigorously in the yard.

"Hi, Mom. We're back. Thanks for seeing after David." She hugs Daphne.

Kissing her cheek, Daphne quietly says, "You may want to check in on David. He's having a tough day."

Angela says, "Who isn't?" She checks her watch. "I only have a couple of hours before my Prince Charming comes to whisk me off for a magical evening."

Daphne, with her hands on her hips, says, "Angela Marie, I did not raise you to give in to your feelings. Put on your boots, shrug off the angst of the day and keep marching."

Angela salutes, "Aye-aye, Ma'am."

Christopher, with Jackson at his heels, runs by and says, "Hi, Gramma. Have any goodies for me?"

She asks, "Been a good boy?"

Christopher says, "Does 'sorta' count?"

Daphne nods toward the kitchen. "Just put oatmeal cookies out to cool. Be sure to..."

Simultaneously they say, "Wash the hands!"

Angela says quietly, "Mom, this is the first night in months that Jonathan has suggested a romantic night out. We do go out for dinner but he's really doing this up."

Daphne smiles and says, "I understand. Go check on your other son. Then you should have enough time to run to the mall and still get home for a nice warm bath before your prince arrives. Meanwhile, I'll feed the bottomless pits and watch them tonight. Stuart's playing basketball with the league and he won't be home until later. Okay, princess?"

Angela smiles and says, "You are the sweetest mother in the world. Do you know that?"

Daphne looks at her and says, "Really? Little old me? Shucks!"

CHAPTER 30

ROWLAND HAS MOVED CARTER'S CAR to the back of the lot so that it can be more closely inspected and left undisturbed. He stops to speak to Jonathan and Mahler. "Sorry that I have to run but there's been an accident up on Highway 49. Spend all the time you like and I'll talk with you later."

Mahler says, "Thanks for your help, Rowland. Be safe."

Then he asks Jonathan, "How, or better yet, *when* did you figure out that I had anything to do with it?"

Jonathan says, "As for how, I'll tell you in a minute. As for when, you just confirmed it."

"You always were the chess player," says Mahler.

"Maybe so, but remember two things. First, I know something about psychology and that lets me understand a lot of things about people; most of it comes from observation. Second, you and I've been friends for a really long time. You learn a great deal about people with whom you've shared a dorm."

"I suppose."

Jonathan pats him on the back and motions for him to follow. At the back of the car he says,

"See the crease between the trunk lid and the bumper. That's a pretty specific crease. See the two indentations here and here?" He points. Mahler nods.

"I don't gamble but if I did I would bet that this is the exact height of your bumper. These two indentations are from the oversized winch on the front of your truck. Right here," he bends to look underneath, "would be from the hook on the front of your bumper that allows you to use a chain to pull tree stumps up."

Mahler looks from the bumper to Jonathan, who holds his eyes. "Like the tree you helped Carter pull up from my backyard a couple of summers ago when we added the deck extension on. Remember that?"

Mahler nods.

"Also, look inside on the driver's side. See anything odd?"

Mahler looks and shakes his head.

"Notice the parking brake? It's on."

"So?" Mahler asks.

"This is just a hunch but I would say that whoever was about to get out of this car wanted to make sure it didn't move while they got out."

Mahler frowns, "I'm not sure that I follow."

Jonathan stands and brushes dirt from his hands.

"See if you agree with any of this. More than likely one of three things happened. One, in reverse order of my thinking, Rowland put the brake on in order to keep it steady on the tow truck."

Mahler says, "Makes sense."

"Except, Rowland pulled the car from the water and from behind... attaching the chain to the axle and loading the car backend first. I doubt that he'd have any need to put the brake on as he was pulling it onto his rig. The car is a rear-wheel drive."

Mahler listens.

"Second, let's say for argument's sake that the car stopped short of tumbling into the lake..." Mahler stares intently. Jonathan continues, "Why would someone put the brake on before pushing the car into the water?"

"I see." Mahler nods and says, "Continue, Sherlock."

"Third, if I were rolling down an incline at the speed I would imagine this person must have been traveling, then you can be sure that I'd do everything in my power to stop the car from leaping off the cliff and into the deep, dark, cold water below."

"Unless of course, I wanted to stop..." He pauses for effect. "And here's the tricky part. What if I wanted to stop, knowing that someone was quite likely to come behind and finish the job for me."

106

Mahler scowls and says, "That's ridiculous, and it's too much of a calculated guess. You've been watching too many CSI shows."

Jonathan asks, "Have I? What would happen if your superiors got wind of your covering this up?"

Mahler's mouth is dry. He fidgets, "That…can't…happen. I'd lose everything. My job, my house…my reputation."

Jonathan chuckles. "The reputation would be the last thing I'd be worried about if I were you. It's the weakest link in your chain."

"It is not."

"Danny. We've known one another a very long time. You've never really given a damn about what anyone said of you. It could be one of the reasons you're pretty good at what you do. But it also could be one of the reasons you're not married, don't appear to have it on your horizon and don't really have that many friends, aside from Reddick. And frankly, he's just a loner with less to lose than you have."

Mahler is angry. "What are you saying, Johnny? You would never…." He peers at him, "Would you?"

Jonathan asks, "Do you think I would? If I were you, I would live by my own conscience and do the right thing." He starts toward the front of the parking lot. "I have to go back to the office, get my truck washed…again, and take my girl out on a date."

Mahler grabs his arm. Jonathan stops, looks at Danny's hand on his arm, then into his eyes. Mahler releases his arm. Jonathan raises his eyebrows questioningly.

Mahler says, "I know what you're thinking."

"Do you?"

"Yup. You're thinking that I killed Carter and should burn for this."

Jonathan laughs heartily. "That's good. You should see your face." He shakes his head and walks away.

"Cut it out, Johnny. I'm serious," Mahler calls after him.

Jonathan stops. "Oh, I know that. You may be as crooked as a fish hook, but you're not a killer. Now, our Jersey-boy, Reddick? That's a whole different story."

Mahler starts to disagree but Jonathan holds up his hands.

"Whoa. I'm not through. I know my brother and I know what my brother's been through. Most importantly, I know what my brother is capable of. And my guess?"

Mahler asks, "What?"

"I'd say that there is a 50 percent chance that Carter is sleeping with the carp."

Mahler asks, "And the other 50?"

Jonathan is frustrated. "Come on, Danny, do I have to do everything? I'm a pastor. I have the church and my family to think about. You're the cop. You think about it and then get back to me."

Mahler stands in the middle of the parking lot with his mouth open. Jonathan gets in his truck, lowers the window and says, "Close that thing or you'll catch flies." He laughs, waves and pulls away.

Mahler closes his mouth, grimaces and stands looking pained.

CHAPTER 31

DAVID IS LYING IN BED watching the solar system rotate on the ceiling above. The remote in his hand controls a tiny projector that bounces the images via a mirror to the ceiling. With the click of another button, the names of the planets slowly fade into view, hovering over the respective planets in the virtual solar system.

A soft knock comes at the door. David quietly says, "Come in, Mom. It's unlocked."

Angela smiles at her son, "Hi. May I approach the inner sanctuary of learning?" Looking overhead she exclaims, "Ooh, that's nice. I feel like I'm in an observatory."

David continues to watch with wonder and says, "Yes, it's pretty cool."

"Did you have lunch?" She makes a funny face then says, "Of course, you did. Gramma's cooking. Much better than mine."

"That's not true. Yours is good. Gramma's just tastes…richer?"

"It's the butter. In everything. Why do you think I work out so much?" She sits on the foot of his bed and rubs his sock feet. "Everything okay, my little professor?"

He clicks another button, changing the scene from the solar system to images of the Northern Lights. "It's okay."

"Anything you want to talk about?"

"No. Not really." Changing the subject, he asks, "Where are you and Dad going tonight?"

"Your father is taking me to an elegant restaurant and then someplace that's a surprise."

"That's nice. You deserve it. You've had a tough time and I think you're due to be happy."

His caring heart nearly takes her breath. "Son, that is so sweet of you to say. You're so precious to me." She hugs him and kisses his cheek.

"I'm saying it because it's true."

"Thank you. I have to run out for a quick errand before my big date, so…unless…"

He interrupts, "Mom, do you love me and Christopher the same amount?"

"Of course, son. We love you and have loved all three of you equally." She moves closer to him. "There is no more love for one than another. Why do you ask?"

He fiddles with the remote and then says, "I guess I was just wondering. I know this may sound silly, but…when it was just Christopher here I'm sure that he was the center of attention."

She smiles.

"Then, along comes Grace. I can't imagine what that was like. The first girl in the family for, well, like forever. Then I come along right after. I realize I'm awesome and all but, I don't know, I guess I feel that just as everything was going right…Gracie dies and…" He trails off.

She watches him closely and asks, "Yes? And what?"

He finally says, "Since I'm smarter than Christopher…and funnier than Dad…" he grins, "I guess I was just wondering if…" He stops.

"What, honey? You can talk to me about anything."

"Well, I know that Christopher is angry with Uncle Carter…but it was an accident, wasn't it?"

"Of course, dear. He didn't mean for that to happen. He loved Gracie nearly as much, probably as much, as all of us. It's just that he did something terribly irresponsible. Something your father had asked him many times to never do."

"Bring the gun into the house," he says so quietly that Angela leans close to hear him. But she knows what he said. Hearing his young voice utter those words and knowing that his heart feels such pain crushes her all the more.

"Do you think that if Christopher hadn't put me down, and then chased Grace into the house that day, then maybe she wouldn't have died?"

She looks at him trying to understand what he's feeling. "Son, do you think..."

"Was it my fault?"

She catches her breath and her heart nearly breaks.

"David, do you think...have you felt this way...all along?"

He lowers his head, reaching for the words. Finally he says, "All I can remember is that we were playing and having so much fun with our friends. Then it was Grace's turn to be 'It' and we were all in the yard..." He looks away, evidently trying to recall something.

"And you and Dad were in your chairs. But for some reason, Grace was really teasing Christopher. Then she said, 'If you weren't carrying that bag of books on your shoulders, you could catch me.' She always called me 'Books' like you and Dad call me 'Little Professor.'"

"But son..."

"I guess I keep thinking that if I'd held onto Christopher, or made him let her tag me...then...they wouldn't have run in the house... and then she wouldn't..." He stops.

"Son, I had no idea that you've been thinking that, and feeling that...all this time. It was no more your fault than old Farmer Tucker's who lives down the road and across the way."

This drew a tiny laugh. "Mom. Seriously? He lives too far away and he's way too old. He could never catch us in a game of Tag!"

She sees a light begin to break through. "That day was what appeared to be a random series of events. All somehow under God's control. He allowed it to happen. The way He chose to create all things. Only He knows why."

"I guess that makes some kind of sense, Mom," he replies.

"It may not seem like it does now, but maybe in time it will," she adds.

"I was just wondering if I was in the way. I don't know. It's confusing."

She squeezes his hand and says, "Life is funny, David. It doesn't always make sense. But what happened was not your fault, or Christopher's fault…and in some ways, it wasn't even Uncle Carter's fault."

He looks at her. "But…"

"He was told not to bring a gun into the house. But because your uncle likes to…"

"Drink alcohol," David interjects.

"Yes. Sometimes one will drink too much, and it clouds one's judgment and sometimes allows them to do unfortunate things." She pauses. "Does that make sense?"

He nods.

"Son, did you know that your father and I prayed for you nearly the entire time after Grace was born? We asked our Heavenly Father for another son."

Propping on one elbow he perks up, "Really?" His eyes sparkle with innocence.

She smiles, "Yes. Really. Your father and I always thought that three children would be perfect. That way, you each would always have a playmate, arguments could be settled more easily and your life would never be boring because each one of you would always have two best friends."

He contemplates this and then says, "That does make sense. And did you always want two boys and a girl?"

"That's exactly what we wanted. We thought it would be best to have a boy first, that way he could be the protector. Then, what could be better than to have a sister right in the middle? This way Mommy could have the little girl that she had always dreamed of having. Dad could have his little angel and she could grow up to be married. Then we could have grandchildren."

David squeezes his mother's hand. In his eyes she can see the anticipation for more.

He says, "And what else?"

She smiles and says, "And then we thought that we would save the best for last!" She grins.

He beams.

"We thought about how wonderful it would be to be a little brother. This way, our daughter would have someone she could take care of. Also, the older brother would have a brother for a best friend, something that we think is a tremendous gift to have. And, we prayed that our youngest would be really smart."

His smile grows bigger. "Why?"

"Why? Because if he were smart, then he would be able to learn and work and do and achieve anything in the world that his bright mind could imagine."

"And that was me," he says.

"Yes. That is you, my precious youngest child. And so you see, your daddy and I are very, very happy and thankful that God blessed us with our three beautiful children, Christopher, Grace and you."

His smile fades and he looks down at his hand in his mother's hand.

"What is it, son?"

"If you and Dad prayed for all three of us then why did God give you three but take one away? We were a perfect family."

Angela fights back the tears, but loses the battle, as several trickle down her cheeks. Taking a deep breath she gathers herself and smiling, she replies, "That's a very good question, son. I don't have an answer but I do have a thought that I would like you to consider."

He nods.

"Consider this. First of all, only God knows the plans He has for us. Right?"

He nods the second time.

"And only God can make the really big decisions of what is best for all of us. Right?"

And again he nods.

"And maybe God decided that after He had given us three perfect children...which He did...that one of them had already accomplished her mission here on earth."

He wrinkles his brow and studies her.

"What I mean is this. You know how Dad's mission on earth is to help people and pray for them? And then help them get married and be a comfort to them when a family member dies?"

He nods in understanding.

"And you know how it's perhaps even more important for him to be able to teach those same people God's word each week, so they can learn to become better people and help others too?"

"Yes."

"By the same token God's plan for me is to be the best mommy for my children to teach them things...like I'm sharing with you right now...and to be a good helper for your father. And think about this. Christopher's job may be to become a singer and inspire people. Your job may be to teach people about outer space..." She looks up at the ceiling. "Or, about investing in the stock market, or how to create new things."

He smiles with understanding.

"And here's the best part. Maybe God wanted you to have a perfect big sister who could teach you how to play tag, throw a Frisbee, whistle with your fingers and things like that. And I think her job was not only to teach her older brother to stand up for himself, but also to share and to look out for his little brother. But you know what I think little Grace's best lesson was for all of us, and maybe the reason God wanted her to be here?"

"What?" David asks.

"I think God wanted us to learn how to laugh more and to play more, as she so loved doing. And also for us to see the absolute best in people. You know how she did that for us all, right?"

"Absolutely!"

"Have you ever noticed that we are happier people who laugh and smile more? We seem to love people more easily, too. Grace showed us how to do this."

He smiles and reaches for a hug.

"Mom, you're awesome. Thank you for helping me understand

better."

She hugs him and kisses the top of his head. "Son, I know no better joy than to know that my children walk in the truth. Anything that I can do to help you is what I'm here for."

He holds up his hand and they high five.

"Now, I have to run a quick errand before your dad gets home. We have a special night on the town waiting and I seem to remember one young man telling me that I deserve it. If I don't get moving…"

He interrupts, "Well, what are you sitting here for? Go!"

At the door she looks at him with the love that only a mother can express.

"Son, I'm proud of you and am so thankful that God gave you to me and your dad."

He beams with happiness.

She blows him a kiss and is out the door.

CHAPTER 32

JONATHAN HANDS THE CAR WASH attendant money and gets in his truck.

"Thanks, Pastor Matheson. You can come in twice a day anytime," the attendant grins.

"You're welcome, but twice every day could get a bit expensive. Today's a special occasion. Keep up your good work and I'll be back to see you soon."

"What a day," Jonathan thinks and then his cell phone rings. He looks at the screen with frustration. It is Officer Mahler. "Yes, Danny."

"I was just trying to watch your back, Johnny," Officer Mahler says somberly.

"There are other ways to watch my back, Danny. Safer and smarter ways."

"I know, I know. It's just that..."

Jonathan's phone beeps. It's Angela. He smiles. "Danny, hang on a second, I've got another call," and clicks over.

"Hi, babe," Jonathan says, "Can you hold one second, I have to end another call."

"Sure, dearest. I'll wait."

He clicks back over. "Danny, we're going to have to chat another time. It's Angela and I need to take it."

Danny says, "Alright. I just want you to know your family is, and has always been, a priority to me. That's what friends do."

"Understood. And I want you to know, good or bad, Carter is family too. Must run. Talk to you later."

"Hi, pretty woman," Jonathan speaks softly into the phone.

"You can call me that anytime you like," she says. "However, not so sure you'd say that if you saw me right now."

"Why? Are you okay?"

"I'm fine. But between setting out plants in the garden this morning and putting out home fires, I'm a bit weary."

"Aw, sorry baby. If it's any consolation, I've had a rough day too. Probably not as bad as yours from the sound of it. Have you had a chance to shop?" he asks.

"No, actually, I'm running out of the house in five minutes. So that we're not completely pushed could we move dinner off an hour? You probably will need to speak with Christopher."

"Sure. No problem. And what's with him?"

"Not really that much. But so that you won't be surprised, Christopher is suspended for two days. Call it a cooling off period."

"Oh, boy." Jonathan feels his blood pressure rise.

She senses this and says, "Now, before my sweetheart gets too agitated, let me just say that you'll understand where he's coming from."

"Okay, I…"

"Tell you what," she interrupts, "And I'm sorry to interrupt, but I really need to say two things to Mom before I leave and then I have to run. Why don't you just try the subtle approach and let him come to you. Maybe toss some baseball in the backyard? You know how he loves it when you two do that. Tell him you've had a stressful day and need to unwind before you spend a night listening to your wife talk your ears off…or something like that."

His anxiety subsides into pure admiration. "Done."

"Great. This way, I can finish my tasks and we can enjoy our evening, just the two of us."

"Sounds good. Talk to you in a bit. Love you."

"Love you too, hon. Bye."

He checks his watch. It's nearly four. He thinks about Carter and the car, the mysterious re-appearance of it, and the possibility of an apparent cover-up. He could only imagine what would have occurred if he hadn't followed his instinct, and he wants to see where the car was found. In only a short time he is due home, then it's off to dinner and the show.

He decides that the car puzzle can wait. Carter is either dead or hiding out. But why and where? Surprisingly, Jonathan doesn't have a substantial feeling of sorrow for what could perhaps be the loss of his only sibling. Something was clearly wrong with that and he knew it.

CHAPTER 33

DAPHNE AND ANGELA ARE TALKING at Angela's car. She is in the car and Daphne stands by the driver's door. "Angela, take a deep breath. You've had a lot on your plate. It will all work out. Everyone is under more than enough stress so nobody should be fretting anyone."

"You're right. I am doing the best I can. Recently it has just been..." She falters.

"Yes, I know. And who's been there with you every step of the way?" Daphne smiles.

"Oh, Mom..." Angela places her hand on Daphne's. You're a saint." She asks, "Wait, why do I always think of saints as being men?"

Daphne smiles, "Angela. Were you not listening all those years?

"What?"

"We were not Catholic but your father's family was. And I've told you this before. Saint Angela was the saint of children and education. Oodles of years ago, Saint Angela built a school for young girls who were not properly taught religion at home. And yes, we did have that in mind when we named you." Daphne sees Stuart riding his four-wheeler across the expanse of lawn.

"Here comes your father." Angela turns and looks, shielding her eyes from the sun.

Daphne says, "He certainly loves that contraption."

"Aw, Mom, leave him alone. It's one of the few toys you let him enjoy. Besides, wait'll you see David's eyes light up when he hears that motor coming. He loves that Gator, or whatever you call it... nearly as much as he loves his Grandpa."

Daphne jokingly says, "Are you kidding?" They laugh.

Angela says, "If I don't get out of here, Mom..."

"Okay, okay. I know. I'm holding you up." She pulls an envelope from her apron pocket. "Now, don't give me any of your sass. Take this and get yourself something extra pretty." She tries to hand it to Angela.

"No! I have it covered. Jonathan told me to..."

"Daughter. Take this. That's an order. This is your Mother speaking." She tries to put it into Angela's purse.

"Okay, okay. Thank you. You're way too kind." She kisses her cheek and Daphne beams.

"I'm going." Angela backs out of the driveway. She calls, "Thank you, Mom. Love you. See you later." She waves at her father and he throws up his hand.

When he reaches the end of the long driveway, Stuart pulls up and shuts off the engine.

"Hey, good looking...whatchya got cooking..." He lifts one eyebrow several times and grins. "How's about cooking something up with me."

Daphne smiles saying, "How's about apple pies?" She removes her apron and starts toward the house as he climbs off his vehicle.

"Mmmm...that'll work." He follows her. She turns and playfully swats her apron at him, saying in a teasing voice, "Play your cards right and..."

"Yeah? Yeah?"

"And I may let you do the dishes later."

He stops in his tracks and says, "Oh, boy."

Laughing, they walk arm in arm into the house.

CHAPTER 34

"I FEEL LIKE I HAVE been in this truck all day long," Jonathan says into the phone as he drives down the highway.

"It's because you have, Johnny. Every time I've tried to chat with you today, you've either been getting into or out of the truck. And going to one meeting or the other. Speaking of which, where have you been all day?" Joshua asks. Joshua Ridge is the Associate Pastor at Mission Grove Community Church. He has been Jonathan's right hand man for several years.

Jonathan replies, "I'll just give you the Cliff Notes. I've been to Dunkin' Donuts, The Derby Diner and Circle K. I was at Circle K once for gas and once for a super sized Coke."

Joshua laughs, "Okay, so a healthy run around town."

"Right." Jonathan merges onto a secondary road and continues his play-by-play.

"There's been a trip to Brown's Body Shop & Tow Service, then to my brother's place on the far side of town, and to the car wash twice...but don't ask."

"Ever thought of turning that truck into a taxi? Bet you could make some nice money on the side and still get your errands, I mean your work, done."

"Smart aleck."

They laugh.

"And if that's not enough before my date tonight with my lovely and wonderful wife I get to have a wise, fatherly chat with my teenage son who was booted out of school today. For what I do not know," Jonathan responds.

"Ouch. And that's just the home life of our beloved pastor. We haven't even touched on the business side of things." Joshua switches into business mode.

"I confess, I am afraid to ask but I will."

Joshua says, "It's not all that bad. We have the Board Meeting that you so judiciously rescheduled to later in the week, not a problem. The building committee will want guidance on the new construction so that we can get that nailed down before fourth quarter."

"Fair enough. It's been a long time in the making and it's about time we erected the new structure. Our congregation is expanding rather handsomely...not as quickly as our friendly competition across town...but handsomely, nonetheless."

Joshua replies, "True."

"And?" Jonathan asks. "Please share. I have five more minutes of near quiet before I'm home."

"Only other thing, and it can wait until tomorrow or the next day, is the Band Competition meeting."

"Yes. Christopher's pet project. This means the world to him. Let me ask you something since you and I are fairly close to the same age. Is the music these days getting louder and maybe a little harder to understand?"

Joshua laughs and Jonathan joins in. In a deep southern accent, Joshua says, "Hey, Grandpa! You could just turn your hearing device down."

Jonathan nears home. Still laughing, he adds, "Oh wait, I'm here..."

They catch their breath and Jonathan wipes the tears from his eyes. "I don't know why that all struck me so funny. Guess I needed the comic relief."

Joshua says, "Me, too!"

Jonathan turns into his driveway.

"You kids have a great and well-deserved evening and I'll chat with you late tomorrow," says Joshua.

"Thanks, partner. I appreciate you."

Christopher and David are in the front yard tossing a baseball back and forth. David is trying to keep up but the power of Christopher's arm is a bit more than he can handle.

"Hey, Dad!" David waves and shouts as he sees Jonathan approaching.

Christopher waves too, a bit less enthusiastically, but he waves nonetheless.

Jonathan can imagine the fear that Christopher has right now, thinking that he will be punished. It is written all over his face. He remembers when he was a boy and got into trouble. The last thing he ever wanted to do was to disappoint his father. Times may change but boys never do. They all want to be loved and respected by their fathers. He watches as they come to greet him. Pride and love fills his heart.

Jonathan rubs David's head and fist-bumps Christopher. "Hello, gentlemen."

"How was your day, Dad?" David asks.

"Good, thank you. Busy but good and it's much better now."

Christopher asks, "Why is that?"

"Because I'm home. With you guys. And Mom."

"Who is upstairs as we speak, dressing to the nines!" David says.

Jonathan smiles, sets his briefcase down and removes his jacket and tie. He puts them over his briefcase.

"Say, David…"

"Yes, sir."

"Mind if I cut in and play a little catch with your big brother before I have to go get ready?"

Christopher's look says, "*You're going to play catch with me?*"

David has already started running to the house. "I'll get your glove, Dad. It's right inside the door." He darts inside.

Christopher quietly says, "He carries all three gloves every single time we come out to play. On the off chance that you'll have time to play."

This hits Jonathan hard.

Christopher lowers his head and kicks at the dirt.

Jonathan watches this and asks, "How was your day, son?"

"I'm sure that you've heard by now," he says without looking up.

"I hear that you have a two day vacation but I have no idea why."

Christopher looks at him and says, "Dad, it wasn't my fault. Really. You should've…heard…" He stops.

"We can talk about it later but right now…"

David runs from the house with Jonathan's glove in hand. His expression is priceless.

"What do you say that we three enjoy this time and play catch?"

Christopher's shoulders visibly relax as a grin spreads slowly from ear to ear. He picks up his glove and sprints across the yard to get into position.

For Jonathan time seems to slow and it is as if an old movie were playing…the sun's golden glow, the fragrance of freshly mown grass and David sitting on the sidelines waiting to see the "World Series" begin. Christopher is David's age again, wide-eyed and innocent, looking at his dad, his hero and watching for one of the most glorious moments of his life. That is when Jonathan realizes that it has been over a year since he's played catch with his sons.

Life couldn't be any sweeter than at this very moment. Except for the day that Grace was born. He looks heavenward and smiles.

"Hey, Dad, here comes the first pitch. Are you ready?" Christopher shouts.

"Let 'er rip," David adds to the excitement.

"Give me all you got, son," Jonathan smiles. He smacks his glove, holding it in front of his face and smelling the leather. He completes a mental checklist: Happy? Check! Proud to be their father? Check! Excited to have Angela by his side? Check! Happy to be alive and well? Check! All senses are present and accounted for.

'Tuck this away in your memory bank," Jonathan Matheson thinks. Check!

CHAPTER 35

INSIDE THE SHERIFF'S OFFICE MAHLER is typing reports. The room is quiet with the only sounds a typewriter, the occasional squawk of a radio and the low mutterings of Officer Reddick across the room. Mahler checks the clock. It's 5:29. On the "Missing Persons" board are four photographs. A white 13 year-boy missing since 2000, a 27 year-old black female missing since 2003, and a gray Labrador named Daisy missing since last summer. At the top is an old black and white photograph of Carter Matheson listed as missing for 30 days. Reddick is still on the phone as Mahler grabs his coffee mug and goes down the hall to the kitchen. He is rinsing the mug when Reddick comes in and drops coins into the vending machine, then stares blankly at the selections.

"Try the Coke. I hear it's especially tasty this season," Mahler says sarcastically.

"You're right."

Mahler puts his mug in the cupboard and turns to see Reddick wearing a peculiar expression.

"That look?" Mahler asks.

"Yeah. What about it?"

"Lose it. Won't do you any good. Won't do any of us any good. Everything is under the radar right now. Let's keep it that way."

"But..."

"But nothing. The only people who have any clue are you, me, Rowland, Jonathan and his wife. Becky thinks it's just another tow. Rowland owes me one. Jonathan is one of my oldest friends..." He rubs his jaw. "And I'm not sure if he's mad, sad ...or glad."

Reddick finishes the Coke and turns to leave.

"The way I see it there is only one weak link in the chain," Mahler lets the words hang, waiting for Reddick's response.

"What?"

The question hangs in the air. Mahler quietly says to Reddick, "Time will tell, my friend." Then adds, "Let's all just get along. And watch out for one another."

He gets his briefcase and jacket, nods to his co-workers and leaves. Reddick stands alone at the end of the hall, left to his thoughts. And imagination.

CHAPTER 36

THE RESTAURANT IS TINY, ELEGANT and very French. The level of noise rarely rises above the sound of tinkling crystal and everyone speaks in hushed tones. The lighting is perfect, artfully directed to the oils and watercolors on the walls. Tiny white candles in crystal vases are on each table. A subtle soundscape, reminiscent of a Parisian Café, plays. The wait staff discretely attends to every need. Angela and Jonathan sip wine and fully embrace the moment without speaking, as though to do so would burst the magical moment.

Angela finally whispers, "Absolutely perfect." She smiles.

Jonathan is pleased that she's happy and raises his glass saying, "All the more perfect...because of you." She smiles as he adds, "Happy Anniversary, love."

He winks. She melts.

Two hours have passed and Angela is still smiling—giggling, actually, and Jonathan is telling a story with great animation.

"...But then Joshua said, 'Hey, Grandpa. You could just turn your hearing device down, you know.' And I don't know which was funnier...the deep Southern accent he was using or the fact that it was Joshua." He laughs more easily. "You know how straight-laced and unfunny he can be."

"Yes. When they say 'dry sense of humor' they mean bone dry, when talking about him.'"

The waiter arrives and quietly clears the table. "May I suggest a dessert wine? It is quite delicious."

Jonathan, clearly relaxed, nods. Angela hesitates, then smiles and says, "It is a special occasion. But only a very small bottle."

"Excellent. I have just the perfect miniature accompaniment. Would you care for fresh roast coffee while your dessert is prepared?"

They both nod. His assistant pours their coffee. They fall into a comfortable silence...the kind enjoyed by longtime partners.

"I don't recall when we've had a meal so delicious," Angela says.

"Or so quiet," he whispers.

"Yes. Today was certainly fraught with anxiety. Did you get a chance to speak with Christopher?"

Jonathan slowly stirs his coffee and nods.

"He told you what the boy said?"

"I didn't think it was necessary. I had a bit of a flashback to when I was a boy and my mom used to say, 'Just wait until your father gets home. Then, you'll be sorry.'" He adds in a very quiet voice, "I never could grasp the logic of that."

"What do you mean?"

"Think about it, a boy can hardly wait until his father gets home. He has high hopes of playing catch, or telling him about his day, or whatever the case. Yet, someone says something like that. How on earth is a child expected to be glad to see his parent then?"

"I see your point. I am surprised, as he seemed rather traumatized. But you know Christopher, he always bounces back. He is certainly your boy."

Jonathan asks, "You have aroused my curiosity. What did the kid say?"

"Honey, I wasn't thinking straight. The wine and all. I'm sorry I said anything. Let's chat about it tomorrow."

Jonathan feels his chest tensing. "Angela. Come on. Nothing could ruin this evening."

She sits quietly, sipping her coffee.

The waiter brings the bottle of dessert wine and shows it to Jonathan, who nods. His assistant serves the dessert.

Angela sips the wine and smiles. "That's good."

Jonathan looks straight at her.

She takes a deep breath. "Some kid, named Peter Vaughan, stopped

Christopher in the hall and asked him…" She pauses. "Asked him… what it was like seeing someone's head blown off."

Jonathan freezes in disbelief. He drops his head and stares at the burning candle.

She watches him knowing that inside he is churning.

"Baby, I'm so sorry. I didn't…I shouldn't…I was just trying…"

He holds up his hand for her to stop and says in a low, ominous tone, "How…in the world…could anyone say…such a thing as that." His breathing is heavy and he clenches his teeth.

Angela tries to think of a distraction. She stands, knowing that he will also. He does.

"I'll be right back, dear. Need to powder my nose. Would you order more coffee?"

He smiles but it's not the happy smile from earlier. This is a smile that could frighten one.

Suddenly, something outside catches his attention. Shock splashes across his face. A darkened, scruffy face peers in a corner of the window. "Carter?" he whispers aloud, confused.

The waiter approaches. "Sir, is there anything I may get you?"

Jonathan answers, "Yes, actually…" He looks again at the window. Nothing. "My wife would like more coffee, please."

He reaches for the wine and takes a large swallow. Another deep breath and another look toward the window. He quickly pours water into the wine glass as Angela returns to the table. He stands to seat her.

"Honey. I'm sorry." She is remorseful.

"Not to worry. As I said nothing could ruin our absolutely perfect evening."

Jonathan glances again at the window. Nothing.

They have more wine and eat their dessert, enjoying the quiet and romantic moment.

CHAPTER 37

JONATHAN DRIVES WITH THE SUNROOF open. The air is particularly crisp and not too cool. Angela, with her shoes off, has her feet on the dashboard. She wears Jonathan's tie as a blindfold.

"Honey, we really need to do this more often. I mean it. This is FUN!" She laughs.

"Yes it is, love. Yes, it is." The stereo plays Miles Davis' *Flamenco Sketches*. "I love this tune."

"Me, too. And I love you!" she laughs, reaching for his hand. With the other hand she reaches for the blindfold. He intercepts.

"No, no, no...it's a surprise. You can't peek. We're almost there."

They drive for another 10 minutes. He changes the music frequently to keep her from getting too sleepy. "Honey?"

"Yes, delicious one." She giggles.

"I like you."

"I like you too. Really."

"And you know that I'm crazy about everything about you, but...!"

"Jonathan!"

"Sorry." He laughs. "The wine was good. But here's the thing.... your feet...come on. Whew!"

He pulls onto an overlook.

"You're playing. Right?"

Patting her, he laughs. "Yes."

He removes the blindfold and she leans to kiss him, as in the old days. Light is coming through the window in the roof...it is a full moon!

"Oh, baby. Look at that."

He says, "Yes. And look at that." He points out the car window.

The moon glistens on the surface of Lake Mitchell. It is beautiful. They are parked at an overlook above one of the few cliffs in the area. The stars sparkle like diamonds.

She takes a deep breath. "Oh…this is so beautiful. And so romantic."

"Yes, it is." And with that he selects the CD of Jim Hall's *Concerto de Aranjuez,* his favorite. "Wait here." He goes to the back of the truck, removes something and disappears.

A moment goes by and then another. He taps at the window and she opens the door. Just a few feet away is a blanket and a portable gas lantern.

He takes her hand and asks, "Shall we?"

"We shall," she murmurs.

CHAPTER 38

OFF DUTY OFFICER REDDICK AND a few buddies amble from their favorite hangout, The Handle Bar. They're laughing, still telling stories. Reddick says goodbye and goes to his car. It's the same model Charger as his official car, but it has a larger engine and an improved 7-speed transmission. His buddies get in four-by-fours or Camaros; some jump aboard Harleys. One by one, they rip out of the driveway. Reddick is last because he's texting a girl.

The night is clear and the moon is full. Because he's young, aggressive and buzzed he picks up the speed. Dennis has become a quick study since his last outing nearly a month ago and now he knows the roads. Heading down the straightaway, not far from the spot where he pulled Carter over, he decides to see if he can make the curve at a few more miles per hour than the last time that he practiced it.

He knows that the curve ahead is a bit more challenging than most but decides to go for it. He downshifts and then as he approaches the dip he guns it. Knowing that he must time it just right, he shifts down to third, hits the dip, then immediately kicks it to fourth, fifth and then to sixth. He has one gear left, so he picks up more speed. He's doing 60, 65 and now 70 in the straightaway.

To hit 70 or better and be able to take that turn would not only take a great deal of skill, something he has in spades, but also a great deal of luck. He pops the clutch the seventh time and steps on it. He has approached the turn called "Dead Man's Twist" about 10 miles per hour too fast. He feels confident since he has high-performance Brembo racing brakes. At the last minute he taps the brakes. The brakes don't work. Panicked he taps them again. Still too much speed. He stands on them, straight to the floor. He realizes that he

135

has about fifty yards to decide. He cuts it left and prays. He spins in ever-increasing circles. Should he come to a stop somewhere in this neck of the woods, or should he keep going straight? One of two things will happen. Either he will become airborne and end up not too far from where Carter took a late night dip; or, if he tries to keep the hood down he will certainly hit a tree and split the car in half.

He chooses the first, assuming that hitting the water would be softer. Wrong! Because of the trajectory of the launch he lifts off the lip of the road, catching a tree in the process, and subsequently shattering the front end's fiberglass enhancement. The transmission catches on another tree. It breaks the fall but causes the nose to drop precipitously. In the blink of an eye, he rips off the front end upon launch, catches a tree in mid flight, flips the car and goes airborne. At about 80 to 85 miles per hour the car crashes down on it's top. SLAP! Within seconds everything is black, cold and wet. Reddick barely has a chance to say, "Father, forgive…"

CHAPTER 39

ANGELA'S HEAD GOES UP! THE sound was loud and foreign. Jonathan says, "What the heck was that?"

They look at one another with sleepy eyes, trying to become reoriented.

"Sounded like a tree fell. Man, I was dreaming," Jonathan rubs his eyes and stretches his body.

"Me too," she looks at him, "or, was I?"

He checks his watch. "Oh, boy. It's after one!"

Yawning, Angela says, "Guess we're not the youngsters we used to be."

"Guess not." He stands, stretches again then helps her to stand. He folds the blanket and they head to the truck.

"I don't know about you, but..."

"I'm freezing!" she interrupts. They laugh.

Jonathan says, "Okay, we are officially old school. Let's get outta here."

"You don't have to ask me twice. Home James," she murmurs then falls back to sleep.

He smiles and pats her. "Nighty night, my Princess."

On the way home he ponders. Where in the world is his brother? Jonathan is still angry and hurt but he is also anxious and concerned. Angela is out like a light and he decides to take a detour.

Jonathan pulls off the main road and into Carter's driveway. Slowly approaching the house he sees no sign of Carter. At the house he parks the truck and whispers to Angela, "Keep sleeping. Just a quick stop."

"Okay," she sighs and is back asleep.

Taking a flashlight he gets out to look around. He finds the key above the window and goes in, flipping on lights and looking around. Sampson greets Jonathan, his tail wagging. Patting him Jonathan says, "I came back for you. You're going home with Uncle Johnny. Let me look around first."

Nothing seems changed but at the back he notices a doggie door. Frowning he says to Sampson, "I didn't see that before. Guess you did come and go as you liked. Well, not to worry, your old playmate is at my house. Okay, let's get home."

He walks through the house, flipping on lights and checking each room. Everything seems to be in order. "Just the way it was."

He returns the key and Sampson jumps into the back of the truck. Jonathan looks at the yard and nearby woods then he gets in the truck. Before he pulls out, his headlights shine on the side of the house.

"Something's different." He runs a mental checklist: no lights, no broken windows, a huge stack of firewood. He hesitates. "Hmm?" He thinks for a moment and then shrugs it off.

Sampson is already curled up asleep. Angela is still sleeping so he covers her with his jacket. She murmurs and he smiles and drives away.

For no apparent reason he stops mid-driveway, rolls down the window and looks back at the house. He hears only an owl in the distance and the late night sounds of the woods.

CHAPTER 40

THE NEXT MORNING JONATHAN AWAKENS with a dry mouth, pounding headache and a heaviness on his chest. A pillow covers his eyes. But the heaviness he can't shake. He shifts his weight and the weight shifts also. He tosses off the pillow and sees Sampson's face right in his. Sampson begins licking furiously.

"What in…" He pushes Sampson off and looks around the room. He still has on his socks and dress shirt. Fortunately, he had removed his suit and shoes last night.

"Morning, Sunshine!" Angela sings as she enters their bedroom with coffee in hand. She opens the drapes.

"Wow…that's bright," Jonathan groaned.

"What a glorious day. And what a precious, handsome, loving husband you were to treat me like your princess last night. It was deeeee-vine!"

Angela places the steaming coffee on the nightstand, kisses Jonathan's forehead, pets Sampson, shoos him off the bed and exits saying, "Breakfast will be served in 15 minutes, love." Sampson is now on the floor beside the bed.

"Wow," Jonathan mumbles. "This is why I don't drink anymore." His arm and leg hang off the bed as he attempts to collect himself.

A wet, scratchy tongue licks his hand. "Sampson!" he says, pulling away his arm. "Thanks, but I'll take my own bath."

His cell phone rings and grunting, he picks it up.

"Hey, buddy. It's Joshua. Of course you know that it's me because you have caller ID." He laughs.

"Yes?" Jonathan replies. "What can I do for you, Mr. Comedian?"

Joshua asks, "Maybe our board meeting that you had rescheduled for this morning? I was going to assume that you were good to go, but on the off chance that you may have forgotten I thought I'd call."

Jonathan says, "Should I remember this conversation?"

Joshua laughs. "You're kidding me, right?"

Silence.

"Oops. You're not. Oooooookay. Here's the thing. Your board members...the people who will decide how our salaries are paid this year, and who will also decide how much...and also where the money goes to build this new extension of our handsome church...THEY will be here in less than 30 minutes!"

"What?" Jonathan springs from bed then stops suddenly, as his head pounds.

"All right. I have to shower, get dressed and get there. Have Claire order the best breakfast from Causby Caterers. Ask for John, the owner. He'll take good care of us. Tell him that I personally requested him to, as he would say, 'put on the Ritz.' Ask him to bill me directly, please."

"I'm on it," Joshua replies.

"Have Claire order French Press Coffee, it's the best blend. But order decaf so that the board won't be overly anxious. This will all make sense to her."

"Good call. I'll even take it up a notch and order fresh flowers!"

"Nice! I must run," Jonathan says, "if I'm going to even pretend to be coherent. And you, my friend, need to be my Number One Second In Command."

"Done. See you in 30...or so." He hangs up.

Jonathan rubs his forehead, opens his eyes wide, grabs the coffee and heads for the shower.

David and Christopher are at the table. David is reading the newspaper. Christopher is reading Rolling Stones magazine. Angela is cooking bacon and eggs and humming a tune.

David and Christopher look at one another. David shrugs his shoulders. Christopher grins then asks a question. "Mom?"

"Yes, son. The bacon is nearly done."

"No. Not that. How was dinner last night?"

"Nice, son. Very, very nice. I felt like a princess. We went to Barrington's. It was…well, divine."

He smiles at David, then asks, "So, Mom, would you say that the evening ended even better than you had expected?"

She stops stirring, holds up the wooden spoon and points it at both of the boys. "Listen, I know what you're up to." She tries to suppress a grin. "But you can just forget it. I'm not telling anything. Now, drink your juice. It's nearly time for school."

She points at Christopher and says, "Not YOU. You are suspended. It will be one day in the stockade for you." She turns to David. "And YOU, smarty pants, will be leaving for school in less than 30 minutes."

They giggle and return to their reading.

"Breakfast is ready in five minutes." She grins.

CHAPTER 41

THE NURSE'S STATION IS FULL of officers. They are gathered speaking in quiet voices. Inside the Critical Care unit, Doctor Blair stands next to the unconscious Officer Reddick. The doctor and Officer Mahler discuss the severity of the situation.

"It's not good. Frankly, it's a miracle that he survived," Dr. Blair says.

"He is a tough guy, I'll say that," Officer Mahler replies.

A nurse enters the room carrying an IV. She looks at Dr. Blair. He nods and she replaces the empty one, adjusts the drip rate and exits as quietly as she entered.

Dr. Blair flips pages on his chart, reading, "Starting at the bottom and working up, looks like Officer Reddick has a broken right ankle—in two places, a cracked right kneecap, a fractured left hip and likely a bruised spleen, three broken ribs, a broken left arm—both above and below the elbow, one fractured collar bone, a lacerated left cheek with sub-dermal bruising—that may require a little plastic surgery—and we top it off with a severe concussion. We're hoping his current state, which resembles a coma, is indeed the first C and not the second."

Mahler frowns, "First C?"

"We hope it's a concussion and not a coma," Dr. Blair reports, "Big difference when you're dealing with this many injuries. As I said, it's a miracle he's alive. From what Officer Scott reported, based upon preliminary observations, he must have taken one helluva flying leap off of Dead Man's Twist." He shakes his head, adding, "He landed head first on the roof. That he didn't drown is a miracle."

Mahler stares at the floor and scratches his chin. Blair notices and asks, "What is it?"

Mahler quietly says, "I don't doubt that it's a miracle that he's alive."

He searches for the next words, "But the larger miracle may be that he survived the kind of impact that created all that damage, and yet when Scott found him, he was lying on a rock nearby."

Blair listens, intently watching Mahler's face.

"Now, he's a strong man, there's no denying that. Heck, I've seen him chase a guy for over a mile at breakneck speed and then come up on him and lift him up in the air—all 250, 300 pounds of him—and throw him down on his back. And Superman here hardly broke a sweat."

"Yeah?" Blair says in a questioning tone.

Still puzzled, Mahler looks at Reddick. "But the fact that he survived that speed," he continues, "from that elevation, sustained that much damage and *still* managed to release himself from a crushed roof, get out of a pinched window opening and swim 40, maybe 50 yards and *then* crawl up onto a rock and lay there for who knows how many hours?"

Doctor Blair finds this hard to believe as well.

"THAT'S the miracle, Doc."

CHAPTER 42

JONATHAN ARRIVES AT THE BOARD meeting 20 minutes late. Claire smiles at him. She whispers, "No worries. They've been enjoying the most heavenly pastries and coffee for the past twenty minutes. Happy as can be."

He sighs with relief. "Thank you. You're my hero."

She adds, "It was your idea. The pastry shop? Kudos to them for pulling this all together in a blink. Go on in and I'll join you in two shakes."

He starts to enter as she says, "And, Pastor?"

"Yes?"

"How was date night?" She smiles.

He smiles, "Perfect."

Adjusting his tie, he mouths, "Thank you," and opens the door to the Boardroom.

"Hello, and good morning, Mission Grove!" he says with a hearty voice and warm smile.

"Good morning, Pastor," they say one after the other. The men stand to shake his hand. He moves through the room greeting each one with a handshake, a hug, or a kiss on the cheeks of some of the older women. Then he gathers them around the table to settle in for what promises to be a pivotal point in the life of the church.

Looking at Jonathan, one would never know he was in pain, either personal or physical. But this is what is required of a pastor-teacher-leader-counselor-therapist-confidant-husband-father-friend. This is his calling and his joy, and it is what endears him to this body of believers.

The meeting is very important to Jonathan and the future of the church, as it represents a   moving forward. It also represents a milestone as he approaches 20 years as shepherd of this congregation. He never takes for granted that it requires a lot of trust in the leader and a lot of sacrifice from the people to make something as profound and life changing as a church succeed. To him the church is more than a building to attend on Sunday. It is more than the combination of scriptural references, intellectual musings and eloquent words to share on any given Sunday. Indeed, it has more to do with how the pastor lives his life as an example of what a man of God should be, so that people who are far from God may experience life in Christ.

Jonathan loves his place in life among these friends, as husband to his wife, father to his children and shepherd to the world in which he ministers.

CHAPTER 43

THE BOARD MEETING IS NEARLY at an end when the office phone rings. Claire excuses herself from the room and goes to answer.

"Hello, Mission Grove Church. This is Claire. How may I help you?"

A familiar voice on the other end says, "Hello, Claire. This is Officer Mahler. Is the pastor available to speak?"

"Hello, Officer. Actually, he is just wrapping up a meeting. He should be through shortly. May I give him a message?"

"That would be great. Ask him to call me. Tell him that it is urgent."

"Certainly. I'll do that. Thank you."

She hangs up as the crowd exits the boardroom. Everyone seems happy. Claire hears mentions of being ready to move on to the next phase of construction, and how this is good for the community at large, and how the time has come for expansion, etc. Jonathan follows the group, smiles at Claire and mouths, "Yeah!"

The group exchanges parting words, promising one another to, "Get in touch soon," and, "Tell them we said hello," and the classic, "Come see us."

Jonathan closes the door and goes to Claire's desk. With a huge sigh, he rubs his forehead and says, "That was tremendous. We are so blessed and I'm thrilled at the outcome. However, my head is pounding. I never really had breakfast and I need some water." He starts back into his office.

"Pastor?"

He sticks his head back out the door, "Yes?"

"Officer Matheson just called and asked for you to call him. He said that it was urgent."

Jonathan stops and says, "Okay. Sounds good. His cell phone or the station?"

She is puzzled. "Hmm, that's funny, I didn't ask. I would guess…"

"His cell," they both say simultaneously and laugh.

"Great minds," Jonathan says, going into his office and closing the door.

A few minutes later Jonathan, with briefcase in hand comes out and says, "Evidently Office Reddick is in critical condition at Presbyterian Hospital. I'm heading over there now."

Claire nods. Jonathan is still talking as he walks away. "I may or may not return. Depends on several things. If you need me just ring my cell. Thanks!"

Before she can respond he is gone.

CHAPTER 44

JONATHAN HAS JUST LEFT THE church when his phone pings with a text message. "Must have left something at the office." He reads the text. "One down. Two to go."

Not understanding, he frowns. He's a bit unnerved but dismisses it thinking that it could be from Claire. But that didn't make sense. Angela? "One Down..." Something about the boys? Then it hits him! Reddick. But who are the other two?

Before he realizes it he's driving over the speed limit. Stress has caused him to...that's it! Speeding. Carter. Reddick. Carter must be next. But wait, Carter's missing. Maybe that's it. Carter is "one," as in gone. Now, Reddick is "two." But who would want them dead? He is puzzled. This makes no sense. And he knows that he has to remain calm and very cool. This is like something out of the movies.

Suddenly, a car pulls out in front of him. Jonathan slams on his brakes. The car behind him nearly crashes into him, but instead veers to the right and comes to a screeching halt.

He waves his hand in the air as if to say, "Sorry."

"I go from a night of bliss...to Stressville," he says. "That'll teach me."

Picking up his phone again, he re-reads the text message, "One down. Two to go." He mumbles, "Who...why? I need to clear my head." He exits, pulls into the only Starbucks Drive-thru in town and orders a triple Caffe Americano and is on his way.

Within minutes he pulls into Presbyterian's ER Parking lot. Because his job brings him to the hospital often, he bypasses the security guards, front desk personnel and hall supervisors. He goes directly to ICU and is in Reddick's area in record time.

Jonathan nods to Mahler and holds up a finger as if to say, "Wait a minute." At Reddick's bed he looks at the badly broken body. A nurse is replacing bandages and she recognizes Jonathan. She smiles. He places his hand on Reddick's, bows his head and prays. Mahler watches. When Jonathan finishes he gestures and Mahler follows him into the hall and to a quiet corner.

"Not sure that I've ever seen anyone with that much damage," Jonathan says.

"You haven't seen the half of it. The other half of the destruction is on the inside," Mahler adds.

"Is he...do the doctors think he'll make it?"

Mahler shrugs. "It's anyone's guess. I mean, that much damage... But then, he's one tough dude. I know that."

"So, was he drinking?"

"Yeah. But that's nothing new."

"And speeding?"

"Again. Nothing new."

"In his car or the station's?"

"His."

Jonathan is deep in thought.

Mahler adds, "Kind of peculiar, don't you think?"

Jonathan snaps back. "Peculiar? How? He'd been drinking and speeding. And if I recall there was a full moon last night so he could certainly see the roads."

Mahler stares at Jonathan. "Look at you, Detective. I could use you on my team." He grins.

Jonathan smiles at the compliment. "No. Call it an occupational hazard, watching the small details and thinking outside the box."

"How was the big date, anyway?" Mahler asks.

"Did I tell you about that?" He recalls. "Oh, yes. It was good. Nice dinner. Great time. She loved it. Then, drove up to The Point...it was just like the old days."

Mahler stops cold. "What? The Point?" Mahler asks in surprise.

"Yes, The Point. Same place we used to go when we were younger."

He taps Danny on the arm, "Matter of fact, it wasn't far from where…" The color leaves Jonathan's face.

"What, man?"

Jonathan remembers something. "That's where you and I used to go diving, remember? High school, senior year." He continues to search for something. Then it occurs to him. "That's where Carter…?"

"Crashed. Yes." Mahler continues, "Nuts, huh? Crazy coincidence."

Something is bothering Jonathan but he can't put his finger on it. They are quiet for a long moment and then Mahler speaks up.

"But here's what I can't figure out. I find it highly peculiar that a former dirt track pro tosses his prized ride…doing only 80…on a dirt road—his specialty, by the way—and with brand new high-performance brakes that are not even a week old." He continues. "Sure, he was drinking. But come on. This guy's rough around the edges and quieter than most but he's sharp as a tack. And he knows how to drive. Most importantly he knows how *not* to crash." He then adds, "I don't get it."

Jonathan considers what Mahler is describing, looks into Danny's eyes and takes a deep breath, "You don't get it?"

Mahler frowns, not following the question.

Jonathan asks, "You can't figure it out?"

Mahler stands frozen.

Jonathan steps to within inches of Mahler's face and very quietly says, "This coming from a guy who orchestrates a plan…to make my brother disappear?"

Mahler doesn't blink.

Jonathan lets this sink in, then turns and walks away without a word.

CHAPTER 45

DRIVING BACK TO THE OFFICE, Jonathan sips the last of his coffee and remembers something. He recalls a time when he and his brother were kids and used to go, what they called "hunting" in the woods. Carter was an Eagle Scout and took it all very seriously. He won all the badges and awards there were to win. Needless to say he was exceptionally learned about many things.

One thing in particular he recalls is how Carter taught him to survive off the land in case of a catastrophe. He had always looked up to his brother because Carter never tried to prove that he knew more, he simply did. Later in life, Jonathan would receive degrees and awards, but Carter? He was a true outdoorsman and a man's man. Just like their father.

Like an old movie, Jonathan revisits memories he hadn't thought of for years. He recalls one day Carter taught him to build a shelter with nothing but two trees, some brush and a vine. Carter found two small saplings next to one another, bent them over, not even breaking the trees, just "borrowing" them. He would pull a vine from the ground, bend the saplings over, and tie them together at the top. Then he pulled them to the ground and tied them to the base of another tree. Gathering limbs, brush and leaves he created a canopy. It didn't seem to take more than 20 minutes and he'd be able to stay dry for days.

Another time, Carter took his little brother through the deepest of woods. And he was smart enough to take him out just before lunch. This way as the afternoon progressed Jonathan would be more inclined to pay attention, from necessity, and not be comfortable with a full stomach. That day's assignment was feeding off the land. Carter showed him which berries were safe to eat and which could kill you, or at the least, make you sick for days. He'd shown how particular bushes made for a nice, natural salad. And finally, the part Jonathan had the toughest time with was which bugs to eat. But again, listening closely and being very hungry had taught him valuable lessons. And satisfied his hunger.

After Carter came back from Vietnam, he recalled stories that Carter shared over beers in the back yard as they barbequed. It was during those summer afternoons that Jonathan understood more about Carter's true survival instincts...instincts he had learned when danger was nothing more than being at the end of an angry father's drunken fist. But Vietnam...that was horrific by anyone's standards. He recalled how Carter talked about escaping the prison camp and being forced to sustain life in the jungle for months. This was before being recaptured by the VC and being tortured to degrees Jonathan couldn't imagine. In fact Jonathan couldn't imagine having to suffer to such a degree.

He catches himself chuckling as he looks at the empty Starbucks cup and says aloud, as if he were chatting with Carter, "Heck, I fall apart if I don't have a couple of Double-Americanos a day." He continues thinking about his brother. "Or what I'd do without this gas-guzzling SUV seven days a week."

He thinks about how grateful he is for all that he has. It makes him question Carter's disappearance all over again. Something doesn't feel right. And again, he teeters on the precipice of anger and sorrow, hatred and guilt. One moment he mourns the loss of Carter, if indeed Carter is gone. Carter had drifted away from Jonathan for some time now as he retreated to his cabin for weeks on end.

He feels for Carter. He's sorry that he is an alcoholic and often a jerk, that he doesn't keep a job, and that he doesn't have a family. And him following in his father's footsteps of violence certainly doesn't help matters, nor does having a restraining order from wives one and two. But how much of this was really Carter's fault. Was it true that the sins of the father are passed down for generations? Maybe it was like the tendency for one brother to become bald like their father, while the other never suffered from a shortage of hair.

True, Carter suffered from post traumatic stress disorder. "But let's not forget one thing," he says to himself, "big brother made a big mess when he left his big gun in the house." And that mess will never be made right. A light has been snuffed out and it no longer shines. Her smile will no longer greet Jonathan at the front door every day, making the stress-ridden aches and pains of the day roll off his back. Her giggle that could turn the worst day in the world upside down was now only an echo of a memory.

The heartache returns, crushing his chest. Tears form in his deeply stressed eyes but do nothing to salve the pain he feels and he can scarcely breathe. Would the pain ever leave? Would his anger and bitterness ever subside? He misses yet despises his brother, an attitude no pastor should have. He is tormented. Why? Why Grace? He has no answers.

The sunroof lets cool air in and taking a deep breath he prays, "Lord, help me." An instant later the image of stacked wood beside Carter's house comes to his mind. Instinctively he frowns as he tries to find a connection. He checks his watch and calls the office.

"Claire? It's Jonathan. I have an errand to run. Please have Joshua cover for me and I'll check in later to free him up. Shouldn't be but a of couple hours."

"Sure, Pastor. It's taken care of," she says.

"Thanks."

"And Pastor, don't forget Joshua and his wife are joining you and Angela for dinner tonight. To celebrate the budget approvals, right?"

He smacks the steering wheel, "That's right. I almost forgot. All wrapped up in my own world. Thank you for bringing this to my mind."

"Surely."

"Claire, come to think of it, I believe I'll take the rest of the day off. This will let me clear my pounding head and also take care of a few matters of business. I'll make it up tomorrow if you would have Joshua cover the rest of the day. In fact, if he could check in on Officer Reddick at Presbyterian that would be great. I checked in on him and he's in bad shape. I'd like us all to be praying for him. Please spread the word."

"Certainly, Pastor. In fact, I'll get in touch with Officer Mahler and find Reddicks' family contact information and send them something from all of us."

He smiles and says, "You are the best. Thank you, Claire. 'Bye now."

With that he decides to dedicate the rest of the day to finding some answers.

CHAPTER 46

THE NOISE FROM CHRISTOPHER'S ROOM is louder than usual. Angela tries to ignore it, knowing that Christopher is going through an especially tough time. But this is ridiculous. From the window she sees her mother walking over and she smiles. A loud discordant note is struck, shaking the kitchen overhead light. Might be a good time for her to take a walk and greet her mother.

Daphne asks, "What is the racket all about? It sounds like you're having a rock concert in there."

"Yes, Mother, we are. In fact, we've been approached by promoters to stage Woodstock Two here." She indicates the various areas of the lawn where the "promoters" will set up. "There on the hill, not far from your house, will be an enormously long row of Porto-Johns." She spins around, "Here on the front lawn will be the main stage. But down along the driveway…"

"Just stop, smarty pants. There is no Woodstock Two and you know it!"

They look at one another and Angela can't decide which is funnier… the thought that her mother may be serious…or the fact that the idea popped into her head so quickly. She tries desperately to hide a rapidly growing grin.

Daphne says, "I like to never…" They both giggle and this gives way to hearty laughs. The music stops. They wait for the next eardrum crushing note. Nothing. They sigh in unison.

"Ah…." Angela says, "That's more like it."

"Yes," Daphne says. "Care for tea?"

Angela nods. And as if on cue, the noise begins again.

"Okay, that is just about it! I've told your father that he should build a garage for you." Daphne marches toward the house, her voice fading, "But no, you insist on...."

Angela stands enjoying the sounds of fall. While she can.

A few moments later Angela decides that her mother may need backup and she goes in the house. As the kitchen door closes behind her she sees that Daphne is in a stand-down with Christopher who is at the foot of the stairs displaying body language that says, "I dare you." Angela's patience won't allow for a great deal more as her late night partying is finally catching up with her. She walks into the room with authority, circumventing any negotiations Daphne may have orchestrated.

"Christopher, I've just about had it with your insolence, your noise and your fighting at school. I have just about had it. I've tried. The Lord knows that I've tried. Sometimes I just tire of trying. Please go back to your room and keep the noise down for the rest of the evening. I promise that in the very near future I will listen to your grandmother, do the smart thing and get Daddy to build you a garage. And then you can play your music as loud as you would like!"

Stopping, she realizes her voice had been slowly increasing in volume with each sentence. Daphne looks sternly at her.

Angela takes a deep breath. "I'm sorry. That was rude but your momma is tired."

Christopher, in shock and anger finally says, "Understood." He then goes upstairs and slams his door.

A voice comes from the living room. "Loudly," says David.

Angela looks confused and asks, "What?"

David peeks his head around the corner, saying, "So you can play your music as *loudly* as you like. You said 'loud' but it's loudly."

Although she wants to be angry, she can't. For fun, she decides to play with David. She goes to the living room with hands on hips and glares at him. David doesn't see Daphne but she is directly in Angela's line of sight. Angela is trying desperately not to laugh.

David looks at her with fear, but sees her nostrils flaring and knows that's a sign that she's about to laugh. He teases her, "Loudly,

Momma. The noise *be* too darn loudly. C'mon now, children. Give your momma a break and shut up, you hear?"

Angela is laughing so hard that she doubles over and nearly falls. Daphne joins in the laughter.

They're having fun until Christopher quietly enters the room. He stands looking at them with no expression. "Thanks, guys. I appreciate that. I'm trying to create my craft. Mom yells at me for doing just that. Then my kid brother starts cracking wise...no doubt, about my music." He turns and leaves.

Angela calls, "Christopher. We weren't laughing at you. Come back."

Too late. They hear his pickup truck start and he's down the driveway before they can get to the back door.

The three watch Christopher whip down the driveway.

Finally Angela says, "Well, that's wasn't so good."

David quietly pipes in, " Well. That didn't go so well."

Angela looks at him and says, "Don't you have homework to do?"

He nods and heads to his room.

CHAPTER 47

CHRISTOPHER SPEEDS OUT OF THE neighborhood and down secondary roads, slowing before he reaches the interstate. He stares ahead and goes into a "quiet place."

Most everything has come easily to Christopher. He's always been good in sports. When he decided he wanted to be in a band he asked a few friends with similar interests and they instantly jumped on board. Girls have always liked him with his laid-back attitude, hair that forever covers his brooding eyes and a quiet intensity that seems to say, "You can try and knock me off my game, but you won't." Most guys think he's one of the cooler kids in school. When they are around him they tend to mirror his body language. Christopher finds that funny but wonders why they don't just be themselves.

Yet since the death of Gracie it's as though some of his charisma has left him. He's more withdrawn and not as gregarious. He's not as competitive. Lastly, he's not feeling as romantic towards Kym, his soul mate. He cares about her and thinks about marrying her someday, but it's as though his life has become black and white. Less color.

Besides his best friend, Jimmy, the only other people really close to him are David, but he's still young and doesn't get the nuance of being a teenager. The other is his mom. It's not that he doesn't love his dad. It's more that he feels he has to try so hard to measure up and to be a super-fantastic Christian, or something.

He used to really love being around Uncle Carter who would take time and teach him stuff. He never felt judged by Carter and enjoyed hearing him talk about the war he was in. It helped him be more appreciative of what he had, especially after seeing so much that had been taken away from Carter. But sometimes he would start drinking and become different. Christopher noticed that if Carter were drinking what his parents referred to as hard liquor, he seemed to get hostile. Yet if he was just drinking a lot of beer, like he and his Dad used to do in the summertime when they grilled out, it wasn't as much a problem. They certainly laughed more when they would drink. But after what happened recently...

A car behind blows its horn and Christopher snaps back to reality. He had drifted over the middle line. He has to pay attention. That was another thing—his attention seemed to be weaker. He was more easily distracted. He knew he had to snap out of it, but he couldn't seem to get a grasp on things. He felt as if he were right on the edge of going to sleep all the time. And when that wasn't happening, then it was just the opposite. He wanted to get into fights and would gladly punch anyone for no reason at all, and at just about any time. Like yesterday. Or was that two days ago? Or, was it a week ago? He didn't even remember when it was that he smacked the daylights out of Peter Vaughan.

Not paying attention, his truck is speeding. 55 then 60. Christopher is angry just thinking about it. 65, 70. He is furious! Why does everything feel so stinking messed up? 75, 80.

Suddenly, flashing lights catch his eye in the rearview mirror. He hits the steering wheel and blurts out, "Damn!" The cop pulls over behind him.

"That's just great. Dad is gonna..." He tries to calm himself and reaches in the glove-box for the registration card. He turns back to see that it's Officer Mahler and cranks the window down.

"Look who it is," Mahler growls, trying to suppress a grin.

Christopher stares. His pounding heart gradually quietens.

"Trying out for NASCAR, are you, Christopher?"

"Hello, Officer Mahler. I'm really sorry. I was just..." he takes his license from his wallet.

"Just going a little fast is what you were just doing. And maybe not a little fast. How's 80 sound?" Mahler takes the registration card and license.

"Sorry. I had no idea."

Mahler looks back at traffic, then at his watch and then at Christopher. He hands him the license and registration. "Christopher, ordinarily I'd write you up. 20 miles an hour over the limit is certainly worthy of a ticket. But you're family and I like to look out for my family, so if you wanna just keep this between you and me..." He lets the words hang in the air, before adding, "I'll let you slide—with a *warning.*"

Christopher brightens. "Yes, sir. Absolutely, I understand. Between you and me. Thank you. Dad would kick my...I mean, he'd give me some serious hurting, especially after..." He catches himself and stops.

Mahler asks, "What? Especially after what?"

Christopher takes a deep breath and says, "I was kicked out of school for two days. So I could 'adjust my attitude' as they put it."

Mahler chuckles. "Let me guess. Fight?"

He nods.

"Good for you. And it must have been about...uh..."

"Yes. It was. But it was my fault. I've been ticked lately. And...well, some jerk...said something that made me lose my cool."

Mahler slowly nods, saying nothing.

"I had to hit him."

"You won't get any argument from me, Chris. Sometimes you gotta let people know who the boss is. Take matters into your own hands." He looks directly at Christopher, making sure he has heard what he was saying.

"Yeah." Christopher, feeling self-conscious, lowers his head.

"Lucky for you I was on this side of town. Just heading over to... take care of some...things."

He starts to walk away but turns to say, "It's probably best if you keep this between you and me, right?"

"Yes, sir. I owe you one."

"Yes, you do," he chuckles. "Be safe. Don't want you ending up on the side of the road...or in a lake somewhere, upside down and all.

You take care, okay?" He goes back to his patrol car.

Christopher sticks his head out the window. "Yes, sir. And thanks again."

Mahler tosses his hand in the air as he tears off down the road.

Christopher sits a moment then sighs. "Man, that was close. That'd be about all I need."

His palms have stopped sweating, his heart is no longer racing and he takes another deep breath before starting the truck. Shifting into gear he checks for oncoming traffic and slowly pulls out.

"Wonder what Uncle Carter would've done," he thinks to himself. "Shot him?"

CHAPTER 48

AT CARTER'S PLACE JONATHAN PARKS and sits thinking. "Am I losing my mind? What am I doing here? Is Carter at the bottom of Lake Mitchell? Or, is he alive and living in the woods trying to torment me and the family? Or, is he trying to drive me mad? If so, what's he trying to prove?"

He looks at the idyllic surroundings, remembering a time when life was in harmony. Where did it go wrong? Did our sinful nature get the best of us? Was it my fault? No! It was Carter's fault. And he knows it. Maybe it was God's way of punishing him for living a life away from God. Or, was it God's way of punishing me for being proud, or arrogant, or maybe loving my work too much?

He slowly walks up the driveway. It is time to figure this out once and for all. Or, forever live in this half-life. The not knowing was for the birds. He was here the other night checking on the house and picking up Sampson. He recalls that Carter's woodpile was stacked high, and he knows that whenever Carter is around he stays in shape by chopping and stacking wood. Yet, the wood was lower than this a couple of months ago. Now the wood is clearly stacked to the window ledge and he wonders what is going on. Someone has chopped and stacked more wood. This makes no sense. He walks around the house looking in the windows. Nothing seems to have changed inside. But outside there is clearly more stacked wood.

A loud crackle sounds and he turns to see Jess, a neighboring special-needs teenager, emerging from the woods.

"Hey, Jess. Pastor Matheson. How are you?"

Jess frowns. Then tilting his head to the side he grins as he recognizes Jonathan.

"Hey, Pastor. How are you?" Jess says slowly and deliberately.

"I'm good, Jess, thank you. Just stopping by to see my brother. Have you seen him?"

"No, sir. I haven't seen him for weeks and weeks. But he told me a long time ago that if he was away, or off visiting friends, or sick in bed, or whatever...that I was to come by here and chop wood and stack it until I got tired. Then, go home. And he would pay me money the next time I see him."

Jonathan smiles, nodding his head. "You're a good man, Jess. Carter is lucky to have you as a friend. Thank you."

"You're welcome, Pastor Matheson."

"Okay, well...I'll leave you to it."

Jonathan starts back to the truck and mourns Carter's probable death. He prays, "I can't take this anymore, Lord. Please help me."

"Pastor?"

Jonathan turns. "Yes, Jess, what is it?"

"Should I play catch up now?"

"What's that Jess?"

"Should I play catch up now?"

Confused, Jonathan asks, "What do you mean by catch up?"

Jess is confused and asks again, "Should I play catch up now?"

Jonathan asks, "Would you like to play catch up?"

Jess nods vigorously, saying, "Yes, sir. Carter says if it's not high enough for me to make it high enough. He must have got tired and quit." He laughs.

Jonathan looks from the woodpile, to Jess, then into the woods and asks, "Jess, has Carter been here recently?"

Jess grins and points to the stack of wood saying, "Can't you tell?"

Jonathan is confused but waits.

"Carter says that wood don't stack itself." Jess laughs. "Today's my first day!"

"Got it!" Jonathan smiles and says, "You're right, Jess. Good man. You're completely right...and smart too. Tell you what, why don't you take off the rest of the day. I'll make sure Carter stacks the rest of the wood. Right to the top," he says, pointing to the roofline.

Jess places the axe next to the house and walks back into the woods, shouting over his shoulder, "Bye, Pastor Matheson. Tell Mr. Carter to chop-chop." He grins, "That's what he always tells me to do!"

His laughter echoes in the trees as he disappears.

Jonathan looks at the woodpile and smiles. The tension in his shoulders eases for the first time in months.

CHAPTER 49

GATHERED AROUND THE DINING ROOM table is Daphne, Stuart, Angela, Jonathan, Deanna and Joshua. They have finished dinner and are having dessert and coffee.

Joshua says, "Daphne, that was one of the best meals I've had in a very long time." He puts his hand on Deanna's, "Not that your cooking isn't exquisite, hon, it's just..."

Deanna interrupts, "Watch those very next words, dear, or we'll be eating your specialty, beans and franks, for a very long time."

Daphne adds, "Well, it certainly wasn't all me. My daughter's a great cook also."

"Amen!" Jonathan shouts.

Angela beams and says, "Oh, stop..." They all laugh.

There is a lull in the conversation. Then Stuart says, "Jonathan and Angela, your Mother and I and these dear friends genuinely care about you both and we want what is best for you. I believe that you know this, right?"

Angela nods.

"This last year has been a bumpy ride what with the economy and all. Then, all of our lives were devastated with the passing of our dear and precious, Grace."

All nod in agreement.

"We've seen heartbreak take its toll on everyone. The two of you, your boys, us and our friends. And while we all need to band together and continue to pray for one another, we think..." he takes Daphne's hand "...that it's time for you to consider some professional help."

Jonathan stiffens. It's hard to be told what to do. He feels that he knows what he needs to do for his family. Angela senses this and tries to buffer the situation.

She smiles and looks at everyone. "Stuart, thank you. And thank you each for what must have taken courage to say, perhaps for fear that we would be offended. And, of course, we aren't." She looks at Jonathan and he nods.

"Angela's right," he says quietly. Turning to Stuart, he adds, "And you're right, Stuart. It has been tough. But with family like you all... and friends like all of those in our congregation...we will get through it."

"And your suggestion is good," Angela adds.

Jonathan interrupts, "But we feel that we have a pretty good handle on things."

Looking at Jonathan and Angela, Daphne finally speaks, "We're not saying that you aren't able to handle things. It's just that we think a 'coach' may be a good way to help navigate the waters. After all, I've been listening and watching your boys, and frankly..."

Jonathan tries to hide his agitation and stands to stretch. He smiles at her, "Daphne, this is a good idea. And actually all of you could be right. But I think I speak for Angela when I say that when it comes to our family..." he pauses, searching for words.

Angela interjects, "Our private life is something that we hold sacred."

Joshua nods, "Jonathan, Angela, we certainly get that. Nobody knows that better than four of your closest fans right here. Here's the thing, a consultant is often brought into a big business to assess the company and offer insight as to its inner workings, as well as an analysis of what makes the company good or bad. Well, a highly trained therapist can help champion your cause, and..."

He hesitates and Dee interjects, "Help make the path to recovery a smoother one."

The room falls silent for the first time this evening.

Jonathan dons his best smile and says, "Right. Good stuff. Well intentioned. Carefully considered and we appreciate it."

Just then, David comes running in the back door, chased by Christopher. David screams just before rounding the corner and stops abruptly at the doorway of the dining room.

Out of breath, he gasps, "Sorry! Chris was chasing me with…" He looks in the opposite direction as a small snake appears. Christopher sticks his head around the corner, grinning and holding the snake.

Angela is surprised. She speaks sternly, "Boys! It's homework time and getting close to bedtime. Please apologize for interrupting our conversation and then go to your rooms."

They start to grumble but Jonathan frowns and they straighten up and smile. Simultaneously, they say, "Sorry."

Christopher says, "It's just a garden snake," and heads upstairs.

David adds, "Our apologies. Very rude of us." And he is on his way.

All six adults chuckle when the boys are out of sight.

Stuart says, "I remember what it was like at that age."

Daphne jokingly says, "Can you remember that far back?"

Jonathan shouts, "Hey, now!" He begins gathering the dessert plates. Joshua follows his lead.

Daphne tries to stop them, "You don't have to…"

Jonathan shoos her hand away, "I know we don't. We just are." He winks at Angela. She smiles and says, "Thank you again for your support and your suggestion. We can look into it."

Joshua interjects, "I have the perfect guy. Armful of degrees. Sharp as a tack."

"Very…unique, with a great sense of humor. He comes highly recommended." Dee adds.

Jonathan says, "Good enough. Thank you."

"Thank you again for caring and for being here for us," Angela adds.

Jonathan and Joshua leave with dishes. Angela quietly says, "While I have a hard time believing that he'll have much fun, or go quietly, it is certainly worth considering."

CHAPTER 50

OFFICER MAHLER STANDS IN THE corner of Officer Reddick's hospital room and looks at the various machines and tubes. A nurse quietly enters the room and checks the patient's vital signs.

"Will he ever wake up?" Mahler asks.

She jumps. "Oh, goodness!" Catching her breath she says, "I didn't see you."

"Sorry. Didn't mean to startle you."

"That's alright. Been a long day and I thought everyone was gone for the night."

"I will be in just a minute. Just running over things in my mind."

"I understand."

"So, what do you think? Will he wake up, that is?"

She smiles, "Well, I'm not a doctor. Yet. But I have a very good feeling about him."

"Really? How's that?"

She pulls down a chart from over the bed. "I've been watching him closely...and considering all the severe damage he's undergone...his vitals are remarkably strong."

"That's good?"

"Oh, it's more than good," she adds. "I shouldn't say this, but his primary doctor didn't think there was any way in the world he'd survive...especially with all the internal damage."

"Yeah, he's a tough one, alright."

"I'd say." She returns to her work in silence, taking his temperature, blood pressure, pulse, checking his fluids and the state of his pupils.

Mahler watches with admiration.

She looks at his wristband, then the clipboard of notes, then to one of two IVs that hang overhead. One is blood and one is a clear liquid. She frowns. Mahler notices.

"Hmm."

He asks, "What?"

"Strange is all. He lost a lot of blood." She nervously states the obvious, "Fortunately, we've been able to supply him with plenty of blood."

"That's good. Right?"

"Well, of course. But the thing is…his blood type is very rare…" She trails off.

"And how is that strange?" Mahler asks.

"AB Negative is the most rare. Only .07% of the nation's population has it. It's the hardest to find and the trickiest to keep on hand."

He says, "But it looks like you have…uh, plenty…"

Before he can finish, she says, "We do have plenty, or have *had* plenty."

"It must be really late, or…" He shakes his head.

She chuckles. "I'm sorry. I'm making no sense. Anyway, here's the thing. Simply put, it's often the hardest to keep around and yet during these past few days, there has been plenty." She looks at him intently. "It's like it came from nowhere."

He checks his watch, suppresses a yawn and rubs his eyes. "Well, I've got to get outta here. Been a long day—long couple of days— and I'm beat. Thank you…" He looks at her name tag, "Brenda. You've been helpful."

She blushes. He notices.

"Thanks," she replies.

He's attracted to her. Maybe it's the uniform, he thinks.

She is finished, yet she seems to be waiting, and accidentally drops the clipboard. He reaches to pick it up and nearly bumps her head in the process.

"Oh, boy. I can be a klutz sometimes," she says.

"No, it's me. Working doubles is tough on the social life."

"Tell me about it. Try working a double and a third-shift." She pauses, smiles and says, "I have to get back to my station." She looks

AVID TEMPLE

at him. "I'll check on him later."

They walk out together.

"Sounds good," he says. He puts on his cap, keeping his hand on the brim and nods. "See you tomorrow."

"Sounds good." She smiles.

He's nearly to the car when it hits him and he says aloud, "Working doubles is tough on the social life?" He smacks his forehead, "Dude, why didn't you just ask her out? She teed it up perfectly."

In his driveway Mahler notices the front porch light is off. It's a dusk-to-dawn light and has been on every night since he bought this place. He puts the truck into park, turns off the engine, and sits quietly with the headlights aimed at the front door. It's then that he notices the front door has been tampered with. He unsnaps his holster and puts his hand firmly on his gun. He eases open the truck door, scanning the area around the house.

The simple, craftsman home is on the perimeter of a suburb. It's not in the city but not quite in the country. On full alert, he listens for anything out of the ordinary. Taking the large flashlight from the truck he flips it on and shines its strong beam at the windows. Nothing. He approaches the house, still listening. On the porch, the creak in the middle would alert about anyone within a hundred yards. The deadbolt has been busted and the door stands slightly ajar. He pushes the door with his foot and holds the light with his left hand directly over the barrel of the gun. His heart is pounding from nerves, not from fright. He's a big man, holding a powerful weapon and he had pulled up in a truck that had enough lights to illuminate a football field. He steps inside. Quiet. Suddenly his Great Dane, Buford stands. He raises the gun, ready to unload it.

"Drat it, Buford. You scared me!"

Buford comes to Danny and licks him on the arm. Then it hits him. Nobody would enter a house with a 170-pound Great Dane inside.

"Go lay down, boy. I'll be right back."

The back yard is park like and has two big oaks with an over-sized hammock strung between them. A small garden shed stands alone in the middle of the property. He nears the shed and reaches inside for a hidden panel. A small black cotter pin keeps the door closed. He pulls it out and opens the door. Shining the light inside he sees its prized contents are still intact.

A crushing blow to his head knocks out his lights.

CHAPTER 51

OVER BREAKFAST THE NEXT MORNING with pancakes for the boys, French toast for Angela and Irish steel-cut oats for Jonathan, the television reports that their good friend and local Sheriff Danny Mahler, was burglarized overnight. An early morning dog-walker noticed the open front door to his house and that the tires on his truck were slashed. When the local news station showed up they found the gagged and bound sheriff with a note duct-taped to his forehead.

A sheriff's department evidence bag, that had originally stored a number of confiscated items, was taped to the front door. Inside the bag was an official document describing all the contents and their origins. The items themselves were scattered around the room. They included three small unregistered handguns, a bag of marijuana and a very large roll of unmarked hundred dollar bills. The camera crew captured his image as he was being loaded into an ambulance.

Within ten minutes of the news report Jonathan's cell phone vibrates, signaling a text message is waiting. He flips the phone open and reads, "Two Down...One To Go!"

Angela shifts her focus from the television to Jonathan's face. He is trying to hide his shock, but is obviously upset and worry is evident on his face. She has seen this look before and had vowed that she would do anything in her power to relieve the stress that caused it. This didn't keep her from fearing the unknown.

"What is it, hon?"

"Nothing much," he says, trying to protect her.

David is watching his every move and this reminds him of his responsibility to be a good example. It isn't always easy. Parenting never is. He winks and David winks back. It was the kind of wink that says, "I want to be just like you, Dad."

Jonathan checks his watch once more before grabbing his coat. "Danny could probably use a friend about now. And from the looks of it..." he glances at the television, catching the very end of the story, "he'll need as many as he can get. I think I'll check on him on the way to work."

"Go get 'em Dad. He's lucky to have a friend like you," David says with wide-eyed innocence.

Jonathan's heart fills with thankfulness and he lifts a prayer to heaven: "Thank you, God, for my family." He kisses Angela, high-fives both Christopher and David and goes out to face the valley of the giants.

CHAPTER 52

DRIVING TO THE HOSPITAL JONATHAN tries to piece together the parts. Several things he knows, others he isn't sure about and a few extra he should learn about soon.

"One down—Two to go."

That was the first message coming immediately after Reddick took a dip in Lake Mitchell.

"Two down—One to go."

That was the second message, arriving within fifteen minutes of Mahler being found in a compromising position. Coincidence? Doubtful. Whoever was sending the messages, and he had every reason to believe that he knew who it was, had an immediate knowledge of both of the parties' predicaments, as well as an axe to grind with both.

"Axe to grind." Funny, he thought.

The clue, if you could call it that, was right in front of him. And who were the last two people to see Carter "alive?" Right, again. This is what he knew. That and the fact two people were hurt but still alive to tell about it. More pointedly one was alive but wishing he were dead, thanks to utter humiliation. The other? He was walking a tightrope between here and eternity. He wasn't sure whether both were meant to be dead, or simply hurt.

This pastor was beginning to feel more like a detective chasing clues and less like a shepherd tending his flock. He had always liked a good mystery, was a good problem solver and wasn't afraid of a little drama from time to time.

But one gnawing element remained: guilt. He felt torn by guilt. On one hand, he felt guilty for being glad there was a chance his brother was dead. If so, his problems would be over, as his daughter's killer, accident or not, would have paid for his crime. But the other side of guilt was sad and more empathetic. The kind of empathy that pastors were supposed to have for others. That part of him cared deeply and had the desire to roll up his sleeves, gather his best men and head out, turning over every leaf in the forest and dredging every inch of Lake Mitchell if that's what it would take to find his lost brother.

Therein lies another equation: *lost.* Jonathan reminded himself that his brother was not only physically lost but also spiritually lost.

CHAPTER 53

JONATHAN CALLED THE SHERIFF'S DEPARTMENT. It was answered on the first ring.

"Mission Grove Sheriff's Department. Office Scott speaking."

"Hello, Officer Scott. Pastor Matheson here. Has Officer Mahler processed yet and would it be alright if I come by to see him?"

"Actually, Pastor, Officer Mahler isn't here. Seems he took a pretty good blow to the head and they have him at Presbyterian Hospital."

"I'll check on him there. Thanks." Hanging up he thought, "Must have taken quite a hit to drop that bear."

As a nurse is putting the finishing touches on Mahler's bandaged head, Jonathan goes around the bed to where Mahler is facing the wall and rubbing his temples.

"You think the guy broke his stick?" Jonathan asks.

Officer Mahler opens his eyes, squints and sits up.

"Ooh...that's a rush," Mahler says, touching the back of his head.

Nurse Brenda says, "Big surprise there, Officer Obvious. We just gave you a half-dozen stitches."

"Ouch," Jonathan says and then laughs. "As I said, the other guy probably ruined whatever he hit you with."

Mahler grunts, "Funny. Very funny. Johnny, you know Brenda, right?"

Jonathan nods, "Of course. Nice to see you again."

"Likewise." She turns to leave.

Mahler looks at her and asks, "Hey, Nurse Brenda, you're not leaving me, are you?"

She smiles, "Oh, I think you boys have plenty to talk about. Besides

I work the third shift, remember? I only hung around so that I could give you a little more pain than you already had."

"Thanks," he calls to her disappearing back.

"Danny. What were you thinking?" Jonathan asks.

He replies, "That's just it, guess I wasn't."

"You've really done it this time. You'll be lucky to keep your job… if you don't do time."

He hangs his head. "I know. It wasn't supposed to get this out of hand. It all started…"

Jonathan interrupts, "I have a pretty good idea where it started. And while I appreciate your caring about my family as you do, you've really pulled a boner. And the evidence, it's been planted, watered and sprouted."

Mahler looks at him. "Good times."

Jonathan checks his watch. "Not sure how you're going to get out of this one." He stops at the door and says to the officer who is about to enter the room, "Just a moment please."

The officer nods and stands outside the door.

Jonathan lowers his voice, "I'll tell you what. Judge Timberlake and I used to play football together. You may recall that. No, you were always too busy chasing the girls. I'll pay him a visit and see if we can do something about this."

As he starts to leave Officer Reed comes in and says, "Alright, Captain Klepto, let's head out."

Mahler puts both wrists out and asks, "Really? Is that the new nickname?"

Officer Reed nods and cuffs on him, saying, "Sorry about this, but you know the rules."

Jonathan says, "Hang in there, bro. Maybe, just maybe, God will smile on you and give that thick skull of yours a break. I'll check on Reddick. Talk to you later."

Mahler nods and Officer Reed takes him by the arm heading in one direction as Jonathan goes the other.

Nurse Brenda is going toward Reddicks' room, but sees Jonathan and motions for him to follow her down the hall. "Have to check on patient number two now."

"Looks like we have more blue in here than on the street," she jokes.

"True."

Reddick is awake and Jonathan exclaims, "Well, happy day! You've had us worried."

Officer Reddick manages a small smile and tries to sit up, wincing with pain. He asks Brenda, "Would you please raise the head of the bed?"

"Sure." Brenda replies, pushes a button and the bed slowly raises. "How's that?" she asks.

"Good. Thanks." Reddick shifts only slightly, as several wires and tubes are still attached to his body.

"You're looking great, Dennis. Considering what you've been through, it's a miracle you're alive," Jonathan says.

"That's what I've been told. Guess your Man's looking out for me, huh?" He lifts his eyes upward.

Nodding, Jonathan says, "He must have some big plans for you."

Reddick snorts, "Well, don't know about all that, but I will say… I'm glad to be on this side of the grass."

Brenda checks his pulse, adjusts the IV and says, "Everything looks good. You gentlemen have a good one. I'm outta here."

Reddick looks at her intently and quietly says, "Thank you. You've been great to me."

She smiles, "My pleasure."

He continues, "Seriously. I know it's not been good. I felt like I was knocking on heaven's door."

Jonathan says, "Thank you, Bob Dylan."

Reddick grins and says, "I actually liked Clapton's version best."

Brenda adds, "Yeah? Guns N' Roses did it for me."

Jonathan says, "Looks like we have at least a couple of generations represented here."

After she's gone, Jonathan says, "Seems like both you boys have eyes for her."

Reddick frowns, "What both? Who are you talking about?"

Jonathan replies, "You and Danny?"

"Oh. Maybe. I'd say I have a better chance than he does. He may be able to walk but I'm better looking."

"And more humble."

They laugh. Jonathan stands at the window, giving Reddick time to gather his thoughts. A couple of moments pass.

"I'm really sorry about your brother," Reddick quietly says and looks at his broken body. "Guess I had it coming," he continues.

Jonathan just listens.

"It wasn't supposed to go the way it did."

"How is that?" he asks.

"I was just supposed to scare him."

Jonathan relaxes and leans against the wall.

"My job was to take him out for a few drinks. Show him a good time—get him sauced up pretty good. Then, Danny was to show up. No hard feelings and all that."

Jonathan nods.

"Then we all leave. Danny was heading home and I was supposed to wait until Carter got down the road, hopefully swerving and/or speeding. Which he did. And I chased after."

"So, I stop him. Ask for, you know, his license and stuff. He was surprised. Guess 'cause I just lit him up and now here I was trying to arrest him again." Reddick sighs deeply.

"I walked to my car, going through the motions, when he just takes off. And I mean, shoots outta there like a rocket. It caught me off-guard, but I just kicked into autopilot."

Reddick's mouth is dry.

Jonathan gets the glass of water and puts the straw to Reddick's mouth. He drinks.

"Thanks. Still dehydrated." He looks at the IV bags and says, "You'd think with all this…" He shifts a bit trying to get comfortable.

"What happened then?" Jonathan asks.

Another deep sigh. "He's going fast. So, I go fast. Then he turns down this side road, one I didn't even know about and of course I chased after. But, then he came to this…gap. He slowed down and just as I was about to catch up, he guns it again, and jumps the ledge, speeding down the side of the mountain. Before I can catch up, he hits the tree, taking it down to the ground, and…"

Reddick stops. He looks at Jonathan who is listening to his every word.

"What?" Jonathan asks.

"It was crazy. I can't to this day decide if he was drunk and went off the side of the mountain, or if it was like some sort of…suicide mission. I have to believe it was an accident."

Jonathan is intent on getting clarification and asks, "So that I get all this straight, what was the reasoning behind all this?"

Reddick takes a deep breath and replies, "We figured the easiest way to get Carter handled, for lack of a better term, was to get him back in jail. And given the fact that he'd just been arrested for drunk and disorderly conduct at your house, it wouldn't be a tough case to argue. Plus, this would have made his third DUI. All in all, things were pretty stacked against him."

Silence.

Jonathan very quietly says, "He's always been a tortured soul."

Reddick adds, "Honestly? This is certainly none of my business, but if I had happen to me what you had happen to you and your family…" After a long silence he adds, "Brother or not, I would've sent him to prison, charging him with negligent homicide."

Jonathan can feel heat rise in his face as pain slowly squeezes his chest and tears beg to flow. But he won't allow it. Suppressing his emotions, he says, "Well, the first order is to get you well. I hear that you'll likely be able to get home in no time."

"Well, not so sure about that, but I will say that I'll sure give it my best."

"That's the best thing you can do."

Reddick smiles, "Yep. And you can be sure, I'll be up and moving full force faster than you can say rehab. I get something in my mind and I won't let it go."

"Good attitude, Dennis. We could all take a lesson from you. I have to be on my way, but I'll check on you in the next couple of days."

Reddick extends his hand, "Thank you for your concern…"

Jonathan takes his hand, "The pleasure's mine."

"And for not throwing me to the dogs."

Jonathan frowns, not understanding.

"It'd be easy to hate me, and Danny, for that matter, for plotting this mess."

Jonathan shrugs. "You know, Danny looks at you as a brother. You and I are about his only friends. While I'm not crazy about the method of justice, I appreciate the heart that's behind it. I'm of the opinion that revenge, if not carefully monitored, can become a slippery slope."

Reddick nods.

Jonathan salutes Reddick.

CHAPTER 54

A COOL BREEZE WAFTS THROUGH the bedroom window. Angela is sound asleep. Jonathan is restless, having a bad dream.

He is running through a dark forest, dense with underbrush. The sound of gunfire echoes through the thick air. Stopping for an instant he tries to gauge how near his captors are. Falling from time to time his knees and hands are bloody but he continues to run. Men are shouting in the distance and he runs faster, looking back to see who it is that is chasing him. He stumbles, falls off a low cliff and lands on his back; the wind is knocked out of him. He tries to catch his breath and fears that his back may be broken. He squeezes his eyes shut, wincing in pain. When he opens them, Carter and his father, Randall, stand over him. The scene is distorted. Carter has a gun in one hand, the same one that killed Grace, and a bottle of beer in the other. Randall has a large gun holstered on his belt and a bottle of liquor in his hand.

"What are you, a sissy?" Carter shouts.

Randall leans over Jonathan. He barks, "Why can't you be a MAN like your brother...and like ME! You are scared and running like a little girl. What do you have to be afraid of; you wouldn't know danger if it bit you!"

Both men laugh. Then Randall pulls the gun from his holster, points it at Jonathan and snarls, "You think you are better than us, all high and mighty. Well, how about you pray to your Maker now, preacher man!"

He pulls the trigger. BOOM!

Jonathan sits up and his heart is racing. He is breathing heavily, drenched in sweat. Next to him Angela is asleep. He gets quietly out of bed, grabs his robe and tiptoes down the hall. Christopher and David are both asleep. In the kitchen he checks the time. It's a few minutes after three. He has awakened at the same time for weeks, but this time instead of trying to go back to sleep he drinks a glass of water and tries to calm his racing heart.

Outside a light is flickering. He mumbles, "What the…" and opens the sliding glass door and steps onto the deck. Hamburgers are burning on the grill and next to the grill is a cooler. The cooler is open and stocked with beer. He looks around but nothing else seems out of place.

But what he sees in the lounge chair takes his breath away. It is a gun…like the one that killed Grace. Taped to the gun is a note that reads: "Three Down—None to go." And underneath is written: "Why not do us all a favor and end this torment. Your choice: you or me."

Jonathan feels faint and sits on the bench thinking, "Only one person would do this. But what does the last line mean, *your choice: you or me?*"

He gets a beer and takes a long drink and it seems to help calm his nerves. He stares at the note and then he cries. He feels that he can't take it anymore. He buries his face in his hands and sobs for several moments.

"Honey?" Angela quietly says.

He sees Angela, straightens up and wipes his eyes.

"Baby, what's going on?"

He says nothing but gestures for her to come sit by him.

"Why is the grill…"

"I don't know."

She sees the gun in the chair and gasps, "Honey…"

He hands her the note. "Here."

She reads the note and groans, "Oh, baby. Who…" She tries not to cry.

He finally whispers, "First, I lose my little girl and then my brother disappears…"

She draws him to her and seeks to comfort him.

"Maybe they are right," he says.

"Who?"

He doesn't answer.

After a moment she whispers, "Right?" She continues to hold him and kisses the top of his head.

"Maybe our family and friends are right. Maybe we need help."

Another long silence and finally he says, "And maybe it is time."

"Time for what, Jonathan?"

"I…need…help."

CHAPTER 55

STANDING AT AN ELABORATE AQUARIAM Dr. Jefferson Long feeds his fish an assorted mixture of food. From the passion with which he feeds the fish to the numerous photos that adorn the handsome office, one knows that Jefferson is comfortable with what he does and the people with whom he works. He wears a sports coat, sweater vest, bow tie and matching pocket-handkerchief. He also has on linen Bermuda shorts and leather flip-flops. His strong, dark legs shine. He is humming a tune when the phone rings.

"Good morning, Eloise. Yes, I have fed the fish but thank you for reminding me. What's on your sweet mind?

Eloise is the demure spinster who has worked for Dr. Long for a decade. She is older than she looks and her youthful appearance is reminiscent of the 60's, complete with form-fitting dress, perfectly coiffed hair and cat-eye glasses.

"Your first appointment of the day is here. Shall I send the Mathesons in?"

"Yes. Please do."

He straightens the desk, gives his office a once-over, stops at the mirror to adjust his bow tie and opens the door.

"Hello, Reverend and Mrs. Matheson. Please come in and do make yourselves comfortable."

They take chairs in front of his large desk.

"I'm delighted to meet you both. I've heard such nice things about you, Pastor Matheson, and also you, Mrs. Matheson."

"We have heard good things about you also," Angela replies, touching Jonathan's hand.

Jonathan smiles politely and says, "Your fine reputation precedes you."

Dr. Long says to Angela, "I hear that you are an accomplished pianist at your church."

"I used to play more earlier but now I am spending more time with the congregational families, some who are trying to cope with the loss of a loved one."

He nods. "May I address you as Angela?" He turns to Jonathan, "And you as Jonathan?"

"Certainly," she replies.

Jonathan says, "Of course."

"It is more informal. And given the fact that we're here to explore personal issues..."

Jonathan fidgets. Dr. Long notices.

"Dig away," Jonathan quips.

Angela chimes in. "What he means is that..."

"He knows what I mean, Angela."

"I do," says Dr. Long. "And I realize that you both have suffered an enormous loss. Something that none of us would ever, ever wish upon anyone."

Angela is subdued and says, "It has been awhile yet feels like forever. We are trying to cope with the loss of our daughter Grace."

Dr. Long nods, "Indeed."

Jonathan and Dr. Long hold one another's eyes.

Dr. Long then asks, "If we weren't ready to try and learn how to cope with our grief then why are we here? Would I be correct in saying this?"

Angela smiles at Jonathan. His discomfort has caused him to stand. He goes to the fish tank and leans close, watching the dozen brightly colored fish swim toward him.

"You like fish, Dr. Matheson?"

Jonathan replies, "Yes, I like fish. And I am not a doctor. I have a master's degree. I'd like to work toward a doctorate one day."

Jonathan looks at Angela and she motions for him to come and sit by her.

Dr. Long doesn't miss the non-verbal communication. "While

you two were creating your lovely family I was spending my time studying and collecting degrees. They are good but what you both have is better, and it is something that I truly admire."

Jonathan studies the floor, then says, "It's more about what is most important to you and how selfless you're willing to become. For me, family is the greatest reward for a life well spent."

Angela smiles and Jonathan reaches for her hand. "Doctor?" she asks.

"Yes."

"May we get right to some of our real issues? We've been putting this off, for one reason or the other, for some time. I'm sure that you can surmise that my husband is well-educated, loved by his family, respected by his congregation and admired by his community."

Jonathan smiles, "Thank you, dear."

She continues, "And we understand the mechanics of sorrow... having dealt with it throughout the years. But when it hit home, where we live...we need to reach out for help. That's why we're here today."

Jonathan says, "Yes." He pauses a long moment then says, "It's one thing to build a family and a church...but sometimes the foundation upon which we build that home gets shaken up by stress... complicated by sorrow..." He stops.

She adds, "Add to that the recent loss of his brother."

Jonathan looks at his hands.

Dr. Long says, " I wasn't aware of that. I'm so sorry. When did this happen?"

"Some time ago. His car went off a cliff at Lake Mitchell and his body has never been found. He appears to have just disappeared," Jonathan says in a subdued tone.

Angela adds, "Jonathan believes that he may still be alive. But frankly, there's been no sign of him. And we have certainly searched for him, but he..." She trails off and lowers her head.

Dr. Long allows moments to pass.

Angela continues, "As you can imagine, all of this is quite a bit for anyone to handle, much less someone with the responsibilities that Jonathan has."

Dr. Long nods.

"Again, the people love him and love our family, but they feel the stress just like anyone else. Sometimes Jonathan gets full of himself and plays the investigator."

Jonathan looks at Angela. "What?"

She continues, "I'm just saying…"

"I do not!"

The doctor speaks. "Just a moment. We're here to repair, not rebuke. To fix, not fixate."

They look at one another. Silence.

"What I'm getting to is this. My husband, while wanting to reach out, frankly doesn't want to be here."

Jonathan interjects, "That's not fair. All I want is…"

Dr. Long holds up a hand. "One at a time. Let's honor one another's feelings."

Angela looks at Jonathan and says, "Honey, I'm not rebuking you. I'm simply trying to, as you would say, cut to the chase with the doctor."

Jonathan nods, "It's just that…" After a pause, he says, "Okay, you're right. I don't want to be here. Frankly, as much as I respect what you're trying to do here…and you evidently know what you're talking about…perhaps you are outside your level of expertise."

Dr. Long says, with a small but kind smile, "Perhaps you're right, Jonathan. But I would much rather err on the side of optimism than on the side of perfection."

Again, silence until Angela speaks. "Doctor, could we simply ease into this? As you have said, my husband and I have been through tremendous grief and turmoil. Frankly, while we need to understand how to cope, and we want to equally understand what we can expect in this grieving period."

"Well put, Angela. I see that you comprehend what it is that I hope to bring out in our sessions. You are way ahead of the curve."

"Really?"

"Really," he answers.

Jonathan looks at them with consternation.

She continues. "We know that in some people's eyes perhaps we should be better adjusted by now. But frankly, Grace was..." She hesitates, "We waited so long for her to show up in our home." She begins to cry softly.

The doctor hands a box of tissues to Jonathan for Angela.

"Thank you," Angela says quietly, and takes the tissues, allowing her hand to linger on Jonathan's.

Dr. Long watches and then says, "I will share what I think, according to the questionnaire that you filled out prior to our meeting, and interpreting what I've seen in our short time together. What you have gone through is not only extremely tragic but also confusing. And here's what I mean by that, it's as though your family has been attacked. Consider it as a random act of pain inflicted upon unsuspecting humans. When tragedies such as these occur we often seek to place blame on something or someone. And what we really need to do is try, to the best of our abilities, to understand that perhaps Angela is making progress."

"Damn!" Jonathan blurts.

Angela looks at him. "Jonathan. Please."

"Angela, you 'please.' We know exactly who is responsible for this...'accident'."

"Jonathan, we don't have all the evidence."

"Doctor, we have all the evidence we need. It's pretty cut and dried, if you ask me," Jonathan growls.

Dr. Long looks from Angela to Jonathan, then to Angela again, before speaking.

"Do you?" he asks.

Jonathan nods at the same time Angela shakes her head no. He then turns to her. "Yes, we DO. We know exactly what and how what happened...happened!"

Silence. They chuckle at the awkwardness of Jonathan's delivery.

Jonathan barely smiles.

Dr. Long replies, "Really?"

Angela says, "Really."

Dr. Long returns with, "Seriously?"

"Seriously."

Finally, Jonathan laughs. The laughter slowly dies and Angela takes a deep breath.

"Feels good, doesn't it?" Dr. Long asks.

Angela nods her head, "Yes, quite. Thank you."

"No, thank you. This is after all your time," Dr. Long replies.

Jonathan is obviously restless and says, " This is all well and good, and I'm trying to appreciate your insight and your sense of humor, but I would venture to say that until you have walked in our shoes you're not likely to be able to fully appreciate what we're going through."

Dr. Long slowly nods.

"Perhaps you're right." He glances at the clock and continues, "And perhaps our time is up. For now."

Angela is surprised and says, "It doesn't seem as though we have been here that long."

Jonathan says, "Long enough," and stands to leave.

Angela says, "Yes. Of course."

Dr. Long says, "There's no rush to our meetings. And though we have just met, I feel we've already made progress in this short time. Let's agree that that's enough for today."

He stands and then adds, "Let's meet again next week and see what progress we can make. Shall we?"

At the door, Jonathan says, "Thank you, Doctor. See you soon."

Angela shakes the doctor's hand. "Thank you, Dr. Long. Give us time. He's having a really tough time adjusting to...not having his little girl. Among other things."

"Understood. And you may call me Jefferson."

She smiles. "Thank you, Jefferson. You're a delight. We'll see you next week."

Jonathan walks down the hall saying, "Should be fun."

Dr. Long says, "Have a lovely week. Blessings to you both. I will see you next week."

He closes the door, crosses to the fish tank and quietly says, "We have work on our hands don't we, my little ones?" The fish gather at the top of the tank, swimming in circles and anticipating food.

"Pain is a pool that you shouldn't swim in too long..." He watches Jonathan and Angela walking to their car and adds, "For fear of drowning."

CHAPTER 56

THE OLD CHURCH BELLS CHIMED a tune heard in this community for over a hundred years. This is one of the twenty oldest churches of its affiliation in the country. Several people cross quickly from the front lawn into Mission Grove Community Church as Pastor Matheson is giving the morning announcements.

"Good morning. Thank you for coming to worship with us in the Lord's house this lovely fall day. My wife and I thank you for your continued encouragement and support since our daughter Grace's passing. These have been difficult times and more than challenging. But our grief and adjusting to not having her smile brighten our lives has been minimized by the prayers and support of you, our congregation...our family. You are what helps to keep us going every day. Thank you."

Sniffs are heard throughout the congregation. Angela lowers her head and young David takes her hand. She smiles at him and he rests his head on her shoulder. She looks at Jonathan. He smiles tenderly at her.

"Let us begin our worship by singing hymn number 114."

Christopher tunes his guitar as his band mates tweak their instruments. The crowded room is stacked with equipment, some borrowed and some new. The garage is filled with the things found in most American garages: yard implements, boxes and other miscellany.

They hit a few discordant notes and as the bass drum is struck the windows rattle. Christopher's best friend, James Garvin, aka "Choppers" because of his oversized teeth, plays the drums. He has a natural beat and an equally natural sense of humor. Everyone likes James, or Jimmy to his friends. Christopher and his band mates are about the only people who use the nickname "Choppers." The group has been friends all through high school and band mates for about a year.

Jimmy asks, "Hey, Chris. You about ready?"

Christopher frowns, "What's your hurry? Going somewhere?"

"Just asking, bro. You're taking longer than usual to get your act together."

Christopher snaps, "Listen, Choppers, if you're in such a hurry why don't you just hit the road? We can manage without you."

Jimmy lowers his head and mutters under his breath.

Ray Foster, the lead guitarist, chimes in, "Chris, chill, huh? We're all here to have fun. Besides, you could pick it up a bit." He turns up the amp and strums a couple of chords. It's loud.

They all laugh.

Christopher wails, "I wanna rock and roll all night....and party every day!"

All the instruments kick into high gear.

Pastor Matheson is trying to detect the source of the noise. "...And bless us, Lord, and the words that we shall hear." The loud noise continues. Clearly distracted, he finishes with, "Amen." He looks at the congregation, notices a few heads turn, but continues to ignore the blare from next door.

"I have a question for you today that I would like each of you to contemplate. Have there been any instances in your life whereby you have needed to forgive someone but can't seem to come to terms doing so?"

Several heads nod in agreement.

"In His word, we're commanded by God to forgive those who trespass against us, those who have caused us wrong. We are to love them, unconditionally, just as Christ loved the church."

The sound in the garage has grown louder, along with the heat, thanks to the energy produced by the jumping and yelling for the past half hour. Christopher stops playing and opens the double garage doors.

"There. Let's get some fresh air in here and cool off. And let our neighbors," he nods to the church next door, "enjoy the music too!"

They all laugh.

Christopher turns Ray's amp, then Scott's and then his own to volume 10.

"I'd crank it to 11 like in Spinal Tap but this only goes to 10." Again, more laughs.

The band breaks into an ear-splitting rendition of AC/DC's *Hell's Bells*.

The church bells announce the end of the service. Pastor Matheson and Angela stand in the vestibule shaking hands with the departing congregation and thanking them for coming. The pastor looks in the direction of the noise and the garage next door. The music stops just as Christopher and the boys see that church is letting out. Angela sees the fire in Jonathan's eyes. He conceals it well, given the presence of the congregation. He continues to shake hands, wishing his members a blessed day.

In the distance, Ray and Scott pick up their bikes and leave. Jimmy jumps on his motorcycle, waves Christopher aboard and they roar down the long driveway and onto the road. Angela's gaze follows the boys into the distance. She is both sad and concerned.

CHAPTER 57

THE MATHESON DINING ROOM TABLE is laden with fried chicken, collard greens, coleslaw, mashed potatoes and homemade rolls. It is a true southern Sunday dinner. All seems well but Jonathan sits drumming his fingers and quietly simmering while looking at the newspaper. David comes in.

"Wash your hands, son?" Jonathan asks his youngest son.

"Yes, sir," David answers holding both hands high.

"Excellent. Know where your brother is?"

"No, sir. Last I saw him, he was...uh..." He stops.

"Playing in his rock band?"

"Uh-huh. I mean, yes, sir." He scans the sports section of the paper and asks, "Dad, have you seen what Duke did to Clemson?"

Jonathan smiles, appreciating his son's attempt to change the subject. He winks. David winks back.

"Dad, I'd go easy on him. He's been suffering a bit lately. Depression, you know. It's a tough thing to beat."

"Really?" Jonathan replies.

"Yep. Really."

"Seriously?" Jonathan adds.

David asks, "Is this 'really, seriously'...thing something that's creeping into the common vernacular? Or is it my imagination?"

Jonathan adds, "Why yes, Professor, I think that it is."

David smiles and says, "Seriously!"

Angela enters and Jonathan stands, kisses his wife on the cheek and pulls her chair out.

She looks at David who is standing behind his chair, straight as a soldier. "At ease," she smiles. "Let's eat."

They all sit. Jonathan looks at his watch and Angela touches his hand, "It's okay. He'll be here eventually."

As Jonathan serves David's plate Christopher comes in the back door. Jonathan and Angela exchange looks. Jonathan stands to face his son. Christopher tries to walk past as though nothing were happening.

"Excuse me," Jonathan says, sternly.

Christopher stops and stands in a slumped "I don't care posture."

Jonathan stares. Waiting. They hold one another's eye and Angela finally speaks. "Son, come on, it's time to eat. Get washed up. It's your favorite, fried chicken."

Christopher walks away, saying over his shoulder, "I'm not hungry."

Jonathan, still standing says, "Son. Look at your mother when she's talking to you. Go wash up and get in here and join us for Sunday dinner."

"But..."

"Not but! Get in here and let's have lunch as a family. I'll not hear another thing about it. Understood?"

"Yup," he replies.

Jonathan glares and Christopher straightens up.

"Yes, sir. Thank you, sir. I'll look forward to lunch with you and the missus, sir." He salutes.

Jonathan is not happy.

"Honey, it's alright. If he's not hungry..."

Jonathan stops her. "He is hungry. He just doesn't know it yet. And if he isn't, he should be. It's Sunday dinner and we always dine together. No matter what. And besides, we're going to honor..." He stops.

"I know, Dad! Why the hell do you think I'm not hungry!" He storms off.

Angela gives Jonathan a "let him go" look. Jonathan obliges and sits down.

Angela is washing the dishes and looking out the window. Jonathan dries. They work in silence.

"You know it undermines me, and my authority, when you do that," Jonathan finally says.

She continues to work silently. "I know. I'm sorry. It's just that he's still a young boy, Jonathan, and…"

"No," he interrupts, "he's a young *man*, and he needs to learn respect and to do the right thing."

"Baby, he is, yes. And he knows, and he does."

Jonathan chuckles, "You're amazing. And you don't miss a trick. BUT, you are entirely too easy on our boys. And…"

She interrupts. "No, I'm not. I'm lenient…in times of trouble. Jonathan, you were raised by a tyrant; a man who lived by a code whereby he destroyed whatever he wished, whenever he wished… and whomever he wished…because he was a…" She falters.

"A bully and a drunk. Yes." He drops his head.

She turns and holds his face in her hands. "Dearest. You are not your father. He was someone who was never able to feel anything unless it hurt. Therefore, he wanted to make sure everyone else around him hurt, too."

Jonathan is silent for a long time then goes out onto the deck. She watches him for a moment before joining him.

"Jonathan, what's wrong?"

He stares into the distance then slowly turns to face Angela.

"Honey, there's something I've been hiding from you. I've meant to tell you. I've wanted to tell you. In fact, it's been on the back of my mind for the longest time, but…"

"What?" she interrupts. "Just tell me. And stop frightening me."

"I don't even now how to tell you."

She grabs his arm. "What is it?"

"Carter…isn't…dead."

"WHAT?"

"He's alive. And, as far as I know, he's watching our every move— otherwise, how could Reddick have crashed and survived. How would Danny have been framed with the information that only two people knew about? One other thing…and I have a pretty good feeling that it is also true...I *think* Dad is alive, too."

Angela's mouth drops open.

CHAPTER 58

JONATHAN AND ANGELA SIT AT the picnic table on the deck for a very long time. Angela gathers herself. "Jonathan Randolph Matheson, I have no idea how you could keep something of this significance from me."

"I'm sorry. I truly am. It's just that..."

"It's untrustworthy is what it is!" More silence. "What else have you kept from me...after all this time? Anything?"

"No. Nothing. I promise."

She looks at him intently and studies his eyes. "I know that some deep-seated thing must have risen to the surface in order for you to bring this up. Is it because of Grace?"

He shifts uncomfortably, "I suppose so. That and maybe I am not the father that I thought I would turn out to be."

She's confused. "Is this about Christopher?"

"Part of it."

"Honey, you know as well as I do that he's a teenager and his hormones are all mixed up. He's trying to figure his place in the world and all that, plus dealing with his little sister's death."

"True. I know that he feels so responsible. Being there, seeing the gun, watching her play with it."

"But how does this make you a bad father?"

"Because I shouldn't have let my brother bring his gun into the house."

"Yes, but you didn't know. Did you?"

"As I said before, I had no idea he was carrying his gun. You know that damn thing never leaves his side, except when he steps on our property. I have no idea why he had it that day." Silence. "And I know that you hate guns."

Angela stands. "Again, WHY on earth would you lead me to believe

207

your brother was dead? And, until just the other night that …your father was dead all these years?"

"Angela, he was such an awful father."

She turns away. "That's no excuse to keep something like this from me! I'm your wife."

"I know. I'm sorry," he quietly says. "He was a drunk, a cheat and..." He stops.

She sits back down and touches his hand. "Go ahead."

"After Mom died he just disappeared, more emotionally than anything else. But he got lost in that damn bottle. I never wanted to subject you to the horrors that I had to live through. I guess I figured it was better for me to protect you from it, than for you and the rest of the family to have to see it and live with it. To add insult to injury he never had any interest in God. And if he did, Randolph would be the kind of man who would pick a fight with Him."

She holds both his hands and moves closer to him. "Baby, that's why I hated it when you and your brother drank. You would change. You'd let your brother's darkness blend with your temper and..." Hesitating, she looks away then thinks better of it.

"What?"

"Well, it would frighten the kids. And me."

"But..."

"I know you don't do that anymore. But your brother..." She shakes her head. "He had...or has the same problem as your father."

More silence.

Then very quietly she adds, "The sins of the father are passed down..."

"Sure, maybe Dad had some reasons...the war, the flashbacks, the stress of being the top dog, but Angie, he didn't have to displace his anger with the Corp to his family."

"I understand. He was a sick man."

"Then there's Carter. MIA in Vietnam. Dad sent me to military school to straighten me up. And then he disappears with some woman. And to who knows where?"

"Jonathan."

"Yes."

"Why all of this now? And why wouldn't you let any of this out when we were talking with Dr. Long?"

His stiffens and pushes away. "Angela, I'm not going to sit in a room with a...with that...man...and have him tell me how to fix my life. I'm a pastor. I'm supposed to do that for others. I'm an educated man. I know what my prob...I mean, what my challenges are. I don't need him to tell me anything."

"Jonathan, if I didn't know better, I'd say you were..."

He interrupts, "I'd say that I was intellectually enlightened and completely aware of the eccentricities that I may or may not have. And, just maybe, those faults are made more complex because of feelings of inadequacy...but only in certain parts of my life."

She looks at him. "Wow. Maybe I should call *you* the doctor." She leans and kisses him. He returns it. It's a kiss like the old days. "Brains are so sexy," she whispers.

"You are."

"Yummy," she sighs.

"Yummy, indeed," he says quietly. They kiss again.

"You know what I think, Mrs. Matheson?"

"What's that, Mr. Matheson?"

"I think we need some 'us time.' Just you and me. No kids. Just the two of us."

"Yes. Yes. Tell me more," she sighs.

"In fact, I think the doctor should prescribe at least an overnight. Maybe even two. Yes?"

"We could use a little romantic rendezvous. We haven't been away for entirely too long."

He stands, takes her hand, spins her around and then wraps his arms around her. "Consider it done! All this emotional soup has wiped me out."

"Agreed." Then, her smile disappears.

"What is it, baby?"

She says nothing.

He nods. "Yep, I can hear her giggle now. That was something that would always bring a smile to our faces...when nothing else could." He held her close.

"Absolutely!"

In the open window above Jonathan and Angela, Christopher slowly steps back from where he has been listening the entire time.

CHAPTER 59

IN THE LATE AFTERNOON JONATHAN stands in the driveway of his friend and colleague, Joshua. Jonathan admires Joshua's sparkling car.

"Yep, being the assistant pastor of a big church certainly has its benefits."

"But I don't pay you that much," Jonathan grins.

"True. It just takes saving. As in every penny that my wife and I make."

They exchange car keys.

"Thanks, Josh. We really appreciate this," he says, admiring the freshly washed BMW convertible. The car looks perfect sitting in front of their handsome suburban home.

"My pleasure, Johnny. And thank you for letting us borrow your truck to move some things for Deanna's parents this weekend." He admires the Cadillac Escalade that he's about to abuse.

"No biggie, as long as you don't mind a little mud and the smell of wet dog. Jackson and I went for a run the other day. His treat was a few laps in Lake Mitchell."

They laugh.

Joshua says, "That'll work. Besides, I have my own dirty work to attend to. Dee's folks were going to rent a van but this will be great!"

"You can imagine how Angela is going to love riding through the mountains with the wind in her hair and not a thing to worry about except what's for room service. And..."

"Enough said."

"Yep, we're looking forward to the escape."

"Hey, Jonathan!" Deanna calls as she walks toward the men.

"Hello, Deanna. I was just telling Josh how much Angela and I appreciate your lending us the 'baby' for a little get away."

"No worries. We'll be with the folks for a better part of the week. Besides, you and Angie do so much for all of us that it's the least we can do."

"Thank you."

Joshua speaks up, "Of course, if you'd like to babysit the twins when you get back..."

Jonathan waves his hand, "No, thanks. Got rid of the diapers a long time ago."

"It's a full-time job, that's for sure," Deanna says. "So, where are you love-birds going, anyway?"

Joshua says, "You know that's none of our business. Pastor has to keep some things to himself, don't you think?"

"No!" she replies. "We girls like all the details. You both should know that by now."

They laugh.

"We're heading up to the Blue Ridge Parkway, then the Biltmore Estate for the weekend."

Dee's eyes light up, "Ooh...that's nice."

"No doubt," Joshua adds. "Dropping a little coin, are you?"

"She deserves it."

They nod in agreement.

"But please don't say a word. She has no idea," he adds.

"Your secret is safe with me." Dee smiles, as she nudges Joshua's side.

"Yeah, right," Joshua jokes. "Listen, you two go, have fun and don't worry. Not a peep." He holds up his hand to indicate "Boy Scout's Honor."

Joshua knows that Jonathan is anxious to be on his way so he nudges Jonathan toward the car.

"Go, get on your way. And I'll check in on your boys. Who's watching them?"

"Christopher's pretty good at watching over David. Angie's parents will likely spend one night there, just for the fun of it."

Jonathan climbs into the BMW-Z4, pulls out of the driveway and waves to Josh and Deanna.

He kicks the car into sixth gear and speeds away down the road.

"Just one more stop before home."

CHAPTER 60

ANGELA CHECKS HER REFLECTION IN the full-length mirror. She turns sideways, sucks her tummy in and spins around for a rear view check. "Not bad for a forty-something year old woman." From her lingerie chest she selects a tiny, silk negligee and puts it into the overnight bag. "Hmm, it has been awhile since I wore this. Wonder how I'll look in it."

She felt like a schoolgirl again, waiting for her date to show up. She and Jonathan hadn't been away for a romantic weekend for too long. Besides occasional flowers Jonathan was good about doing small things, but they had let entirely too much time pass without doing things that help keep romance alive.

Sitting on the bed she remembers their final days of school and then their wedding day. Jonathan had graduated a semester early with a double major in Religion and Psychology from UNCC. He planned to attend graduate school in the fall and earn his Master of Divinity at Duke Divinity School. She would finish her last semester on time with a degree in Sociology from Queens College and would begin work with the city in the fall. She also planned to spend her last summer as a single touring Northern Italy with her two best girlfriends.

Those plans changed when they decided to get a jump start on married life and were wed the first week of summer. They honeymooned in Paris. She couldn't believe how romantic it was, and she felt that as a clergyman-to-be those days would be numbered. He had worked the entire last year saving for the wedding and the honeymoon. She remembered that he always said he wanted to do it right, the first and only time. The wedding was small and elegant with just the family and some of their closest college friends. They were married at Manor Park Community Church. The wedding party was then hosted at the nearby Manor Park Country Club. Her father had been a member there for many years. Then Paris! That was something she would never forget.

Angela snaps back to reality and realizes that it's getting dark outside and Jonathan isn't home. It is six o'clock. He had assured her that he would be home hours ago. Where was he? She went downstairs to see if he had come in and perhaps she hadn't heard him. David was at the dining room table doing homework.

"Professor, have you any idea where Daddy is?"

"No, ma'am. Just little old me, trying to figure out if this math may be beyond my ability."

"Son, you are the smartest young boy that I have ever known, and if there is anyone who can do it, it will certainly be you." She pats his back and goes to the kitchen window.

"Your dad should have been here hours ago."

Suddenly the phone rings, causing Angela to jump.

"Mrs. Matheson?" the husky voice on the other end said.

"This is she."

"This is Officer Mahler. Jonathan's been in an accident and I need you to come to Presbyterian Hospital and get him. Can you do that, please?"

She sits down. David looks at her and mouths, "What?"

"It's your daddy. He's in the hospital."

She continues. "Is he alright, Officer?"

"Yes, ma'am. More shaken up than anything. He got a bump on his head when he slid off the road and into a ditch, up off of 59. The Snake Loop?"

"But he's okay?"

"Yes, ma'am," he assures her. "May I expect you soon?"

"Of course. I'm leaving now. It shouldn't be more than 15 or 20 minutes."

"Good enough. I'll wait for you. And don't worry, he's in good hands. See you in a bit."

"Yes, of course. Thank you. I'm on my way."

She gathers her things and then kisses David. "Your dad's been in a little accident. Want to go and keep me company?"

"Sure." He clears the table and goes to his room. "I'll dump these in my room."

Christopher is coming downstairs as David heads up.

"Pop's been in a fender bender. We're going to the hospital to get him. Wanna go?"

Christopher grunts, "What's he done now?"

"Watch yourself. Your father's been hurt and needs our prayers that everything will be okay."

He mumbles, "He needs more than prayers."

"What was that young man?" she asks sternly.

"Nothing. But in answer to David's question? No. I'm heading over to Jimmy's to practice. I'll grab a burger on the way." He walks past her.

"You could show a bit more sympathy. Your father could have been seriously injured."

"Sorry that you're upset Mom, but he'll be fine." As he leaves he says, "Probably up to his old tricks again."

She doesn't understand him and let's it go.

"David, come on!" she shouts but he's standing right there.

"Mom, I think they heard you in Davidson." He laughs.

She gives him a big hug and says, "Thank God for you, my son."

CHAPTER 61

INSIDE THE EMERGENCY ROOM DR. Blair and Officer
Mahler stand on either side of Jonathan. He sits on the edge of
the bed as the doctor finishes putting a large bandage on his head.
Officer Mahler closes the curtain, partitioning them from the public
area.

"J. M., I don't need to tell you that this could have been a lot
worse," Mahler says quietly.

"No kidding, Johnny," Dr. Blair says. "You're lucky you just bent
the fender and creased your forehead. It could have been the other
way around."

"Thanks guys. Really." He turns to Officer Mahler and says quietly,
"Danny, if you could keep this quiet, I'd really appreciate it." There's
a long pause before Jonathan adds, "I owe you."

"You're damn right you do."

Blair looks directly at Jonathan, "Johnny, we've been pals a long
time so I can say this and you'll hear it. I can put a band aid on your
head and you're on your way, but if you don't keep your head on
straight it'll take a much bigger bandage to..."

Pushing the curtain aside Angela comes in and wraps her arms
around Jonathan. "Honey, are you okay?" They hug one another
tightly.

"I'm fine, baby."

Over her shoulder, Jonathan winks at David and says, "Hi,
Sport."

"Hi, Pops. Glad you're okay."

Dr. Blair says, "Mrs. Matheson, your husband will be fine. The
fender of that very fast car took the brunt of the damage. His head?
Nothing a couple of painkillers and an ice-pack can't cure."

Officer Mahler chuckles, "Yeah, some people need to realize the speed limit is a law, not a suggestion. He's one lucky guy."

Angela whispers, "It's more than luck," as she hugs him tightly.

As the doctor leaves, he points his finger at Jonathan with a *watch yourself* look. Then, Mahler points two fingers at his own eyes and then two fingers at Jonathan, does it a second time and leaves. David watches with curiosity.

Jonathan pulls David close and says, "That was close."

Angela quietly adds, "What matters is that we are all together."

Jonathan nods, "You can say that again."

David interjects, "What matters is that we are all together."

They laugh. David adds, "May we go now? I'm starved."

"What's new, right?" Angela asks.

Jonathan stands. A little light-headed, he reaches for David to brace himself. "I'm okay, son. Thanks for being such a handsome crutch."

"Yup."

Jonathan reaches for his jacket but drops it to the floor. Angela picks it up and says, "I'll get it honey. David, help your father. I think he's the one that's nearly faint with hunger."

She smells the jacket and thinks, "That's strange." Then she calls to them, "Hey, wait for me. I'm hungry too!"

They leave the ER, arm in arm.

CHAPTER 62

CHRISTOPHER AND JIMMY PLAY VIDEO games as they sit on the couch. Their feet are on the coffee table in the family room of Jimmy's parent's house. Their eyes are riveted on the screen. The competition is fierce.

"Dude, what's up with you?" Jimmy asks without taking his eyes from the screen.

Christopher slowly responds, "Nothing."

"Yeah, right. You've been weird the past couple of days. I mean, more weird than usual." He laughs.

Christopher attempts a laugh, tosses his gaming console on the coffee table and picks up Jimmy's guitar, strumming out chords.

"I was kicking your butt."

"As if," Christopher quietly replies.

"Man, just when I was getting close..." He waits a moment before asking again, "What's wrong?"

Christopher says, "It's nothing, bro. Just...thinking. And pissed, I guess."

Jimmy takes a soda from the mini-fridge and asks, "What about? You have a great life, cool parents, even though a little preachy at times." He punches Christopher's arm. "Get it? Preachy?"

"Yeah, brilliant." Pause. "And original."

"Dude, you have a hot girlfriend, you drive a cool truck and you'll be graduating soon which means you'll be able to get outta this tinker-toy town. Then before you know it, you'll hit it big with some band in a hip city like Chicago or LA, or something."

"Give me a break," Christopher mumbles.

"What could you possibly be sore about?

Christopher sits at the drum set. Picking up a set of sticks, he taps out a series of beats. "Choppers, are you stupid or both? How long have you known me? Like..."

Jimmy interrupts, "Like all our lives."

"Right. Then, you would know where my head is. And my heart too, for that matter. And yes, Kym is hot. Who knows, she might be my wife someday, but that's not what I'm thinking about right now." He stops.

"What?" Jimmy asks. "What's bugging you so bad?"

"It's my dad. Actually, my grandfather."

"Huh?"

Christopher says. "It's whacked, bro."

"Dude, I thought your grandfather was dead."

"Me, too. That's just it. Come to find out he's alive and has been. Like, my whole life."

Jimmy is floored. "What?"

"And my dad never even told us. How do you like that?"

Jimmy stares. "That's freaking nuts. There has to be some reason, right? I mean..."

Christopher interrupts him, "What it means is my dad's a jerk for making me believe that I didn't have a grandfather. When he's been alive my whole freaking life."

"Wait," Jimmy says. "How do you know this? And why now?"

"Remember Sunday, when we were practicing?"

"You mean when you were skipping church."

"Yeah, well, I've heard most of my dad's sermons. Anyway, after church, we were having dinner...or trying to have dinner...and Dad was really riding me about stuff."

"Yeah? So, that's new?"

"Part of the rules of parenting, I guess. Anyway, he and Mom were out on the deck talking about stuff and I was just hanging out. My window was open and I heard him tell Mom that his dad was still alive. And some other stuff, but man, I couldn't believe my ears!"

"You musta freaked."

"Duh. I mean, what would YOU have thought. All this time, Dad kept that from us...because his dad was supposedly such a creep.

Okay, so evidently he was not the nicest guy walking the planet. Had a bit of a…problem." He motions like he's drinking from a bottle.

"Yeah, so? My old man likes to tilt a few from time to time."

"Right, but I'd bet he doesn't beat your mom."

Silence. Jimmy shakes his head. "No, dude. That's just not right."

"True that! Booze is one thing…which I don't even like…but to do it all the time. My Uncle Carter can put it away. I mean, like drink until he just can't…" He stops and heads for the door.

Jimmy is confused. He tries to lighten the moment but fails. He follows Christopher toward the stairs, "Listen, Chris, I'm sorry. I just realized it's been like, what…" His voice trails off.

"It *feels* like it's been a year. And we just can't seem to move on."

Christopher stares at the floor, "I don't know why everyone is moaning. It wasn't them who stood there and watched their little sister…blow her brains out…when I…" he points to his chest with two thumbs… "could have stopped it."

Jimmy starts to hug Christopher but Christopher pushes him away.

"Dude. Seriously? It's cool. That was a long time ago. I'm so over it. I just wish my dad wouldn't lie to us. To me. He's a preacher."

"Yeah, but he's human too," said Jimmy.

Christopher stares at him.

"Yep. Right. Sure." He slowly nods. "Good talk. Nice support there, dude." He leaves saying, "I'll check ya later. Gotta call Kym."

Jimmy meekly says, "Yeah, okay. Later."

Christopher is gone and Jimmy stands alone.

CHAPTER 63

IT IS LATE WHEN CHRISTOPHER drives his old pickup truck into the driveway and turns off the lights. He sees that everyone is at home and he starts walking toward the house. Suddenly, the hairs on his neck stand up. He feels as though someone is watching him and he slowly looks around. The neighborhood is dark and quiet but something seems out of place. Then he notices a car parked down the street, facing this direction and a tiny light inside the car glows bright, then dims.

"Who would be sitting in their car smoking a cigarette at this hour," he thinks. Motionless, he observes the car. "Wait," Christopher mumbles, "Tim and Tina don't smoke."

Strange. There's enough light from the moon to reveal that someone appears to be watching him but he doesn't recognize the car, and he starts walking toward it. Suddenly, the car leaves with the headlights off, makes a U-turn and speeds away.

He shudders. "Okay, that's just freaking creepy," he says and goes inside.

Jonathan and David are finishing what appears to have been French toast, bacon and eggs. Angela is cleaning the counter. Jonathan looks up and says, "Hello, son."

"Hey," Christopher says quietly. "Nice hat," he adds as he looks at the bandage on Jonathan's head.

"Yeah, it's all the rage. You should try one."

David wraps his dinner napkin around his head. "See? They even make the high-fashion, low-brim style for kids like me."

Everyone laughs except Christopher.

Angela chimes in, "Come on, son. That was funny, you have to admit."

One thin strip of bacon is left on the plate and he snags it as he passes through the room. He finally says, "Yep, it's a regular Matheson Comedy Hour around here. Funny stuff."

Jonathan faces Christopher and asks, "Not even going to ask how your dad is doing?"

"I give. How is my old man doing?"

Jonathan takes the last bite of food on his plate. "Just fine. Thanks for your concern."

Angela senses the tension and changes the subject. "You know, Christopher, your father and I have talked about it and we want you to join us for a little outing tomorrow."

"May I come?" David asks.

Jonathan says, "Sure."

Angela adds, "It'll be fun."

Christopher asks, "Before or after school?"

"Actually, right in the middle," Angela answers.

"Sounds like a plan to me," David says.

"What is it?" Christopher asks.

Angela looks at Jonathan then says, "A…surprise. We'll all get something from it."

David chirps, "Sweet. A field trip!"

Jonathan and Angela laugh. Christopher sighs.

CHAPTER 64

INSIDE DR. LONG'S OFFICE JONATHAN brushes lint from his jacket and straightens his shirt cuffs. David's face is pressed against the side of the aquarium, mesmerized as he watches the fish. Christopher is slouched on the couch, staring at the ceiling with his iPod blasting music through small earbuds. Angela looks at David, then Christopher and smiles. She checks her watch and taps her foot. Across the room, a clock ticks.

"What a really nice field trip," Christopher mutters.

"Hello, hello, hello. What a wonderful surprise to see you all!" Dr. Long removes his coat and hat.

Christopher takes one look, grins and says, "Sweet."

Dr. Long counts, "One, two, three and four shining faces. Nice to be greeted with such happy people. Please excuse my tardiness. I had an unexpected delay. And not to worry, today is on the house."

"That's not necessary. We realize this is an unscheduled visit but we wanted the boys to meet you. You are a very important part of our recovery."

"Thank you, Angela, for those kind words." He shakes Jonathan's hand, "Hello, Jonathan." Jonathan nods.

Dr. Long extends his hand to Christopher. "Nice to meet you, Christopher. I've heard a lot about you and I can't wait to hear some of your band's music."

Christopher perks up and smiles.

Dr. Long continues, "I'd say from your handshake that you play either the guitar or the drums."

Christopher looks at his parents. "Actually, I play both but lead guitar is my favorite."

"And I'll bet that you are equally great at both. In fact, I'm sure of it."

He reaches for fish food and joins David at the aquarium. "And you must be 'The Little Professor'."

David beams, hearing his nickname. "That's what they call me. Guess it's because I'm intelligent," he smiles.

"I would say that you are. I've heard that you will be college material when you are a little older."

"I hope so. I sure do like school."

"Yes, I did also," he says. "Now, let's feed the fish. Something tells me that you could probably name every one of them." He hands the food to David and opens the top of aquarium.

"Yes, sir. This one's a…" he looks at Angela. "I guess I can share more of that another time."

"Right. Then will you please feed my little friends?" He pats David's shoulder. "And I'll see if I can help my other friends."

Seated at his desk he asks, "Is all at peace with the world?"

Angela answers, "Not exactly." She indicates Jonathan's bandaged head.

"Yes, about that. I couldn't help but notice. Personally, I thought that perhaps you were trying to start a new fashion trend, Jonathan," Dr. Long jokes.

From across the room David says, "See, Dad? I was onto something, right?"

All laugh, except Christopher. He turns up the volume on his iPod.

CHAPTER 65

CARTER DOESN'T LOOK LIKE THE same man that he was months earlier. He's lost weight but is in better shape. His skin is tan, his hair is short and he sports a salt and pepper beard. His cool blue eyes are clear, thanks to not drinking for several months. The near-death experience had seen to that. Working reconnaissance was also sure to clear one's head. A deep scar stretches from above his left eye, through his eyebrow and down his left cheek. If it weren't for his Vietnam training, he would be dead by now.

Now all he thinks of is how to stop the madness that his life has become and how to bury the guilt that weighs on his shoulders. Every day he seeks to calm the blinding fear of things that are outside his reach. He knows deep within that his father is still alive and he looks over his shoulder at every turn. The agony of what happened to his niece, because of his negligence, is nearly unbearable. People had tried to make Carter go away. He has only gone under their radar.

He drove through the night to get to Palm Beach. He has been trying to bounce between the two places for months. In one locale he watches to see how things play out. He has found out that Palm Beach is the hidden, secure enclave of his father, Randall Christian Matheson. He sees his father's middle name as the biggest of ironies.

He needed to orient himself to the area, for he would be watching that tyrant for the next several days. It had taken time to find him. He stopped in Mobile, Alabama, months ago, following up on a tired trail that Randall had left years ago. Funny their parallels. Dad: Marines. Son: Army. Son Number Two: would have been Navy. Talk about an interesting time at family reunions.

Carter had stopped in Mobile one weekend and while there he ran across Richard "Dickie" Nolan. Dickie had smelled the alcohol on his breath. Before he knew it he was living at Dickie's, in a room over the garage, and attending AA meetings. What had begun as a search had turned into one of the best things that had ever happened to Carter. He was off alcohol. At least for one day at a time.

In West Palm Beach, Carter had found the cheapest hotel he could. It was Ye Olde Knights Inn near the airport. It was shabby and cheap. Since he didn't know how long he would be staying he decided that it was the lowest maintenance and the most under the radar that he could find. It wasn't far from his father's home, the gated community of Blowing Rocks Marina, which was between Jupiter Inlet and Jupiter Hills Golf Club.

He drove through the community at 3 miles under any posted speed limit for he did not want to attract any attention. He was driving a Metro Secure Home Installation & Watch Service van and he should be safe. The residents wanted to be safe. "No worries," he thought, "you'll be safe with me."

Carter had found the neighborhood on his last trip, a month ago. It had taken this long for his head to clear and to figure what he would say to his father. He looked at the matchbook lid that he had scribbled the address on. It read: 12779 Prestwick Lane. It was just ahead.

Pops must have done something right all these years. The house was easily 5,000 square feet, with a 3-bay garage, a swimming pool, and of course Metro Secure was their home security companion.

Here he was at the end of his emotional road. Randall would have no idea who he was. Wrap-around Maui Jim sunglasses completed his look. The tidy bow tie was a nice touch harkening back to a simpler time. It seemed that in the old days everyone trusted you if you wore a tie. He thought, "I'll walk right up in broad daylight and confront my fears."

It had been a dozen years since Carter saw him last, but he still knew that the 6 foot, 4 inch, barrel-chested, buzz-cut of a grizzly bear would as soon snap his neck as to look at him. Especially after knowing what Carter had known all these years. Something that would not only haunt him until the day he died but would also help bury a stake into the old man's heart.

He approached the house slowly, pretending to check the signs in the yard and compare them to the clipboard in his hand. Instead, his shaded eyes watched the windows looking for movement of any sort. Bingo. In what appeared to be a second-story library a hand pulled a curtain back. He pretended to jot some notes, then took the cell phone from it's holster and pretended to take a call. A hand was now pulling back a curtain from a downstairs window. Someone was watching. Someone was pretending. Which was which was anyone's guess.

The hand pulling back the curtain reminded Carter of a time in Vietnam when he had been locked in a bamboo cage. His body was kept in water up to his neck until the guard came to inflict more pain. The cage was kept in a cold river and his teeth had chattered until they were nearly broken off. Leeches, the size of silver dollars, latched onto him and slowly sucked the blood from his frail, emaciated body. Interrogators would pull him from the water, often with a clawed hook, and whip him and his comrades with a cat-of-nine-tails. Flesh would be torn from their skin. The enemies laughed at their pain. The men seethed with hatred, plotting their demise. The captors mocked their pain, their country's flag and their honor. It meant nothing to them. The men meant nothing to them. They simply gambled, seeing who would last the longest and could tolerate the most pain. Carter nearly always won. Or did he? The screams of his teammates echoed in his mind even to this day.

Suddenly the front door opens, startling Carter. He looks into the eyes of his nemesis. He can't believe what he is seeing. The man who had once stood proud, erect and muscled now stands slight, hunched over and shriveled.

"Hello!" the shrunken old man barks, immediately breaking into a raspy cough.

"Mister…" Carter looks at his clipboard, "…Matheson?" he asks.

"Yes!" he coughs, "Who wants to know? I didn't order service from you."

Carter steps closer. He is amazed at the size of the former, overgrown bully who doesn't look directly in Carter's eye and he shakes ever so slightly with tiny tremors.

"Yes, Mr. Matheson. I've been instructed to visit your lovely community and tell you about the upgrade of services this month."

Randall squints at Carter. "Wait a damn minute. That was last month." He hesitates, "Wasn't it?"

A woman comes to the door. She is a much younger and prettier version of what would formerly been hanging on the arm of who this man once was. She has a pleasant smile, scant clothing and too much perfume.

"Hello. How may I be of assistance?" she asks in a sultry voice.

"My name is Charles and I'm with Metro Security. We have a special this month for upgraded security for the life of your account."

She is attentive, uninterested, but polite.

"I think we're pretty secure, but since you are here, we may as well listen to what you have to say," she says, motioning for Carter to enter.

Randall stands motionless, squinting. Carter can't decide if the squint represents an inability to see clearly, or an eye that is about to make a connection, identifying his long lost son. Either way Carter enters the home, being careful not to get too close. Yet.

CHAPTER 66

DAVID AND CHRISTOPHER SIT ON opposite ends of Dr. Long's waiting room. Eloise types quietly at her desk. She looks at the two boys from time to time, smiling each time as though it were the first time she was seeing them. It makes David feel happy. It makes Christopher feel weird and he doesn't know why. David is engrossed in MSNBC-TV. Christopher texts on his phone.

"Damn," Christopher says. David looks at Christopher, then at the receptionist and then frowns at Christopher. She smiles.

"What?" David asks.

"James can't make practice tonight," Christopher replies.

"So?"

"So, we have a gig at the church auditorium in less than 3 weeks and we're not ready."

David smiles, "You'll be fine, bro. You guys rock."

Christopher stops and enjoys the moment, appreciating the admiration from his kid brother. "But that's the second time this week that he's a no show. This gig is important."

David picks up a magazine and flips through it. "Say, dude. Remember when you and Kym first met?" David asks.

"Yeah. So?"

"Well, didn't Jimmy just meet Jennifer recently?"

"Oh. Right. Good point," Christopher grins.

David tosses the magazine down, takes mints from a bowl on the counter and sits closer to Christopher, placing an extra mint on the arm of his chair. He then continues, "And, if I recall, you and Kym were inseparable for the first three or four months that you dated."

Christopher picks up the mint and puts it in his mouth, "True."

"Besides, he did write most of the songs, right?

Christopher nods.

"Well, I'm pretty sure that he has it all dialed in. Don't you think?"

Christopher says, "Yes, up until recently. Actually, I've written 5 new songs. And I think they're pretty good."

David nods. "Actually."

David nods again. Then asks, "May I hear them?"

Christopher searches his iPod for the tunes. "Sure. You might like them." He finds one. "Here, check out this first one." Christopher anxiously, yet quietly, waits for David's response.

David listens, nodding immediately. They fist-bump and both nod. The secretary looks over and smiles.

CHAPTER 67

DR. LONG WAITS FOR THE information to settle. Jonathan is frazzled, adjusting his shirt cuffs. Angela is emotional. "I can't help but feeling that something is off between us," she says quietly.

"But I was getting the car as a surprise. I wanted this weekend to be special," Jonathan adds.

"I understand that. But sliding off the road? That's not like you. You're a good driver."

Jonathan chuckles, "Yes. I'm an excellent driver."

"And that is your best friend's new car. It's not like you to be careless with something as important as that." She trails off.

He becomes defensive, "Accidents happen." He looks at Dr. Long, who gives no response. "They do. Come on."

Finally she responds, "I suppose so."

After a long silence, Dr. Long speaks. "It's true. Accidents do happen. Tell me something, Angela. You and Jonathan have been married twenty years, right?

"Yes."

"This year, actually," Jonathan adds. She smiles at Jonathan and he touches her hand.

"Good. And in those two decades, you've pretty much grown up together, right?" the doctor asks.

She thinks about it. They both nod.

"Excellent. Then it would be safe to assume, would it not, that you both know one another pretty well?"

Again, they nod. She asks, "Why?"

"It is my opinion that habits, mannerisms, routines and such would all be things of which you both would be intimately aware."

They nod together.

Jonathan asks, "What are you getting at?"

"Just confirming. Jonathan, since you both know one another so well, I suspect that you know when your wife is anxious."

"Yes," Jonathan replies.

"When she is anxious, and I'm sure it isn't that often, you have a pretty good idea of what..."

"Substantiated," Jonathan adds.

Dr. Long nods. "Yes, that's it. Substantiated. Furthermore, we could likely assume that she's not prone to just be poking at a sleeping bear to see if she can awaken it. Is this correct?"

Jonathan is quiet. He looks from her to his hands, then at the clock. Finally he looks at Dr. Long.

Angela says, "I'm not following you."

After a long pause Dr. Long speaks, "Simply put, you are extremely compatible, loving, comfortable companions who are still *in* love after all these years. You both know who you are and who the other is?" He gestures questioningly.

Jonathan adds, "To quote my boys, 'Uh, yeah!'" The three chuckle.

Dr. Long continues, "I suppose the feelings Angela has are ones of caution, or distrust. There must be something that has raised a flag."

Jonathan nods and shifts in his seat. Dr. Long notices.

"I've said this before and I mean no disrespect, but until you've..."

Dr. Long interrupts, "Walked in your shoes? Sorry Jonathan, but we are here to repair, not rebuke. We are here to fix, not fixate as I have said before."

"I'm just saying, you have children and then lose them. Then, see what happens to you." Jonathan lowers his head.

Dr. Long says, "Understood, Jonathan, and an excellent point. I'll keep that in mind. Thank you."

Jonathan nods, "This is good information and I want to understand it better, but..." He pats Angela's hand, "I need to get back to work, and the boys are out of school on a half-day, so we need to get them back."

"Of course," Dr. Long quickly responds, "Yes. It's all good. We'll stop and pick up here next time. If you both agree." They nod.

Angela adds, "That would be nice. And quite helpful. Would you agree, Jonathan?" She turns to Jonathan for support.

"Would you agree with that, Jonathan?" Dr. Long smiles.

Jonathan hesitates then smiles. "Yes, of course. Thank you for your time."

Angela says, "That's good. Thank you." She touches Dr. Long's arm and he pats her hand.

In the reception room David and Christopher join their parents and Dr. Long.

"Nice to have met you, Christopher," and Dr. Long gives Christopher a fist-bump.

David joins in with his small fist. "Same here, Doctor," he says with a smile. "Thanks for letting me feed the fish."

Dr. Long chuckles, "Glad that you could, David. Come see me again. Maybe we can delve deeper into fish species."

He smiles at his receptionist and says, "Nice family." Then he retreats into his office, closes the door and sighs, "Deep secrets."

CHAPTER 68

THE FAMILY DRIVES IN SILENCE, as if to allow the past hour to genuinely sink in. All that can be heard is music coming from Christopher's tiny earphones. Then he says, "That was... interesting."

Surprised that Christopher spoke, Jonathan looks at him in the rearview mirror.

Angela says, "It was, wasn't it?"

David adds, "I liked the fish," he pauses, "and Dr. Long was nice and..." He pauses again.

"Colorful?" Christopher suggests.

David thinks a moment. "Yes. He was nice. And...colorful too."

David turns to Christopher and whispers, "Is he gay?"

Christopher bangs his forehead and whispers, loudly, "Ya think?"

"Boys! He's a very intelligent man who helps a lot of people," Angela interjects.

"Whatever," Christopher adds.

"You boys know that we don't judge people, we love them. And if we disagree with them, or their philosophies, or choices of religion... or otherwise, we pray for them. Right?"

Jonathan looks at Angela, then at the boys. In unison, the three men say, "Right."

She adds, "Dr. Long is giving part of his life to help us get through a rough patch. We should all be thankful for that and embrace him as one of God's children." She stops. Looking at them, she says, "Okay, enough preaching. I need to leave that to your father."

They all laugh.

"Nicely done, hon. Now, I know who to call on when I have to be away. You'd make the perfect substitute for me in the pulpit." He winks. She smiles, placing her hand on his.

Christopher changes the subject, "So, this is our big outing, huh? Great way to burn a half-day."

Angela turns to confront Christopher, "Son, please take your headphones out of your ears. I'm beginning to think they're permanently attached." They smile.

"Thank you." She continues, "Your father and I needed to talk some things out with a neutral party. To see if we could find peace amidst the tragedy that continues to hang over our heads…and cloud our hearts."

"Good luck," Christopher adds, sarcastically.

Jonathan taps the breaks, "Son. Stop that. Show respect to your mother."

He straightens up and says quietly, "Yes, sir."

"Your mother is saying that we all have different ways of coping with life, and that's perfectly fine. But sometimes when I have a noise in this car I need to see a mechanic for a tune-up. In much the same way, we need... an emotional tune-up."

David says from the backseat, "Yeah, but without getting put on a rack!"

Christopher adds, "Maybe that uncomfortable, skinny couch in the doc's office, but no racks."

They all laugh.

Angela says, "Emotional tune-up." Nodding her head, she adds, "Spoken like a man."

Jonathan looks at her, his mouth agape, with a look of *What?* She winks.

"Nice," he says quietly.

"Anyway, you get the idea. And now, I have an idea! Let's play hooky for the rest of the day. Sound good?" she asks, and puts her fist out for a fist-bump. "This is how you do it, right?"

David obliges with a reciprocal fist-bump. "That's it, Mom!"

Christopher perks up, "Hooky?"

Jonathan says, "Yes, why not? You guys are doing well in school. Besides, sometimes you just have to bend the rules."

Angela adds, "Sounds like a plan to me. I say we grab lunch, then go play somewhere."

"Sweet." David shouts. Christopher grins and nods.

"In fact," Jonathan continues, "I say you boys choose what you want to do and we'll make it happen. Within reason, of course."

David suggests, "How about miniature golf?"

"The batting cages at the park!" Christopher shouts.

"Go Karts?" David chimes.

"How about white-water rafting?" Christopher shouts.

"White-water rafting? How about an African safari, while we're at it!" Jonathan says. He grins at Christopher in the rearview mirror. Christopher nods.

"Whoa…let's not get carried away," Angela says, "And we need to include shopping!" she laughs.

Together, Christopher and David say, "What?" All three guys simultaneously moan. They all laugh.

Jonathan finally says, "Okay. Let's pick one where we ALL can play together."

Christopher, David and Angela shout, "Go Karts!"

Jonathan nods, "Done. Lunch, then Go Karts." Then adds, "But you boys get ready! Your old man is gonna have to kick your skinny little butts."

David pipes up, "You mean the skinny butts we inherited from you?"

As they speed down the road they laugh together, as a family, for the first time in a very long time.

And it felt good.

CHAPTER 69

SITTING OUTSIDE BIG MACK'S SPEED Shop Restaurant & Bar, the family enjoys lunch at a picnic table. They feast on ribs, burgers, fries and sodas. Shoving a handful of fries in his mouth, David stops long enough to say, "Man, we don't get to eat like this very often."

Christopher says, between licks of several fingers, "No kidding. I could get used to this."

Jonathan finishes the last of what was an enormous burger, wipes his mouth and adds, "But then, if we ate like this every day, it wouldn't be special."

"Good point," says Angela. "Now, please pass the ketchup. The fries are awesome."

"Never seen you put away that many fries, Mom," David says.

She stops and with a guilty smile replies, "Yes, guess I'll have to do double-duty at the gym tomorrow."

The Victory Lap Go Kart & Sports Center is on the outskirts of town. It is part of a large sports theme park developed and donated by NASCAR driver, "Fast Eddie" Montgomery. He chose the small-town atmosphere, far away from the regular hub-bub of the NASCAR world. In fact, he lives not far from the Mathesons. Rumor has it that he is a big kid with lots of toys that includes his own indoor kart track, like the one Christopher, David, Jonathan and Angela are about to terrorize. He also has a regulation dirt track, a 10-acre dirt-bike track, as well as a 100-acre hunt preserve. All this is part of his 200-acre property, some 20 miles away. He called his enclave Montgomery Sports Mountain, or Mo-So-Mo for short. His race team is Race Monkey Motor Sports. He figured if former NASCAR Champ, Dale Earnhardt, Jr. had Dirty Mo Acres and the late pop-star Michael Jackson had Neverland Valley Ranch, then he, as the winner of last year's NASCAR Verizon Wireless Cup Series, deserved his own playground.

While Jonathan and Angela don their race outfits, eager for the day's competition, Christopher tugs at a jumpsuit much too small. "This isn't going to work so well." He sees David who is trying on a helmet much too big. They laugh at one another. Angela uses her digital camera to capture the antics for a future scrapbook.

On the track, Jonathan is instantly in the lead, but Christopher comes from behind, passes and turns to taunt him. But, as he looks back around, Angela T-bones him, making the way clear for David to pass, clear the finish line and win the race. Christopher grimaces. Angela slams on the brakes and looks at him with a scared expression. Christopher stops, then shouts, "Let's hear it for the kid!"

At the Mo-Miniature Golf Course, Jonathan stands over the putting tee. He waggles his golf club then strikes the ball squarely for a nice, long putt. He misses by a foot. "I was robbed!" he shouts, slapping his forehead.

Next up is defending champ, Christopher, who steps in attempting the same long putt across a perfectly manicured green. It is brilliantly executed but misses by just an inch. David goes for the same putt and misses it but taps it in with his foot. Christopher gives him a big high-five.

Angela has a nice and easy swing, looping it through the windmill and bouncing off a rail. It spins through a second loop and rolls directly into the hole at just the right pace. All the boys look at one another with mouths wide open. She receives high fives from each of them, their mouths still agape. Christopher and David are bent with laughter. Jonathan and Angela smile at each other as they haven't in a very long time.

At the Mo-Batta Baseball Batting Cage, Angela steps up to bat. Jonathan shouts, "Swing batter, batter, batter," and the two boys join together as they all shout, "Swing batter, batter, batter…Swing!" The ball rockets out of the machine nearly hitting her. The boys laugh. She gives them a faux frown.

Jonathan sheepishly adjusts the speed. "Sorry."

She sets herself again and awaits the next rocket. The ball barely dribbles out. They laugh again. She puts her hand on her hip and yells, "Smarty! Give it to me. I'm one home run away from kicking all your butts!"

He re-adjusts it. This time, it's the perfect speed. But she misses. Then she misses again. And the third time she misses with a foul ball, nearly hitting the boys. They duck. David steps up to bat. He taps his left shoe with the bat and points it to center field. The machine discharges the baseball and he misses.

Christopher comes over and pats him on the back. "Slow down. Take a deep breath. And keep your eye on the ball." He steps away. David waits. Here comes the ball. He misses. Then, he misses again.

David shouts, "Animal Crackers!"

They all look at him.

Jonathan steps up to the plate. "Okay, guys. Step back. The force of this swing is liable to take heads off shoulders. Give your old man some room." He swings and misses.

"No worries. Just warming up." He chokes down on the bat a bit and takes a perfect stance. Here comes the ball. He swings and it pops up high then straight down right in front of them. Everyone laughs.

Grabbing his shoulder, he says, "Must be the old college football injury acting up again." And looking at the sky he adds, "Must be getting ready to rain."

Christopher pushes him off the plate, "Whatever. Give the kid some room." He grabs the bat, assumes a great stance, takes a deep breath and nods to his dad. "Let 'er rip, Pops."

It comes out of the machine and straight down the middle. He misses. "No big. Just jumped the gun is all. Give me another one." He misses the second time.

"Okay. No big. Dad, give me just a bit more. I got one more in me." He takes another deep breath and the machine fires. Straight down the middle. He's ready. Swing. Bang, right over the left field sign. He homers it.

They all look in amazement then do "the wave."

He high-fives each one.

CHAPTER 70

THE SUN IS LOW ON the horizon as the Mathesons head home. It has been a perfect day, the best day they've had in a really long time. It has been good to get away and spend time in harmony instead of hatred, with laughter not lethargy and optimism instead of oppression.

At home everyone gets out of the van, still energized from the day. As Christopher gets out he sees the same car, sitting in the same place down the road, as the other night. He can't make out who is in the car. Jonathan sees him staring, follows his gaze and recognizes the car. He looks at Angela, motions his head toward the car and speaks quietly but sternly to Christopher and David.

"Boys, we had a really fun day. And that's not going to stop now. But I need you to go inside and get to your homework, if you have any. We'll have dinner in about an hour. Can do?"

They both nod.

Angela extends her arm to help David who is lugging a heavy backpack.

Christopher looks at the car then at his Dad. "Who is it? Need me to go with you?"

Jonathan smiles. "No, but thanks. I have it, buddy. You go on inside. I'll be in shortly."

He heads toward the car then stops and calls to Christopher, "Hey, Christopher."

Christopher, nearly in the house, turns, "Yes?"

"It really was a great time today, right?"

"Yes, sir. It was. Thanks, Dad."

To Angela he says, "I'll be right back, babe. No need to worry."

"Okay, boys, let's get homework done, rooms straightened and I'll start on dinner."

"Sure, Mom," David says and goes to his room.

Christopher asks, "Who is that, Mom?"

She says, "Come on, honey, your dad's taking care of things."

"Mom?" he sternly asks.

In the kitchen she looks out the window and sees that Jonathan is nearly to the car.

"It's your Uncle Carter."

Christopher reacts with anger, "If he hurts Dad, or any one of us, I swear…"

"Son, he's not going to hurt anyone," she assures him.

"I swear to you, Mom. Uncle Carter touches any one of us and I will kill him." He storms out.

"Son."

Silence.

"Christopher Allen."

Silence.

At the kitchen window she says quietly, "That makes two of us." She takes a deep breath, exhales, bows her head, and holds the edge of the counter. Then whispers, "But for the grace…of God."

CHAPTER 71

JONATHAN APPROACHES THE CAR AND Carter looks through the front windshield at his brother. He whispers, "Oh, boy."

At the driver's open window, Jonathan says, "What in heaven's name are you doing here?"

Carter tips the brim of his baseball cap, "Afternoon, Pastor."

He gets out, stamps his cigarette on the ground and hugs Jonathan. It's not a warm embrace but it is a hug, nonetheless.

Jonathan looks at him closely and says, "Man, you're a sight for sore eyes."

Carter nods. "Surprised?"

"You could say that. I can't decide whether to kiss you or kick you. I think I'll go with the..." He motions as if he were going to kick him. Carter flinches.

"Been awhile," Carter says. "Didn't know if you'd want to see me or not."

Jonathan says, "Well, I specifically recall telling you to stay away from my family..."

Carter looks at Jonathan's house and sees Christopher at a window.

"I don't remember it that way," Carter replies.

"Well, make a new memory." Jonathan looks at the house and then back to Carter who is staring at him. "Then again, I did think you were dead...for a couple of days."

Carter pulls off his baseball cap and tosses it in the car and rubs his head. "How's that?"

"I know you. I also know that you are a survivor. Plus, the fact you just...*Poof*...disappeared? That was too much."

"Yep."

"The deal with Reddick?"

"Mmm-huh…" Carter barely grunts.

"You could have killed him."

Carter thinks a moment then says, "Don't you think that if I had wanted him dead, he'd be dead?"

Jonathan is silent.

"Notice that he took a high-flying dive…into the same lake, I might add… that just days before he drove me into?"

Jonathan looks at him skeptically. "Is that how it happened?"

Carter nods. "For sure."

"But…"

"Notice how he ended up on the rocks?"

Jonathan nods.

"Did you see the car?"

Jonathan nods again.

"Did you really think he could've crashed, trashing the car, and then swim from the car to the rocks?"

Jonathan ponders this, then slowly smiles. "Ohhhh…"

"And Danny?" Carter adds.

"Yep."

Carter continues, "He deserved that set-up. The lying rat lives two separate lives. Good cop but bad person. Give me a break. And I knew it was his idea to try and run me back in again. But I wasn't going to do it."

Jonathan says, "And you thought you could outrun a former dirt track racer…who happened to be an officer of the law?"

"He got lucky. And I didn't."

"No doubt," Jonathan says.

They are silent again for a long moment. Finally Jonathan speaks, "Tell me something, Carter."

"Shoot."

"I had a feeling…a really strong feeling…that you were still around, but I couldn't figure out how you were living."

"In the woods for awhile. Just to stay under the radar."

They stand in silence, then Jonathan says, "You know what gave it away?"

Carter's cockiness turns to confusion as he frowns, "You didn't know."

Jonathan nods. "Yep."

"How?"

"The wood stack."

Carter slowly nods. "Yeah. Guess some habits die hard." He chuckles. "Thanks for looking out for Sampson."

"No problem."

Carter says, "Brother, I know that you still hate me. I get that. You can push me away all you want but this is still my family. And you're still my brother. Nothing can change that."

"I can die trying," Jonathan responds.

Carter has a mock look of surprise. "Why, Pastor, that's not a very Christian thing to say."

Jonathan starts to move closer to Carter but turns and very quietly says, "I'm not feeling very Christian right about now."

"Amazing how an innocent accident can separate blood," responds Carter.

"Not when it's by the hand of someone who has no respect for authority."

"That's mighty pompous thinking, brother."

Jonathan looks away. "Carter, you disappeared months ago. We all pretty much got used to your not being here. And, on top of that, our family just had one of the best days we've had in a very long time. For the first time we could be making some actual headway toward healing."

Silence. Then Carter says, "Good." He nods. "Good for you."

"I don't want to take two steps forward and one step back. And I'm afraid that your being around my family right now could do just that."

Carter speaks very softly, "The sad thing, brother, is you'll never let me around them again, will you?"

Jonathan says nothing.

Carter continues, "And the extra kick in the shorts is that you know that I don't have anyone else. And no place to go."

"And for that, I'm sorry. Truly I am. I want to forgive you. I'm trying to forgive you but honestly, Carter, it's not looking real positive right now."

"But you have to know that I'm in a bad place right now and I need your help," Carter says.

"Where you are is knee deep in your addiction. The same addiction that brought you to this place. And it'll likely be the same one that buries you."

Carter snorts.

Jonathan interjects, "Just like Dad."

Carter stands straight. "But Dad's not buried."

"To me he is," Jonathan says solemnly.

"Damn it man, of ALL people..."

"Don't talk to me like that!" Jonathan shouts.

Carter continues, "You of all people. How can you stand here, a man of the cloth, and not forgive me? I really...just don't get it."

Jonathan responds, "Maybe that's because you don't have what I have."

"And you don't think I want that? Johnny, all I have ever wanted was a family. A nice, normal family just like yours. Two boys. One girl. And the perfect wife."

Jonathan absorbs this. "But you let things get in your way. Anger against Dad. Alcohol to dull your senses. One wife after another."

Carter interrupts, "But..."

"But nothing. You can't gamble with sacred gifts like family. And that's exactly what you've done."

Carter leans against the car, "You're a piece of work."

Jonathan says nothing and turns to walk away.

Carter says, "Have you ever stopped to think..."

"What?"

"About why you and I are both still so angry with Dad...after all these years?"

Jonathan says, "I choose not to dwell on it."

"Maybe you should…"

"What are you getting at?"

Carter sighs, "He's alive. And yet you and I are the ones who continue to suffer. Us. Not him. And Mom?" He hesitates. "She gave up while the giving up was good."

Jonathan becomes outraged. "Wait just a minute. She had NO choice. Boozing and beating have a way of breaking."

Carter sarcastically chuckles, "Sadly…but eloquently, put."

Jonathan pushes Carter against his car, then turns away. "There you go again. Right in the middle of the deepest pain, you like to slide your knife in just a little further, don't you?"

"Just calling it like I see it, brother. Always have. Always will."

"You're a piece of work." He stops to catch a breath. "That tyrant! He always took what he wanted…whenever he wanted…no matter who it hurt or what it broke."

Carter breaks the long silence. "Looks like the therapist is helping you more than you know."

Jonathan gasps, "How did you…"

"Come on." Carter holds up one finger. "You're my brother and you always fall back on that "pop-psych" lingo. It's the way that you're wired." He holds up a second finger. "Special Ops, remember? I can see, go and be anywhere I want."

Jonathan is not surprised as much as he is caught off guard.

"Christopher told me that he saw you out here the other night."

Carter disagrees. "No, he didn't. He probably said he saw someone out here. He had no idea it was me."

Jonathan says, "Okay, James Bond. What were you doing here?"

"Watching."

"Watching what?" Jonathan asks.

"What it used to be like."

Jonathan laughs sarcastically.

"What it could again be like," Carter adds.

Jonathan shakes his head. "Not here. Not now. Not us."

"Johnny, how long are you going to hold this against me?" asks Carter.

Jonathan replies, "I don't know. As I said, I'm trying. Six months ago I would have said…as long as you were alive."

"Man, you've gotten cold."

"Whatever." And he walks away.

Christopher hesitates at the door. Angela is looking out the window as she prepares dinner. He clears his throat as he comes into the kitchen.

"Oh, you startled me," she says.

"Sorry, Mom. Just wanted to see if I could help."

"How nice. Thank you."

He joins her at the window and simmers, "They're still at it?"

"Or each other," she whispers.

"I heard that." He winks.

"Your father does that," she says with a smile.

Self-consciously, he retreats. "I need to get up with Choppers and the guys for practice…"

"I appreciate your help. Will you set the table for me?"

He says, "Sure. Mom you would think that they would just beat each other senseless and get it over with." He looks at her. "Sorry."

"I understand what you're saying. But fighting never gets anyone anywhere. Besides, your father has deep feelings of resentment towards his brother." She hesitates then continues, "As you can imagine. And we all feel…what am I saying…you know better than anyone." She cries quietly.

"Shhh…" he puts his arm around her and consoles her, "No one should ever have the memory that's burned in my brain. Every night. Every dream. I just want that image to go away."

She embraces him. "It will, baby. Time heals all wounds."

CHAPTER 72

JONATHAN TRIES TO FEEL COMPASSION as he walks to the house. But recalling Grace's smile, or remembering the feel of her small arms around his neck, and knowing that he will never see her again; that is all that it takes. His memory flashes back to the aftermath of the gun blast that afternoon. And he begins to seethe.

Carter shouts from the car, "None of us can bring her back."

Jonathan stops.

Carter slowly comes to him saying, "Nothing will bring her back. But you could help me heal, Jonathan. YOU could help me honor her memory...and be an uncle to your boys."

Carter glances at the house. Christopher and Angela are standing on the deck watching.

Jonathan looks from them to Carter and says, "Yes, I could. But I'm afraid between your post-traumatic stress disorder, your abuse of booze and..."

He walks to Carter and pats his hip. Nothing.

Carter says, "What the?"

Jonathan looks in the car. There it sits. The .44 Magnum in the holster, sticking out from under the front seat. He turns, with fire in his eyes.

"Tell me one thing. How in hell can I ever trust you again...when that damn piece of armor never leaves your side?"

"It's for protection."

"From what? The Vietnamese? They're gone. Terrorists? We're in small-town America."

Glaring he says, "You think Dad's going to come back and hunt you down?"

Carter trembles as tears flood his eyes.

Jonathan is confused. Only once has he seen his brother cry. It was when they buried their mother several years ago.

Carter doesn't say anything. He doesn't move. His jaw is clenched. His nostrils flare. He tries to hold back the fear.

Jonathan finally asks, "Is that what..." he nods toward the car, "that's all about?" Jonathan is trying to put two and two together.

Carter finally speaks, "Mom."

"What?"

"It was him," Carter whispers.

Jonathan is confused, "What? Her death was an accident."

Carter shakes his head slowly. Tears spill onto his cheeks.

"Yes, it was," Jonathan adds, "I saw it in the report."

Carter continues to shake his head, slowly and repeatedly.

"Carter. He may have been a lush, but he wasn't...a killer."

Carter is silent. He gets in his car, looks at Jonathan one last time, and pulls away.

Jonathan watches until Carter is out of sight. Angela, Christopher and now David are standing arm in arm on the deck, watching and waiting.

CHAPTER 73

DR. LONG SITS ALONE IN the library, one of the first buildings in the small town of Mission Grove. The high ceilings and marble floors are a testament to the history that the walls surround. Many an intellect was formed here as the pages of history and knowledge opened to eager minds.

Several people prepare to leave as lights near the back of the library are turned off. Dr. Long is surrounded by several books that are stacked around him. He is engrossed in study.

The books vary in topic: *Transactional Analysis Redefined, Post-Traumatic Disorder in Veterans of Vietnam, The Passive Aggressive Nature Defined* and *Hypnosis: The Cause, Conundrum and Cure.* The most influential authors on Psychology of their time are stacked, one atop another, from Jung to Freud to Mesmer.

As the last remaining visitors leave, the librarian approaches and says, "Dr. Long, we'll be closing soon."

He jumps. "You startled me."

"Sorry." She smiles. He notes the empty library and checks his watch.

"Of course, Samantha. I had no idea it was so late. Thank you." He slides several books toward her. "I'll take those, please. And I'll be finished here in just a moment." He resumes reading.

"Of course. And doctor?"

He looks up, "Yes?"

"My friends call me Sammy."

He returns to his books, "There is just one more thing..." He looks up. She's gone. He gathers his notes and briefcase and goes to the counter.

"Tell me, Sammy, do you still have microfiche?" Dr. Long asks.

She smiles. "It's a bit old school but yes, we do. However, let me show you a new technology. It's called a computer." She motions for him to follow her to a bank of computer screens.

"I guess I am old school."

She pats his hand. "I like it. What specifically is it that you're looking for?"

Dr. Long responds, "A death record. Actually, two. Same last name. Different ages. From the same family lineage."

She is puzzled. "This should be interesting."

"You have no idea."

She takes his notes and begins inputting the information, commenting, "That's a lovely name."

Looking at her closely he smiles, "It is, isn't it? I'm sure they were both lovely people."

She stops typing, looks at him and then says, "We need more of that."

"Grace?" Nodding, he smiles, "Yes, we do. Indeed, we do."

She inputs a few more items, then frowns at the screen.

"What?" he asks.

"Okay. Two deaths. One," she glances at the calendar, "was a year ago. She was...nine years old. The other was several years ago."

"Yes?"

She continues, "Both were blunt traumas to the head, one more severe than the other, needless to say."

He watches intently and listens.

She punches a few more keys. "Wait." She looks at him.

He raises his brow, "Yes?"

"Have you dug any deeper into this?"

"That's why I'm here now. I have a hunch about something that I can't...quite..."

She interrupts, "Put your finger on?"

He nods.

She looks around, and then smiles.

"What?"

She continues, "It's strange but I feel as though someone were watching. Almost as if we were in some kind of a movie."

She continues entering more data into the computer. "I have access to the Police Department database. Don't ask why. I suppose it's because I'm an information junkie." She stops, "Okay, now I'm just babbling."

"No, Sammy. You are not. You're delightful. And I love your enthusiasm for knowledge. Reminds me of myself when I was your age. Knowledge is power. And, as we all know, a mind is a terrible thing..."

She chimes in, "To waste. Yes." She continues typing rapidly and delving more deeply. "This is very interesting..."

"I'm all ears, Sammy."

"Are you aware?" She stops. "Of course you're not. You wouldn't have access to this." She continues to read, "Alice Grace Matheson. Maiden name, Baden. Was treated at the emergency room one, two... three..." She stops and looks at Dr. Long in shock, "SIX times she was admitted to Presbyterian Hospital's ER for one accident after another, covering a period of nearly a year!"

Watching intently he moves behind the counter pulls over a chair and asks, "May I?"

She nods. He reads silently.

She says, "Here," pointing to the screen, "next to the on-call nurse. B-F-T."

He inches closer, "BFT?"

"Blunt Force Trauma," Sammy says, motioning a hit to the side of her head.

He continues reading, "Mrs. Alice Grace Matheson was admitted to ER at 12:43 a.m. in what appears to be BFT to posterior cranium. Results found: dizziness, black eyes, bleeding from nose, sporadic vision and overall feeling of light-headedness accompanied by severe headache. Notes: possible hematomas from what seems to be repeated BFTs. Will keep for overnight observation due to severe headache, dizziness and overall malaise. Will recommend Doctor Bluementhal attend at first shift...blah, blah, blah..." He stops reading aloud and becomes immersed in deep thought.

"You know what it looks like to me, right?" she asks.

"Spousal abuse," he replies.

"Damn straight, Skippy." She stops. "Ooops, excuse please, Doctor Long." She smiles sheepishly.

He pats her hand, "You're good. You mentioned six times. Where do you see that?"

She points to the screen. "Here. You see this is in January, right after New Years. Then, in the spring..." She pauses to think. "Right around St. Patty's Day. Then, Memorial Day. See a pattern?" He nods.

She continues.

"But here is where it gets really strange. There were two more visits within a week of one another around the fourth of July. Then three days before Labor Day...she's dead."

Silence.

She continues, "She was either mighty accident prone..."

"Or we're looking at a classically severe case of spousal abuse."

Under her breath, "The S.O.B."

He nods. More silence.

She stands suddenly. "Wait a minute." She goes to another screen and types several entries. "I'm opening another screen so that we can look at them side by side. Here." Again, she points to the other screen. "Look at the date. She dies the day before Angela Grace Matheson is born."

He removes his glasses, leans back and sighs. "Remember the hunch that I couldn't quite figure out?"

She nods.

"The pieces are beginning to come together."

"But...I mean, why?" she asks.

"Who knows? But there is something to consider."

"What?"

"Coincidences like this? Never are."

"I hear that."

"I'm curious who brought her to the ER."

She types and finds nothing. "No idea."

He starts to gather his things and reaches for the books, "These ready to go?"

Still trying to make sense of it she hesitates a second, then says, "Yes. All ready." She looks at her watch. "Oh! It's nearly 10. I was supposed to be closed and gone an hour ago."

"I'm sorry. I shouldn't have..."

"No, that's fine," she interrupts, "This was interesting. Well, helpful. I hope it was helpful."

"It was. You have NO idea. You're quite the investigator."

She blushes. "My secret passion. This gig? Just to pay off school loans. Next year this time? Private Investigator Samantha Brooks at your service."

"Well, good for you. I think we could do some great business together." She turns off the last of the lights, locks the door and they leave.

"Listen, Doc, if you need anything please don't hesitate to ask. I love this stuff and I'm here six nights a week. So, lean on me, brother." She high-fives him.

He responds enthusiastically. "You can count on that."

"In fact, before this week is out you and I, dear lady, have a date. Right here. About this same time. I'll email you before I head over. Sound good?"

They approach her old Honda Civic. She opens the back door and tosses in an oversized backpack.

"Count on it. Ciao for now, Doc!"

She takes off. He waves then walks to his shiny black Jaguar.

What he doesn't notice is the only other car. It is on the opposite side of the parking lot and hidden by several low-hanging tree branches. The glow from a cigarette isn't visible to him either.

CHAPTER 74

CARTER LOOKS AT HIS CIGARETTE with disgust and says, "What a stupid habit." He tosses it out the window, starts the car and follows Long. His headlights are off until he merges into oncoming traffic and he leaves enough room between Long and himself so as not to draw attention. Long pulls into an all-night diner. Carter follows and parks on the opposite side of the lot. He watches the doctor enter and take a seat by the window.

Carter remembers the first time that he came to the old diner seven or eight years ago. He and Jonathan had brought Christopher here after a Pony League ballgame. They had a great time over chocolate shakes and laughs.

Going inside, he takes a seat at the counter and casually glances around at the few patrons. The waitress comes over and asks, "What can I get you, honey?"

"Coffee. Black. Thanks."

A voice from behind him says, "Carter."

Carter realizes that Dr. Long is talking to him. He turns and Dr. Long motions for him to join him. Carter is caught off guard but tries not to show it.

"Thought that was you," Long says.

Carter says, "How do...I don't think I know you."

"I'm the therapist. You're the brother. We're both looking for the same things."

The waitress brings the coffee and Carter sips his, studying Long.

Long holds out his hand to shake, "Jefferson Long. Nice to meet you."

Carter shakes his hand, noticing how strong his grip is. "Carter... but obviously you know that."

Long smiles, nods and motions the waitress over.

"Yes, hon."

"I'll have a three-egg omelet but with only one yolk. Two slices of rye toast, no butter, and any fruit that you may have."

She scribbles, "Pretty particular, aren't you?" she asks.

He replies, "Yes, thank you." She leaves and he wipes the silverware and the rim of his water glass.

Carter watches all of this and says, "Pretty particular, aren't you, hon?" They chuckle.

"Okay. We're off to a good start. I like that," Long says. He takes a thick file from his briefcase and lays it on the table, unopened.

Carter eyes it for an instant then looks out the window.

Long sips his hot tea and waits. Carter drinks his coffee and waits. Then they wait some more.

Long finally says, "About that good start, it looks like I'll be responsible for taking the next step."

Carter nods.

"Here is what I have surmised. Incidentally, none of this abuses the client confidentiality agreement with your brother and his family. I'm not talking about that but about your family dynamics. During my visits with your brother and his lovely wife, I have surmised that much of the angst...if not all of it...is as much about the past as it is about the present. I'm not talking the recent past." He pats the folder, "This tells me that."

Carter finally looks at the file, then at Long, observing his colorful outfit. "I figure that you're about the most unique therapist that I have ever seen."

Smiling, Long says, "Thank you."

The waitress brings the food, sets it down, pauses a second and leaves.

Long takes a small container from his briefcase, opens it and puts some of the spread on his toast.

"Homemade stash?" Carter asks.

Long doesn't miss a beat, "You could say that."

Carter continues, "I am curious as to where you are going. I'm also trying to figure out why my brother continues to be such an ass with me. I know that I was responsible for this tragedy. But of all people, I would think that he would give his brother some latitude. Maybe, a family discount based upon the 'I'm-A-Selfish-Drunk Act.'"

Long says, "Clever."

"Not trying to be clever. Well, maybe a little bit. What I'm really trying to do is to see if you can help me get to him."

Raising his eyebrows Long says, "I see. You do want something from me and you think that I can help."

"I know you can help. Whether you will...that's a whole other thing."

"Yes, it is."

"And, if you want to sit here and play word games, or whatever it is you think you're up to..."

"Sir. You were following me. You must want something. You came over here to sit."

Carter is angry but takes a slow breath before continuing. "A, I was looking for a hot cup of coffee and you happened to be here. B, I got what I needed. C, You invited me over."

Long chuckles and says, "Excuse me one moment."

He stands and walks to the end of the counter, turns and comes back to his seat. Looking surprised, he says, "Hello. I'm sorry that I'm so rude. I should have asked if you were sitting here. Dr. Jefferson Long." He extends his hand to shake and Carter looks at it. "Thought I'd start over. See if we could try a different tactic."

"Nice try. Verdict's still out on whether it worked or not. But I'll give you this, you have some kind of style about you. That's for certain."

Long eats a few more bites, pushes the plate aside, wipes the table and then opens the file.

"First, forgive me for not saying this right out of the gate, I am so sorry for your loss."

Carter quietly responds, "Thank you."

"Second, I see that you and your brother...and you can feel perfectly free to stop me at any time if I go too far, which I'll try not to do... have very likely experienced a long history of violence."

"Yes, I will." Dramatic pause. "And yes, we did."

"Your mother, God rest her soul, suffered the brunt of it, of that I am sure." He catches himself, puts his hand over his mouth, closes his eyes and lowers his head. "I am so sorry. That was…"

"A Freudian slip?" Carter interrupts.

"I apologize."

"Don't. It was a long time ago."

"But I would imagine that you still carry much of that angst."

Carter nods.

"Carter, I know that you didn't come to have a session with me. If you should wish to, I would be happy for you to call my secretary and set one up."

"I don't really want one."

"Understood. And with that said, I shall try to keep my observations more neutral."

"You're fine." Carter gestures to the waitress for more coffee. Carter asks Long to close
the files that are on the table and he obliges.

The waitress pours his coffee and asks, "Is there anything else I can get you two?"

"Not right now," Carter says.

"No, thank you," Long adds.

She leaves. Carter watches her. Long watches him.
Finally, Long asks, "That scar over your eye?"

"Yes."

"From the crash in Lake Mitchell?"

"Yup."

"How did you survive that?"

Carter is confused, then says, "That's what a couple of years in 'Nam will do for you. Teach you to survive. No matter what."

"I cannot imagine." Long pauses, then adds, "They would have eaten me alive."

Carter, sipping his coffee, nearly chokes. Without missing a beat, Long hands him a napkin.

"Thanks. Yes, they would have. Me? They just wanted to see how long it would take to kill me. Dragging it out was like a sport for them."

They sit in silence until Carter speaks. "Let's get away from me and back to my mom. You said you learned something. About the violence that Jonathan and I saw."

Long is now all business. "Yes. Looking at the medical records for just the last year of her life, it was recorded that she experienced multiple BFTs."

"Blunt Force Traumas," Carter interrupts.

"True. What happened to her is similar to what happens to boxers. If you repeatedly receive trauma to the face, and or head, you actually suffer TBI, or Traumatic Brain Injury. They're similar. But what happens is you're tearing the membrane away from the skull. You keep doing that. Then over time you could do something as simple as hit your head on a cabinet, or the trunk of your car while getting something out, and then, Bang!" Dr. Long looks questioningly at Carter.

"Is that what…?"

"That's exactly what happened. She was taking groceries from the trunk of the car. Then she raised up and bumped the back of her head… and…" Carter is quiet and looks out the window. He takes a deep breath, "She died right there on the driveway. Right in front of me. We had just enjoyed the greatest day together. She loved to shop. We were laughing. It was Jonathan's 4th birthday. He was just a kid." He shakes his head.

Long watches him then says, "How did Jonathan handle it?"

"He may have been too young to remember many things in one way, but in another way he was so very sad. He loved her so much, way more than my dad did. Randall." He snorts, "He has never been anything but an arrogant and hateful drunk."

Long says, "Not easy to deal with."

"Hell, no. Especially as a kid! Your parents are supposed to love each other. But them? She was the maid and the babysitter. His real wife was the Marine Corp."

"How did he cover up the…" Long trails off.

Carter is boiling now, with fire in his eyes.

"The Marines watch out for their own. And just so that you'll know, I was in the Army. The Army watches out for their own, too. It's just the way the machine is. SO, I'm not really bashing the Corps. But what I am saying is, you can get away with whatever you need to get away with."

"It was just an accident. She hit her head," Long quietly says.

Carter looks straight at him, eye to eye, and nods, "Yes. Sir."

Long says, "And you must have seen all the damage being done, one hit stacked upon another, until…"

Carter's locked gaze has not shifted from Long and he slowly nods.

"And you've tried to protect Jonathan all these years by never telling him the truth," says Long.

Again Carter nods.

"What a burden to bear," Long says quietly. "And now you wonder why Jonathan can't cut you a break and feel the pain you are going through. The guilt. The anger…"

"You're good," Carter says, reaching in his pocket for money to pay the tab.

"No. I'll get that."

Carter says, "I'm not your responsibility."

"I know that. I want to. It's just a cup of coffee. I'll get it."

Carter nods. "Thanks. And thanks for listening."

"My pleasure."

Silence.

Long asks, "May I ask you one more thing?"

"Why not? I've told you more personal stuff in…" he looks at his watch, "40 minutes than I've ever told anyone."

"This may sound silly, but did your father know that you had ever seen him hit your mother?"

The color drains from Carter's tanned face. It is replaced by a hot flush of color as his fear turns to anger. He takes a long and controlled breath and slowly exhales.

"That is exactly what I've tried to keep hidden from Jonathan for so long." He pauses. "But more importantly, that's exactly why I have wanted to kill my father for all these years."

CHAPTER 75

JONATHAN AND ANGELA ARE IN bed. The lights are out. Angela whispers, "Are you asleep?"

"No."

"Still upset with Carter?"

"What do you think?"

A long silence.

"It was a good day today, right?" she asks.

She can hear the smile in his voice as he says, "Yes. It was perfect."

"The only way it could have been more perfect..." she trails off.

"Yes."

Another long silence.

"Your brother's had a tough time."

"Haven't we all."

"But you're glad he's alive. And well."

After a long moment, Jonathan says, "Yes."

"Jonathan?"

"Yes, babe."

"You're such a good person."

He quietly snorts, "I'm not so sure about that."

"I am."

"Thank you."

"And, I'm proud of you."

"Again. Thank you."

"And you and I both want to find harmony again...in our lives... and in our son's lives."

"Agreed. Absolutely."

"Would you be willing to visit Dr. Long, just one more time?"

Silence. "For me?"

Another deep breath and then, "If that is what it will take to make you happy, and if you think that it will help. Yes. I will do it for you," Jonathan says.

"You're my hero."

"Then please give your hero a goodnight kiss, will you?"

CHAPTER 76

SUNLIGHT FILLS THE KITCHEN AS Angela prepares breakfast. The stereo plays softly. She's humming a tune and all seems at peace. David runs down the stairs, yelling at his brother. "I told you I had a big science fair project and wouldn't be able to go to your concert this weekend. I'm sorry, but this is more important."

Angela is shocked, "What are you talking about?"

Christopher takes the steps two at a time and glares angrily at David.

"You have *got* to be kidding me! I've been practicing for this gig for months and months. You said you liked my music."

"I do. It's great. But my grades...they can't suffer, Chris. Sorry, but this is just more important to me." David turns to Angela.

"Son, you know how important..."

David winks at Angela. She catches on instantly.

"Mom!" David shouts.

"This is important but, well, so are your grades," she says.

David tries his best to suppress a laugh and still facing her says, "But Mom. This is science. He's talking about...what...punk rock?"

Christopher shouts, "What?"

Both Angela and David can't contain the laughter any longer. David high-fives her and shouts, "PUNK'D!"

Christopher's shock turns to hilarity and he chases David who falls on the floor in laughter.

Jonathan comes in and sees the silliness. Angela says with a big smile, "You have a church meeting, too, right?" She winks, "Right, honey? You can't make the concert either."

"Right! Sorry, Christopher. Maybe next..."

"Stop! Alright, already. Very funny."

Christopher stops wrestling with David and looks at all of them.

He says, "That was kinda funny. But seriously, if you all don't go…I will be supremely unhappy. And you don't want that."

"Oh...no! We don't want that!" Jonathan winks at Christopher, then David. He fist-bumps Christopher and high-fives David. Then he grabs a cup of coffee.

Angela says, "Okay, boys. Breakfast in five minutes. Not 15. Not 25. That's five minutes."

David salutes, Christopher waves. "Be right back," they say in unison and run up the stairs.

Angela puts her arms around Jonathan. "Whew. Those boys of yours…"

"Mine?" he says, with mock surprise. "They're yours."

Checking the time he says, "Doing a quick drive by to see our esteemed Dr. Long. Then, off to the salt mines. I'll call you later." He kisses her.

"Please do. I need your sanity in my life."

"Love you." He's out the door.

She replies, "Love you more."

She hears him shout from the driveway, "Love you most."

She turns and David is standing there. He says, "You two are such romantics."

She picks up the dishtowel and throws it at him.

CHAPTER 77

JONATHAN SITS OPPOSITE DR. LONG and stares at the wall of degrees, plaques and certificates. Jonathan shifts uncomfortably. Long waits quietly. Jonathan studies the clock. Long follows his glance.

"Seems to be ticking loudly today, doesn't it?" asks Dr. Long.

Jonathan doesn't respond. He looks at his nails, first one hand then the other. Long adjusts papers on his desk. Jonathan watches every move and then examines artwork on the far wall. Long clears his throat.

Jonathan jerks his head back and asks, "What's that?"

Long smiles but says nothing. Another long period of silence follows.

Finally, Jonathan says, "Okay. Point taken. And I get your quote." He points to the plaque over the door. "If it is to be, it is up to me."

"Yes," Long says quietly.

"It's different without Angela here."

"She's a buffer?" Long asks.

"Yes. Well, actually, more like…" He stops and looks at the ceiling. Long's eyes follow Jonathan's. He looks back down and Jonathan is watching him. Long smiles. Jonathan does also. "I'm trying," Jonathan says.

Dr. Long asks, "You are?"

"Yes."

"I can see that."

Jonathan goes to the aquarium and watches the fish.

He quietly says, "Grace loved fish. She had a small aquarium in her bedroom. She especially liked it when I would come in and turn off all the lights except the one in the tank. And then I would act out a funny little play. I would give each fish a different voice. She loved that. She giggled every time as though it were the first." He pauses. "Children are beautiful. They can find the most pleasure in the smallest of things."

Long quietly echoes, "That is true."

Jonathan asks, "Do you miss the fact you never had children."

Dr. Long's soft smile disappears. His voice is so quiet that Jonathan scarcely hears him when he says, "I did."

Jonathan tries to hide his surprise but he can't. "Oh." He is frozen in place.

"She died. She was younger than your Grace."

Jonathan feels saddened and sits. Long removes a picture from his desk and looks at it before handing it to Jonathan.

"That's Giselle. She was five years old in there."

"She is beautiful." Jonathan points to the woman in the picture, "Her mother?"

Long nods, "That picture was taken a month before they died."

Stunned Jonathan says, "I had no idea…"

"Why would you?"

Jonathan looks at the picture again and hands it back to Dr. Long. "They're both so very beautiful."

"Thank you. It was a car accident. They were coming back from Natalie's parents in Virginia. It was late at night. Pouring rain." A very long pause, then he says, "Drunk driver."

"Oh, no. That's horrible."

"Only one small problem," Long says. He removes his glasses, cleans them and puts them back on.

"What was that?"

"Two drivers. One was drunk in the oncoming car. The other was my wife. She had only had wine. But evidently it was just enough to slow her reflexes."

"I am so very, very sorry, Jefferson." Jonathan looks at him with intensity. "All this time…I've thought…"

276

"No worries, my friend. You're not the first."

"When I said you wouldn't understand…"

"Until I walked in your shoes," Dr. Long says.

"That certainly brings us to a more even playing field."

Dr. Long rubs his hands together, smiles brightly and says, "Enough about me. This is your session. You're the patient. I want to hear just one thing from you today that shows me you're getting closer to understanding and acceptance."

"Me, too. Trust me. I have played the scene over and over and over in my mind. It ends the same way every time."

"You mean, Grace's birthday party?"

"Yes."

"Jonathan, may I try something with you? I promise that you will get it."

"Yes. Sure."

Dr. Long says, "This couch is more comfortable than it looks. With your training you can appreciate what lying on one's back and closing one's eyes can do for relaxing the mind and opening one's memory bank."

Jonathan looks doubtful.

"I promise it will not hurt. And we only have 20 minutes or so."

"I'll do it. After all, that's what I'm here for." He lies down.

"Feel free to remove your shoes if you would like, it's up to you. I'm going to sit behind you, out of your line of sight."

"Okay. Let's start with three long, deep breaths in." Jonathan follows this. "And slowly breathe out." Dr. Long instructs.

Jonathan begins to relax.

"And one more time," Long says and Jonathan follows suit.

"Now, let's go back to that afternoon. Take your time and paint the picture for me. Tell me as much or as little detail as you wish. However, I would suggest sharing as much detail, no matter how large or small, in order for us both to see that day clearly. Trust me, you'll be fine. The pain can't be worse than what you've already experienced." He squeezes Jonathan's shoulder.

Jonathan quietly says, "Okay."

"Where were you and Angela and what did that day look like?"

Jonathan begins…

"It was one of those perfect days. The sky was a brilliant blue. The few clouds were enormous and pure white. Angela and I were in lounge chairs. It was a great day for a nap. Actually, I was zonked but she was reading a magazine. The kids were playing in the yard. It was Grace's birthday so she got to choose what she wanted to do for the afternoon. That is, besides eating all the ice cream and cake that she possibly could. Christopher and David, and about a dozen friends, came to enjoy the day. Daphne was in the kitchen. She helps Angela a lot."

He takes a moment to remember the day. Dr. Long sees the whisper of a smile on his face.

"I can practically smell the freshly mown grass. My tradition every Saturday is to mow the grass and then reward myself with a cool drink and a long nap. That afternoon Carter had come by. We did what we did most times that he came by, throw meat on the grill and have a few laughs. Usually over a cold beer or two. Or, in Carter's case, he'd have a beer or six. But that's a different story."

He pauses. Long sees a wrinkle appear in Jonathan's brow.

"Anyway, we were talking about this and that…and watching the kids play. No, wait. Actually, the kids were playing earlier while I mowed. Then, I stopped to play with them. That must have been about the time Carter showed up. Anyway, they were playing. Then, Angela and her best friend, Deanna, took them for ice cream. Evidently, we had run out. Some of the kids had to go home. It was Labor Day Weekend and several parents wanted to have their own barbeque before the kids headed back to school."

He stops and thinks. Dr. Long quietly waits. "Carter and I are grilling. Brats and burgers. He loves brats and I love burgers. He was miffed about something. I think we were talking about Dad. Boy, that used to rile him up. And fast. If Carter gets riled up, especially if it involves conversations or memories about Dad, he usually pulls out the hard stuff. Which he did. He always carried an old gym bag. Kinda half-mooned shape. Two-tone. Almost like a bowling bag. Two things were always in that bag. And they weren't a good combination. Booze and a gun. A loaded gun at that.

I always, always, always told Carter to never, ever bring a loaded gun around the house. He promised me time and again that it would stay in the car, usually in the trunk. So, we've already had a couple of beers apiece. In case you didn't know..."

Jonathan starts to sit up to explain. Dr. Long touches his shoulder and gently nudges him back down.

"Well, Angela doesn't like me to drink. An occasional drink, like wine with dinner isn't bad, but nothing harder than beer. But whenever Carter came around we would sometimes have a little too much. Usually the hard stuff. And this day, we did. It was vodka. It messed us up fast."

Jonathan slows. Dr. Long watches. Jonathan is processing something.

Quietly, Dr. Long says, "Keep going Jonathan. Just a few more minutes. What happens next? Deep breath and relax."

Jonathan takes a deep breath and slowly relaxes. "We cooked, ate some, but mostly drank. Seems like we drank a lot. I think I passed out, we passed out, for a few minutes. Oh...then, I heard a car door slam. I sat up and gathered my thoughts. I couldn't let Angela and the kids see us like that. I picked up Carter, he was passed out on a deck chair, threw him over my shoulder and hustled inside. An out-of-sight Carter was much better than an in your face, drunken Carter.

I could hear noises from the kids at the end of the driveway. We had blocked off the driveway with some blow-up, bouncy thing. I'm hurrying through the house to get Carter into the guest room. It's at the far end of the house. I took him in there and tossed him on the bed. I remember that when he hit the mattress, his shoes fell off."

Jonathan is very quiet. "Wait…something was…" Jonathan stops. Long notices that his breathing has increased.

"Something dropped. I thought it was his flip-flops. I ran back outside and plopped on the lounge chair."

Jonathan suddenly sits up and stares straight ahead. Panic crosses his face. His eyes fill with tears. He buries his face in his hands, resting his elbows on his knees.

"No…No…it can't be…"

Dr. Long says very quietly, "Jonathan. What is it? What happened?"

Jonathan takes very deep breaths. "I didn't go right back out. I tossed my brother on the bed, something clanked and I looked around and saw it."

He begins to sob.

Dr. Long asks, "What?"

Jonathan tries to steady his breathing. "Carter's gun. It was on his belt. When he fell on the bed, it must have fallen on the floor. I saw it. I could hear the kids running up the driveway. My head was spinning. I was angry about the gun. Scared to have Angela come in. I'm not thinking clearly, so I picked it up…"

Horror covers his face and vibrates through his being.

"What, Jonathan?"

He squeezes his eyes shut as if to force the reality away. "I heard the kids. Looked out the window. I picked up the gun and slid it under the pillow. Then I ran outside and laid in the chair before they could…"

He sobs. Tears erupt, emptying months and months of grief.

Finally spent, he looks at Dr. Long. "I killed my Gracie. It was *my* fault. Not Carter's. She's dead because of *my* hand." He is exhausted.

Dr. Long hands him tissues, puts his hand on Jonathan's shoulder and waits.

Jonathan places his hand on Long's and says, "Thank you." He continues, "All this time…Carter has been carrying this guilt…I've been driving the stake in deeper…without even thinking about forgiving him. Just blaming him."

"It's time for you to forgive yourself, Jonathan. It was a senseless accident. Don't focus on who is at fault. Focus on the fact that events transpired that triggered other events."

Dr. Long continues, "Don't misunderstand me. I am not minimizing what happened. And I'm not saying that irresponsible adults were at play here. What I am saying is that the most important thing to understand is this: forgiveness is paramount to anything else."

Jonathan gathers himself and starts to leave.

Long quietly says, "Let it go. And move forward." They look at one another and they embrace.

"Now, get out of here. Mrs. Switzer has a schnauzer that's driving her nuts. And I need to give her my attention."

In the waiting room Jonathan sees David. He closes his book and asks, "You all good, Dad?"
David's expression is precious.

Jonathan says, "I'm all good. Let's get you to school."

CHAPTER 78

AT THE DRIVE-THRU WINDOW at Starbucks, Jonathan orders a triple-Americano and asks David, "What'll it be for my co-pilot?"

"How about a triple Hot Chocolate with some…espresso whip cream," says David, with obvious delight.

"Can you do that?" Jonathan asks the server.

She says, "Yes. We do that. Just a minute."

Jonathan says to David, "I am so proud of you, son."

"Why? I haven't done anything."

"Are you kidding? Straight A's…helping your Mom around the house…building an interstellar solar system in your bedroom… supporting your big brother's upcoming music career. You've been quite the entrepreneur."

David beams with pride, "Well, maybe."

The drinks arrive and Jonathan hands David his. "All this before school. I'm rich!" David says with a big grin.

They drive in silence and David enjoys downing his large hot chocolate. He wipes cream off his mouth and asks, "Dad, in the Bible it says something about God loving the world so much that He gave us His son. Why would He do that?"

"Well, son, that is a mighty good question. Where did that come from?

David shrugs. "I was just thinking…what would it be like if you had chosen to give up Grace in order for me or Chris to be happy and healthy."

Jonathan waits.

"I mean… I can fathom math. I can do Sudoku. I can do a lot of the crossword puzzles in the newspaper. But I don't understand that."

Jonathan finally says, "Son, that is the single most profound observation I have heard in my years of study. That will most likely be the topic for this coming Sunday's sermon."

With enthusiasm and joy he asks, "Really?"

"Really!" Jonathan answers.

Jonathan drives in silence until the phone rings.

"Hello. Matheson here."

"Hey, Johnny. It's Danny."

"Well, if it isn't the Caped Crusader. How are things?"

"Good, good. How are you?"

"I'm managing. Going through some stuff but most of it's good. Frankly, it's helping. Both me and the family."

"Cool," says Danny, a happy tone in his voice.

"I just dropped David off at school and I'm running errands. You?"

"Actually, things are good. Same but good. I'm not going to keep you. I'm actually heading out of town on much needed vacation, but I wanted to call and apologize."

"Apologize for what?"

"Well, I don't want to be all sappy and stuff...especially with my girl here with me in the car." He blows Brenda a kiss, "I wanted to say, for the record, that I was wrong. And I'm sorry."

"Hey. Water under the bridge. Or would that be water under the lake?"

"Very funny. Seriously, I guess between everything that was going on...Gracie...you and me...Carter being, well, a problem...and my wanting to watch out for you, as I always have, I just wasn't thinking straight."

"I get it. We have history and that won't change. But our attitudes, how we choose to approach life...that needs to evolve all the time."

"Right to what you just said. You were always better with all that mumbo-jumbo. I wanted to say that I hope we're good. Again. And will be. For a long time."

"We're good. Count on it. Have fun. Be safe. And I expect to see you in church some day, okay?"

"Promise. Actually, Brenda is a church going type and she asked me to go."

"As long as it's mine."

They laugh.

"I'll see ya, Johnny. I'll check back in when I get back, if I come back."

Jonathan laughs. "You will. The prodigal son always comes home."

Danny signs off with a hearty, "See you, bro."

Jonathan smiles.

CHAPTER 79

CARTER SITS IN HIS LIVING room looking at old photographs of Jonathan and himself. An occasional photo of Randall shows up. A rare picture of his mother is in the album. He smiles.

A bottle of unopened scotch sits nearby. A pack of cigarettes sits next to the bottle. They remain unopened. But the gun, sitting beside them, is perched loaded, alongside a box of bullets that has been opened. He glances at the tools of death then at Sampson who sleeps in front of the glowing fire.

Carter whispers, "Hey, buddy."

Sampson slowly stirs. Carter says, "Who would really care, old boy?" Sampson sighs and returns to his dreams.

"We're all just one single heartbeat away...from the other side."

He looks from the gun to the pictures, then pats his leg and says, "Hey. Let's go out and chop some wood. It ain't gonna stack itself."

Outside he starts chopping and works up a good sweat. He takes off his shirt, tosses it aside, looks around and smiles. A horn blows. It blows a second time then a third time and he recognizes Jonathan's truck.

Jonathan gets out and says, "Hi, Carter."

Carter looks at him suspiciously, "Hi, Johnny. What's up?"

Jonathan tosses his jacket on the truck hood, rolls up his sleeves and says, "I wanted to stop by and check on you. Haven't seen you. I mean, I've missed seeing you around."

"That's mighty neighborly of you."

"What are you up to?"

"Chopping wood."

Jonathan nods. It's an awkward moment. Carter swings his axe but misses the log and it falls over. He stoops to pick it up and Jonathan sees several deep scars on his back. He winces. Carter replaces the log and notices Jonathan's strange expression.

He asks, "What? What's that look for."

Jonathan says, "Your back. I guess I've never seen your back before."

Carter tries to brush it off. "Yeah, those gooks really took it outta me. Can't even hear the sound of certain things without being reminded. My back is a reminder of just how much pain I can withstand." He resumes chopping.

"Stop," says Jonathan.

Carter looks up. "What?"

They lock eyes. Jonathan finally speaks. "I'm sorry. I'm very, very sorry. You know, there's something that I've never done before...as long as I've been pastor here...that I should have done. I can't believe I haven't. What a jerk I have been."

Carter asks, "What's that?"

"Of all the times since I've been pastor, and all the times I've busted your chops for not coming, I've never invited you to our church.'"

"That's true."

"Would you like to come this Saturday night?"

Carter grimaces.

"It's not regular church. There will be a short message but lots of music. Christopher is playing and he'd be thrilled to have you come and see him and his band perform."

"Christopher?"

He nods. "Yep. He misses his buddy."

Carter says, "I'll think about it. Might be busy."

"That's fine. Whatever. Love to see you there."

A long silence and Jonathan starts to leave, then turns back.

"Carter, I'm truly sorry. I never stopped to think about how everything affected you. And I guess I just tried to suppress things. In order to cope and protect."

"Tell me about it. Easy to do, bro. Easy to do."

Jonathan looks at Carter, from head to toe, then at the stack of wood. He looks into Carter's eyes. "Dad would be proud of you. And me." Long pause. "I think."

Carter slowly nods.

"And if not...too bad." He smiles, then winks at Carter and gets into the truck. Jonathan waves as he drives away.

Carter watches him go down the long driveway and out of sight.

CHAPTER 80

THE DINNER TABLE IS SET as if it were Thanksgiving. Jonathan is at one end and Stuart at the other. David, Kym and Christopher are next to one another on one side. Angela and Daphne are opposite them. At the place between Angela and Daphne, a small candle burns. The family holds hands as Jonathan prays.

"We certainly miss our little girl but we know that she is probably sitting on Your lap, telling you one of her wonderful stories. We thank you, Father for this delicious food. We thank you for the gift of family and what each means to another. We are eternally grateful for the love of your Son and the sacrifice He made. We know that it is by grace that we have been saved. We thank you for our daily bread. Please forgive us our trespasses as we forgive those who trespass against us. Keep us from temptation but allow us to enjoy Mama Daphne's fried chicken."

And they all said, "Amen."

Jonathan gives David a big wink. He winks back and says, "Amen, dive in."

As the food is passed, Christopher notices that Stuart isn't filling his plate with fried chicken. He asks, "Granddad, what's with the no chicken? It's your favorite."

"Well, son, as much as I love it…" he takes Daphne's hand, "and you know that I do. The doctor says I have to cut back."

Daphne adds, "I believe that he said no more."

"Yes, no more. Fried food. Or, pretty much anything that's really good." He looks at his steamed veggies and salad.

Angela says, "Dad, you can have an occasional hamburger. Like maybe once a summer."

Stuart grins, "Thanks."

David pipes in, "Look at it this way, Grandpapa. Think how *good* that burger will taste when you do get it."

They all laugh.

"Speaking of burgers and cooking out, do you think Carter will ever come around again?" Christopher asks.

Jonathan looks at Angela and says, "Yes. I think so. Maybe soon." He smiles.

Christopher smiles.

Kym speaks up, "And speaking of coming around, do you think that after you have won the Band Competition you'll fly in on your private jet and still come around us little people?"

"Oh, I don't see why not. After all, it's you, my real fans, that have made me the great artist I am today," Christopher jokingly responds.

David, reaching around Kym, pops him on the back of the head.

Christopher says, "Hey, watch the hair." He turns to shout, "Makeup." They laugh.

Kym says quietly, "I'm kind of serious."

Christopher asks, "Seriously?"

She nods.

"Who knows, I may have to take you with me! You've been an awesome groupie so far."

She pokes his arm. David laughs and Angela gives him a *mind your manners* look.

"I am looking forward to hearing you play tonight, son," Jonathan says.

Angela interjects, "Well, your Grandmother and I can vouch for one thing."

"What's that?" Christopher asks.

"It's loud."

Daphne nods her head vigorously.

Kym is not eating and is only moving food around on the plate. Christopher quietly says, "Kymmie, you know this is what I have to do. No matter where it takes me. And I would want you to come."

"But this is home. I can't imagine living anywhere else," she says.

Christopher is frustrated. Lowering his voice, he says, "But record deals aren't done in towns as small as Mission Grove."

"If you're that good then you can make millions and move back here."

The family tries not to listen but they are.

He whispers, "Let's talk about this later. Okay?"

"Sure."

Jonathan says, "Who's interested in dessert?" He looks at Stuart, "Well, besides you, Pops."

"Very funny."

Daphne announces, "It's double-fudge brownies with ice-cream." Patting Stuart's hand, she adds, "And low-fat vanilla pudding for whomever would like some." She smiles.

He winces but says, "Sounds yummy."

Laughter and the sounds of clearing the table note the end to a perfect family meal.

CHAPTER 81

CARTER PLACES HIS PLATE ON the floor. Sampson is ready, poised to initiate cleanup duty. Carter watches Sampson's eyes shift from the plate to Carter without moving his head. He awaits the command.

"Are you hungry, boy?"

Sampson's tail thumps the floor. He doesn't move.

"Left a little something extra there."

Sampson wags his tail, waiting.

"Okay. Good boy."

Sampson attacks the plate as if it were his last meal. In minutes he finishes and looks up. Carter rubs his head. "That's it. All gone. Well, I do have a little more where that came from. Come on."

In the kitchen he puts more meat in a bowl, adding dog food.

"You weren't expecting a whole steak, were you?"

The phone rings. He is puzzled. His phone never rings. Sampson is clearly more interested in the bowl in Carter's hand than any noise from the other room. It rings again. Carter stands thinking. Ring. He sets the bowl down, saying, "Have at it."

Ring. "Okay, okay." Ring. He reaches for the phone that's hung mostly silent for decades.

Ring. "Hello."

"Carter Matheson?" a man's voice croaks.

"Yes. It's me."

"It's your old man."

Carter feels faints and leans against the wall. "What?" Silence. "Is this Johnny?"

A dry laugh comes from the phone, "Very funny. He doesn't sound this good and you know it."

Carter asks, "Dad? How did you get this number."

"Oh, Carter. I may be banging on death's door but I'm not stupid."

Carter tries to make sense of this.

"Hello?" Randall barks.

"Yeah. I'm here. Just trying to figure out…"

"Special Ops, son," Randall interrupts. "You know as well as anyone that if you have a little bit of info and a whole lot of know how, you can find anything on anybody, anywhere and at any time."

Carter snorts, "Heard that before."

"Well, you should have. You were a soldier once."

"Still am," he replies, adding an emphatic, "Sir."

The crackling cough on the other end sounds serious.

"So, I'm guessing you didn't buy the whole get-up."

"Ha! Like I said, I may be kicking the tires on the grave, but I'm not in it yet!"

"Yeah, you didn't look so hot."

"Damn. You were no beauty pageant contender."

"Thank God," Carter mumbles.

"Oh, boy. Now you sound like your brother." He coughs several times then says, "What is 'The Preacher Man' up to these days?"

"Are you kidding me? You and I haven't spoken in 10 or 15 years? And you just ring me up on a random Saturday night and say, 'Oh, how's the family. They good? That's good. How are you? Good? Good. I'm good, too.'"

Randall laughs and it causes him to cough. He laughs some more. Then coughs some more.

"You sound like hell," Carter says.

Randall clears his throat and barks, "You would too if you were dying from lung cancer. You better tell me you stopped your nasty habit. I waited too long."

Carter absently pats his pocket for a pack of smokes. "Yeah. Nasty alright. And from the sounds of you it's a good thing that I have stopped."

"No kidding."

Silence.

"Hello?" Carter asks.

"The reason I tracked your sorry ass down was to tell you when you do 'recon' you need more than a couple of weeks beard and cheap sunglasses."

Carter flushes with embarrassment.

"What were you thinking anyway? That my eyes would be gone? You're my son, for crying out loud."

"I have no idea."

"Right." Randall pauses, allowing the extra moment to send the message.

He continues, "You were always one of the brightest stars in the Army. Just because we were on opposite teams, so to speak, we all still knew it."

"Thanks," Carter says softly.

"What's that, soldier? If you're grateful, let me hear it."

"Yes, sir. Thank you, sir." Carter shouts. He stands at attention and salutes for added effect. Sampson walks past him and takes his place by the hearth.

That same guttural laugh echoes over the miles and through the phone. "Well, I won't keep you. I just wanted to say…"

Silence. Carter waits.

"I wanted to say that…it was…good to see you, son. Even though you looked like some laundry delivery boy. What was with the bow tie?"

Carter can't help it. He laughs out loud. Randall joins him.

"It was the best I could come up with on short notice."

"Well, it was certainly colorful. I was looking out the window and I said, 'Honey, go get the shotgun, the Mormons have hit the neighborhood.' She didn't think it was funny."

"Yeah, well." He pauses then adds, "Speaking of which, she's a lovely woman. Is she number two, three…?"

Randall laughs, "Try four. Guess it took me this long to get it right."

That struck Carter hard.

"Wait just a minute…"

Randall interrupts, "Sorry. I didn't mean it that way, son. Your momma was a good woman. We just weren't a good fit."

Carter is angry.

Randall continues, "Don't get me wrong, you boys were the best things that came from that time of our lives. But, your momma and me…"

"Save it," Carter blurts out. "I don't want to hear one single word of disrespect about my mother. You arrogant fool."

Silence.

"You're right. Absolutely right."

Carter is caught off guard. He's never heard his father admit a wrong. Ever.

"What? I thought I was talking to Randall "Razorback" Matheson. Toughest guy in the Corps. Did I just hear…what do they call it?"

"An apology. Yes, you smart aleck kid."

Carter snorts, "This kid is pushing Medicare."

"You're still a kid to me. I got twenty and change on you." He coughs. "And I'm better looking."

Carter smiles. "Not from where I was standing." Carter is torn. Anger, from all the bad years, or happiness from hearing from his dying father.

"Son? You still there?"

"Yes, sir. Still here." He looks at his watch. "But not for long. Gotta run out for awhile."

"Oh. That's right. Saturday night. A good time for bad boys to raise a little hell."

"No, sir. Got off the bottle, actually."

"You what?" He thinks about it and says, "Good for you. It's nothing but trouble. Trust me."

"I know…and no, I don't."

Randall is confused, "Huh?"

"What I mean is, I know it's all trouble. And no, I don't trust you."

"Not a surprise. Well, listen, I best be…"

Carter interrupts. "In fact…Pops?"

"Yeah?"

"Aren't you curious about why I showed up after all this time. No words between us for decades and then I just pop up out of nowhere?"

After a really long silence and a handful of wet coughs, Randall's scratchy voice speaks. "If I were a betting man…and I used to be…I'd say you came looking to kill me."

That's the second time that Carter has nearly dropped the phone. He is speechless.

"And I'd surmise from your silence that I'd win the bet. And you know what, son?"

"What?"

"You'd have done your old man a favor. Between this damn cancer sucking the life out of me by the hour, and me rotting from the inside out for what I did to your mother, you would have done us all a great big, fat favor."

Carter searches for what to say. He isn't used to being blindsided.

"Yep. I thought so. It's okay, son. I'd have done the same if I had seen what you saw for all those years."

"Pops."

"Look. I know I'll burn for that. I'm sure there's a special place reserved in the Hot House for me. I just wanted to hear your voice one more time."

"It was good to see you, Pops. Not that you looked good but, well you know."

"Yep. I do. Listen. Tell your little brother that…well, tell him I said hello."

"Will do."

"And that I asked about the kids. How is Chris, Dave and Gracie?"

Carter feels a wave of sadness wash over him but tries to hide it. "Christopher is about to graduate high school. He wants to be a rock star. David is a brilliant little boy. And Gracie…"

There is a long silence as Carter gains composure.

"Carter?"

"Yes, Dad. Gracie passed away."

"What? Oh…that is terrible. How?"

Carter fights back the tears.

"It…was…an…accident. I'll let Jonathan share more with you another time. Pops, I really have to go. It's important…"

"No. Understood. I am very sorry to hear about your brother's loss. I should…uh…" He trails off.

"I'll give him your regards, sir."

"That would be nice, son. You take care. And…well, take care."

"You too, sir. Keep in touch. I'll check in on you in a couple of weeks. That be okay?"

"Sure. Sounds good. Bye now."

The line goes dead. Carter takes a very deep breath, wipes his eyes, checks his watch, grabs his coat and heads for the door. Looking again at a picture of his family during happier days, he smiles.

"Be good, Sampson. Be back after while."

Sampson flaps his tail and lays his head back down as Carter leaves.

CHAPTER 82

JONATHAN, ANGELA, DAVID, DAPHNE AND Stuart enter the auditorium of Mission Grove Community Church. The house is packed. Dozens of band members fill the orchestral area, as well as the wings of the large stage. Joshua and Deanna approach the Mathesons.

"Hello, everyone," Joshua says, shaking hands with Jonathan, Stuart and David.

"Hi," Deanna says as she kisses Angela on the cheek and hugs Daphne. She pats Stuart's shoulder and rubs David's head.

Jonathan says, "This is fantastic. What a turnout."

Joshua excitedly says, "No kidding. We have ten finalists here tonight."

Dee jumps in, "Yes, we started with 27 initially, then narrowed that down over the past two months to these ten. It's so exciting!"

Angela looks at the side of the stage and nudges Jonathan.

"Look, it's Kym." She waves and Kym waves back. Kym holds up a handwritten sign and carries it from one end of the stage to the other. It reads: "Find your seats. Then park yourself." She flips the board over and it reads: "Show begins in 20. Get ready to rock!" Her image is broadcast on a large screen that everyone can see.

Jonathan smiles at Angela, "That's our girl."

Angela smiles at him and turns to Daphne. They both raise their eyebrows and shrug, as if to say, "Well…"

CHAPTER 83

CARTER RACES THROUGH THE OUTSKIRTS of town. Checking his watch, he taps the steering wheel of his new car. Then he looks in the rearview mirror and sees flashing lights.

"Oh, great!" He pulls over, reaches in the glove compartment and gets the registration. He lowers the window, revealing Officer Reddick. Their expressions are priceless.

"I cannot believe it," Carter says.

"No doubt."

Carter says, "I can't believe that you're back on duty."

"Why not? Nothing else better to do. I can't chase bad guys like I used to." He pats his thigh. "What with this titanium hip and a rod in my leg. But I can still chase speeding Neanderthals like yourself."

Carter is still holding the papers for Reddick and says, "Really sorry about the hip and all that. But you did get me drunk."

"So."

"And set me up."

Reddick shrugs his shoulders. "True."

"And nearly killed me."

"Yep. And then you nearly returned the favor."

"True," Carter says. "But if I had really wanted you dead..."

Reddick puts his hand on his gun and takes a mocking stance, "Whoa, Cowboy." They laugh.

He looks at the papers that Carter still holds and says, "Put that away."

Carter obliges and says, "Thanks."

"I'm sorry about all that. It was stupid."

Carter nods, not saying anything.

"I need to redirect my energy to other things, as my dad used to say. Not sure what yet, but something."

Carter says, "Good." Then something occurs to him, "I have an idea. But…" he looks at his watch, "I really gotta get to this thing…"

"Go ahead. Just not as fast, okay?"

"Sure. What say that we grab coffee sometime? I have an idea that I think you'll like. Something that you're already good at but with redirected energy. Could be a win-win."

"Sure. You know where I work." Reddick tips his hat and walks away.

In the side mirror Carter sees that Reddick walks with a slight limp. He puts the car in gear and drives away.

CHAPTER 84

KYM ON THE FAR RIGHT side of the stage holds up a large sign. It reads: "Show starts in 10. Grab a seat." There are cheers as she flips it over. "You Ready To Rock…Or What?" The cheers grow louder.

The Matheson family is seated in the middle of the front center section about five rows back. David removes a *'Reserved'* sign and shoves it under his seat. He sits next to Jonathan who pats his leg vigorously. Jonathan cranes to see Christopher in the orchestra area.

Christopher blows a kiss to Kym as she crosses the stage. He holds up one finger, picks up a large piece of white cardboard from the edge of the stage and an enormous marker. He scribbles then holds it up. Kym sees it just as she reaches the end of the stage and her face lights up. She nods vigorously.

Angela smiles as she sees Kym beaming at Christopher, who holds up a sign. It reads: "U R MY LUV. R U MINE?" Jonathan and Angela look at one another and squeeze hands.

Jonathan scans the audience; it's a packed house. There are many from the congregation and he beams with pride, as they are his family. He waves Dr. Long over to join them but sees that there are no extra seats.

David sees his Dad's dilemma and says, "Dad, I wanna stand. Is that okay?"

As Dr. Long approaches Jonathan says, "Thank you, son. You're my hero."

David grins and high-fives Dr. Long. Jonathan stands to greet him. "Hello, Dr. Long."

He grins, "It's Jefferson. And how are you, Jonathan?"

"Great, thanks."

Angela greets Jefferson with a hug and whispers to him, "How will I ever be able to repay you for all your help."

"I hear your kitchen serves the best fried chicken in these parts." They laugh.

Kym holds up another sign. It reads: "For Those About To Rock... We Applaud You." The crowd cheers. She flips it over, "Lights Out & Bodies Up in 5!"

The crowd gets louder still.

Carter circles the block looking for a parking space and finally finds one in the parking lot of a bar. Its sign says, "Hot Wings & Cold Beer. Come Early & Party Late."

He sets the security on his car. It beeps, flashes, honks and then beeps again.

The ushers lead stragglers to the last remaining seats. Angela whispers to Jonathan. He stands and faces the crowd, waving to familiar faces. He scans the room from one side to the other. The house lights blink once, then twice and he sits. The music starts with a rumble that grows louder and louder.

Kym directs a group of eight onto the stage. They take their places, holding the same kind of large cardboard signs that Kym has been carrying.

They hold them against their legs.

Then one by one, they pop up one sign after the other.

They read: For Those About To Rock We Applaud You! They flip over them over.

They read: Tonight 10 Bands 2 Runners-up 1 Winner All 2 B Blessed Are You Ready?

The crowd goes wild.

David stands in front of Jonathan. He jumps up and down and

yells, "Chris is gonna rock this place!"

Jonathan shouts, "Yep! You're proud of him, aren't you?" David nods.

Jonathan leans close and says, "You take my seat, buddy. I have to head backstage. Watch after Mom." He high-fives David and heads down the aisle.

The associate pastor, Joshua, steps onto the stage and into the beam of a solo spotlight. The cheering crowd settles as he raises his hand.

"Thank you for coming tonight. This is a very special occasion. It's our First Annual Band Competition." The crowd cheers. "And it's not just any kind of competition for a statue, or a plaque or something like that. But for..." He cups his hand to his ear and waits for the audience to fill in the blank.

They shout, "Five Thousand Dollars!"

"Exactly. Five grand goes to just one band, along with having their latest work recorded at Ramsey Recording Studios."

The crowd cheers.

"The runners up will get brand new band equipment of their choosing, within reason, from Helms Audio & Equipment."

The crowd cheers again.

"And last, but not least the third place band will share $1000!" The crowd cheers once more.

"Now, without any further ado put your hands together for a man that we all know and love. The leader of Mission Grove Community Church, Pastor Jonathan Matheson."

Jonathan takes the stage and waves to the clapping crowd.

"Thank you so very much for coming out tonight and supporting all these very talented musicians. It's an honor for me to be your pastor, and I'm grateful for each and every one of you. You are family."

He smiles at his family, blows a kiss to Angela and a thumbs-up to David.

"There have been some real bumps in the road for many of us, but you know what? God is an awesome God."

They clap.

"And He is worthy of our praise."

They clap more.

"And we are here to celebrate Him."

They clap even more.

"And, just as important, we are here to honor these talented artists."

He spreads his arms, indicating all the band members on both sides of the stage, down in front and along the orchestra pit.

"I want to share one other thing...and he'll want to get me later...but I'm a proud father. My son Christopher is very talented." He looks at him and then the audience. "When he asked me if he could have first a guitar, I said, 'Well, okay, as long as you practice.' Later that year, he asked for a drum kit. I said, 'Oh, boy. The noise ratio's about to grow, but okay, IF you practice.' Then last year, after mastering both of those instruments, he asked for a bigger...better...louder... sound system. And I said...'

The audience in unison shouts, "Practice."

He laughs. "Actually I said, 'Okay, on one condition, you have to learn to keep it under eleven.'"

Some of the crowd claps and others laugh.

"For the Spinal Tap fans...you will appreciate that. Anyway, I wanted you to know that I am proud, as I am sure that you all are, of these young people."

Jonathan raises his hands and shouts out a mini-prayer, "Dear Lord, bless the talents that are before You. Allow them to perform at their optimum and let us always be grateful for You and Your love for us."

The crowd claps and several loud "Amens" are heard.

Jonathan shouts, "Now, let's do this!"

The stage lights blaze on, the sound kicks in, and the crowd jumps to their feet as Band #10 performs their number.

CHAPTER 85

TWO HOURS LATER

JOSHUA IS CENTER STAGE AS the audience finally stops clapping and takes their seats.

"What a night this has been. Ten bands in just two hours." Turning to the band members, he says, "Thanks to all you guys and gals for working so hard the past several months and for tonight, making things move so quickly and smoothly. And now comes the hardest part of all...deciding the winner of tonight's First Annual Band Competition. Thanks to our four talented judges who had tough choices to make since there was amazing talent and showmanship displayed. However, they narrowed the choice to three bands."

The crowd claps.

"And now YOU, the audience, get to pick... by noise level alone... who are the top three winners. All you have to do is give a loud shout as I move across the stage. I will hold my hand over the lead singer of each band and you do the rest. You decide who the winners are. I'm going to ask Pastor Jonathan to come back to the stage while we get ready to present the awards. To refresh, the bands are: David & The Goliaths."

The crowd roars.

"Next up: Song of Solomon."

The crowd gets louder.

"And the third in our top three: Solstice."

The crowd unleashes a thunder of applause, whistles and shouts.

Jonathan's smile broadens as Christopher, the lead of Solstice, looks at him. They nod at one another. Angela is radiant and David is jumping up and down. He whispers to Angela, she nods and he runs to join his brother on stage.

Joshua says, "Pastor, it's all yours," and hands him the microphone. David runs onto the stage and joins his big brother. They high-five, fist-bump and hug.

Jonathan says proudly, "These are my boys. And I'm their proud father." He removes a check from his pocket.

"First, I'd like to present this check for $1,000 to David & The Goliaths."

The lead singer comes forward and the crowd claps. He waves and shouts, "Thank you!"

Reaching for another envelope Jonathan says, "And if the lead singer for Song Of Solomon would come forward, I have this check for brand new equipment for the entire band."

Sarah comes forward and Jonathan hands it to her.

"Thank you so much, Pastor. This is fantastic. We all thank you."

The crowd cheers.

"And last, but not least...okay, I'm more than a bit biased...accepting for Solstice, Christopher Matheson."

Christopher steps forward. Jonathan puts out his hand and Christopher shakes it and hugs him.

The crowd joins in a big "*Aahhh,*" then roars with a standing ovation.

Christopher takes the microphone and waits for the crowd to quiet down.

"You know, first of all, I thank you for believing in me...in us," he beams with pride and turns to the band gesturing for them to join him.

"These are my best of friends and some of the most talented cats I know."

Looking at the rest of the bands he continues, "And honestly, we're not any more talented than all these others. We were just... uh, prettier?"

The audience laughs.

"Anyway, this is awesome. Thank you." Holding the envelope high in the air he says, "And we will make you all proud."

His band mates congratulate one another and Christopher hands the microphone to his dad.

"Thanks to everyone who came here tonight," Jonathan shouts with pride.

Behind him, several band members pick up large signs and write on them.

"As you can imagine this will be an ongoing event at Mission Grove."

Joshua comes and nudges Jonathan to look at them.

Band members of David & The Goliaths move to one side and display their signs that read:

"To God Be The Glory" on side one and on side two, "Great Things He Has Done"

Song of Solomon members are now writing on their signs.

A sign reads: "I was getting wasted and losing my talents"

Flipside: "Now I don't waste them but share them with others"

Another sign reads: "Before, I feared the unknown"

Flipside: "Now, I know no fear"

Jonathan watches the hushed crowd and says, "This is awesome, isn't it?"

Heads nod, people shout and many clap.

Kym comes over with her sign. It reads: "I wondered if I were loveable"

Flipside: "Then I found my true love." She holds up her hand then pulls up a second card: "My one love is God"

Flipside: "And Christopher"

The band members make their way back to their places.

It is then that Jonathan sees Carter at the bottom of the steps, holding similar cards under his arm. Jonathan was about to continue, but he stops as Carter steps up on stage.

The camera swings from Jonathan to the cards that Carter holds as he stands, saying nothing.

Jonathan says to the audience, "This is my long lost brother,

Carter."

They clap.

Carter holds up a card. It reads: I WAS AT THE END OF MY ROPE

Flipside: SO I TIED A KNOT AND HUNG ON

The crowd laughs.

The second card reads: SOME PEOPLE CALLED ME A KILLER

Flipside: BUT IT WAS MYSELF THAT I WANTED TO KILL

The crowd grows quiet.

Carter says to Jonathan, "This is for you." He then turns to Angela and says, "And you."

The next card reads: I WOULD GIVE EVERYTHING I HAVE TODAY

Flipside: TO HAVE GRACE BACK WITH US TOMORROW

The crowd is silent. Then sniffs are heard.

There is one clap and then another. Then, several more, until the whole audience is standing, clapping.

Jonathan and Carter are still standing on opposite sides of the stage. They slowly walk toward one another until they meet in the middle and embrace.

CHAPTER 86

THE LAST OF THE CROWD is on the sidewalk in front of the theatre. Jonathan's Escalade is parked at the curb and David is laughing with Stuart. Christopher and Kym hold hands and joke with several band members. Carter and Angela are to one side, talking.

Christopher joins Jonathan who is helping Daphne into the truck. He says, "Dad, we're all going out for awhile. So...I guess that I'll be seeing you in the morning. Had fun tonight." He starts to walk away.

Jonathan says, "Yes, it was fun and I'm proud of you. Oh, and I'll need you in by 1:30."

"C'mon, it's a special night..."

"Want to make it 12:30?" Jonathan interrupts.

"But, Dad..."

"11:30?" Jonathan asks.

Christopher stops, holding up his hands, "Nope. Got it. 12:30 is perfect. Thanks."

Starting to run after his friends, he waves.

Angela hugs Carter, who had started to slowly walk away.

Whispering, she says, "So good to see you again, Carter. Welcome home."

He looks deeply into her eyes and whispers, "Thank you."

He helps her into the truck, closes the door, and turns to see Jonathan standing and smiling at him, "Glad you decided to hang around awhile longer."

"Me, too," Carter says, "It's good to be home."

They warmly embrace and Jonathan pats him on the back. "Say, Carter."

"Yeah?"

"Why don't you come to the house tomorrow. We can barbeque,

play catch with the boys and just hang out."

A huge smile lights Carter's face. "I'd like that."

Jonathan grins and says, "Me too."

As the Mathesons pull away from the curb, Carter sees that David is turned to wave and grinning from ear to ear. Carter smiles and waves.

He sees Jonathan's license plate.

"By Grace…"

EPILOGUE

Our Father in heaven, may your name be kept holy.

May your Kingdom come soon.

May your will be done on earth, as it is in heaven.

Give us today the food we need.

And forgive us our sins as we have forgiven those who sin against us.

And don't let us yield to temptation, but rescue us from the evil one.

If you forgive those who sin against you, your heavenly Father will forgive you.

But if you refuse to forgive others, your Father will not forgive your sins.

Matthew 6:9-15 (New Living Translation)

DAVID TEMPLE

David has been honing his storytelling skills for years. He has been a radio deejay in the top markets, has enjoyed acting in feature films, network television and commercials, and makes part of his living as a voiceover artist. He has recently written and directed several films, garnering him awards as a filmmaker. David hopes to make his passion for writing a lifelong work.

Discovering Grace represents his first novel. To see what stories come next and to stay in touch, please visit: www.davidtemple.tv.